The Herring in the Library

The Herring in the Library

L. C. Tyler

FELONY & MAYHEM PRESS • NEW YORK

All the characters and events portrayed in this work are fictitious.

THE HERRING IN THE LIBRARY

A Felony & Mayhem mystery

PRINTING HISTORY
First UK edition (Macmillan): 2010
Felony & Mayhem edition: 2011

ISBN: 978-1-934609-76-7

Manufactured in the United States of America

Printed on 100% recycled paper

Library of Congress Cataloging-in-Publication Data

Tyler, L. C.
The herring in the library / L. C. Tyler. -- Felony & Mayhem ed.
    p. cm.
ISBN 978-1-934609-76-7
1. Murder--Investigation--England--Fiction. 2. Novelists, English--
Fiction. 3. Literary agents--Fiction. I. Title.
PR6125.Y545H45 2011
823'.92--dc22

                            2011003696

To Ann

Author's Note

The site of Muntham Court is now occupied by Worthing Crematorium, developers having formed a view of it that was closer to Elsie's than to Ethelred's. The Muntham Court I describe in this book is not, however, very different from the one that existed until the middle part of the last century. If it still stood, it would probably be owned by somebody much like Sir Robert Muntham. All characters in this book are, however, completely fictional. I now accept, on Elsie's assurance, that Miss Scarlett was in no way to blame for the murder of Dr Black and unreservedly apologize for, and completely withdraw, any remarks that I may have made to the contrary.

Other "British" titles from

FELONY&MAYHEM

MICHAEL DAVID ANTHONY
The Becket Factor
Midnight Come

ROBERT BARNARD
Corpse in a Gilded Cage
Death and the Chaste Apprentice
Death on the High C's
The Skeleton in the Grass
Out of the Blackout

DUNCAN CAMPBELL
If It Bleeds

PETER DICKINSON
King and Joker
The Old English Peep Show
Skin Deep
Sleep and His Brother

CAROLINE GRAHAM
The Killings at Badger's Drift
Death of a Hollow Man
Death in Disguise
Written in Blood
Murder at Madingley Grange

CYNTHIA HARROD-EAGLES
Orchestrated Death

REGINALD HILL
A Clubbable Woman
An Advancement of Learning
Ruling Passion
An April Shroud

A Killing Kindness
Deadheads
Exit Lines
Death of a Dormouse

ELIZABETH IRONSIDE
The Accomplice
The Art of Deception
Death in the Garden
A Very Private Enterprise

BARRY MAITLAND
The Marx Sisters
The Chalon Heads

JOHN MALCOLM
A Back Room in Somers Town

JANET NEEL
Death's Bright Angel

SHEILA RADLEY
Death in the Morning
The Chief Inspector's Daughter
A Talent for Destruction
Fate Worse than Death

LESLIE THOMAS
Dangerous Davies

L.C. TYLER
The Herring Seller's Apprentice
Ten Little Herrings

LOUISE WELSH
Naming the Bones

The Herring in the Library

O what can ail thee, knight-at-arms,
Alone and palely loitering?
The sedge has wither'd from the lake,
And no birds sing.

John Keats,
'La Belle Dame Sans Merci'

Chapter One

There is nothing more tiresome, when you are about to expose a murderer, than to discover that you have been wilfully misled by the one person that you had thought you could trust.

Elsie had, since mid-afternoon, been cheating at *Cluedo*, at first subtly but now with little or no pretence of following the same rules that I was.

'If,' I said, 'you really do have Miss Scarlett's card in your hand, then remarkably nobody has committed a murder and Dr Black has died in the library of natural causes.'

Elsie, immune since birth to irony, simply nodded at this self-evident truth. 'That seems reasonable to me. Natural causes in the library. That also means I win.' She picked up my piece (Colonel Mustard) and flicked him back into the box, where he spun for a moment before coming to rest in sad and friendless isolation. The other five pieces, all now happily cleared of any suspicion of guilt, were allowed to remain in their various locations on the board.

The game was clearly over, but there were one or two minor issues I still needed to clear up. 'Ignoring for a moment the impossibility of that outcome, why do *you* win, when I said it first?'

'You said it ironically. I said it in earnest,' said Elsie.

Long experience has taught me that the more ridiculous an assertion is, the more difficult it is to argue against it. Unwisely, I persisted.

'You win only if that's what the cards say,' I said, with impeccable male logic. Though I was confident that the cards could not say that, I immediately regretted my generosity in conceding even this much. Elsie could do a great deal with a very small concession.

Her plump hand was already on the envelope in the middle of the board that concealed the three murder cards. She peeked a little too quickly and put them back. 'Yes,' she confirmed, as if I might really be stupid enough to believe it. 'Natural causes. You lose.'

'Except Miss Scarlett is in fact the murderer, isn't she?' I said. 'So when I asked you whether you had Miss Scarlett and you said you had, you were basically lying, weren't you?'

Elsie assumed a look of wide-eyed innocence, to which she was not even remotely entitled.

'I *am* Miss Scarlett,' she said, as if explaining something that should have been obvious even to me. 'Look, there's my piece, in the library, where you put it.'

'You have to have the card in order to deny Miss Scarlett is the killer,' I said.

'Not if you *are* Miss Scarlett. You could hardly expect Miss Scarlett to admit to the murder and then continue to flounce around the board for the rest of the game as if nothing had happened. Obviously she would deny it right up to the last. It's in the rules.'

I wondered if there was a way of continuing the discussion that wouldn't make me sound silly and pedantic. Probably not. One of Elsie's roles as my literary agent was, I had learned long ago, to remind me of my many inadequacies. We had established two or three new ones that afternoon. I doubted there could be any more to discover, but it seemed wiser not to take chances. Best, then, simply to agree with her that the Fifth Amendment applied to *Cluedo*, and no character could be required to incriminate himself or herself. In any case, I badly needed her to answer a question that I had asked shortly before.

'Yes, Ethelred,' she said when I reminded her. 'I was listening to every word.'

'And what was I saying?' I enquired.

To be fair to her, she didn't look embarrassed. She simply busied herself switching the cards in the envelope, neatly fitting up the absent Colonel Mustard as the murderer (with the dagger in the kitchen). 'You were telling me that Amazon rankings are a plot by the Freemasons, the Jesuits and Dan Brown, and are based not on actual sales but on the dimensions of the Great Pyramid at Giza.'

'No,' I said.

'Then you were probably complaining about the multi-squillion-pound advance to that supermodel for her so-called novel. Actually, I know the agent who negotiated the deal and the advance was scarcely more than your lifetime earnings. And at least ten per cent will have gone to the ghostwriter who really produced it. So, nothing to get excited about there.'

'Elsie,' I said. 'Have you actually listened to anything I have said for the past half-hour?'

'Maybe. Maybe not,' she said. 'Though, come to think of it, I do remember you unjustly accusing my piece of murder. I'm not sure I have forgiven you for that. In any case, writers really only have three subjects of conversation, two of which I have covered. So, it has to be the third one, whatever that is.'

'I was asking you, as my agent, for some advice on my next novel. It's what you get your fifteen per cent for.'

'Ethelred, one hundred per cent would not compensate for having to listen to you rabbiting on. I get my fifteen per cent for selling your books to unsuspecting publishers. My advice has to be free of charge—you couldn't afford it at market value.'

'If I can't work this out, there'll be nothing to deduct fifteen per cent from.'

'So third possible topic of conversation—all genre fiction is sadly underrated by critics and the public, and you want to embark on a great literary novel,' she said, showing she might have been listening in on the conversation after all.

'But whenever I sit down at the keyboard, I just get nowhere.'

'Look,' said Elsie, patiently, 'you are a second-rate crime writer.'

'I'm not sure that's true,' I said.

'Very well,' said Elsie, equally patiently, 'you are a third-rate crime writer, occasionally aspiring to the second-rate. Your fingers are used to typing out straightforward plots—basic characterization, sound accounts of police procedures, accurate descriptions of pubs and dimly lit back alleys—no unreliable narrators, no flashbacks or anything else that might cause confusion for the sort of person who reads your books. Ask your fingers to produce something swanky and obviously they get worried. They start to question whether this is wise. They're good intelligent fingers, those are.'

'I'd hoped for some sensible advice,' I said in clarification.

'Well, why didn't you say so? My sensible advice is as follows. Don't confuse your loyal readers by doing something different. You'll piss them off.'

'Are you saying that crime-fiction fans are incapable of appreciating good literature?'

'I'm not talking about *all* crime-fiction fans,' said Elsie. 'I'm just talking about...well, never mind.' She patted my hand across the *Cluedo* board. 'It's time you wrote another Master Thomas. If you leave it too long between books, people will stop buying them. Don't forget your readers aren't as young as they used to be. You need to get another book out there while they can still remember your name or indeed their own names. Have you checked your Amazon rankings lately?'

'Maybe. Maybe not,' I said.

'If I were you, I'd get down to another historical detective story this evening. After all, there's no time like the present.'

This made me look at my watch.

'You know as well as I do—we're due at Muntham Court in an hour. We'd better get changed.'

'Changed?' asked Elsie.

'Clothes,' I said.

Elsie pointed to what she was wearing. This summer she had gone a bit peasant for no obvious reason. I'd seen one or two actresses photographed in something similar for the Sunday colour supplements, but they had known roughly where to stop. Elsie's costume was sort of Gypsy Rose Lee meets Vivienne Westwood—though it didn't look as if they had been pleased to see each other. I'd hoped she had something else in the small bag she had deposited in the hallway of my flat. I was still hoping.

'Look, *clothes*,' she said. 'I am already wearing clothes. I accept that you probably wouldn't have noticed if I'd shown up naked, but I flatter myself others might.'

'Didn't you bring anything else?'

'Such as? It's just dinner with your mates in their flat,' said Elsie.

'What makes you think that?'

'You said: they live on an estate.'

'They *own* an estate,' I said. 'Muntham Court.'

'Muntham Court? Still sounds a bit Local Authority to me,' said Elsie.

'Sir Robert and Lady Muntham,' I said, 'of Muntham Court, in the county of West Sussex. That's who we are having dinner with.'

'And who else is on the guest list?' she asked. 'Lord Snooty and Bertie sodding Wooster?'

'Just a few friends,' I said.

'For whom I apparently have to dress up?'

'Black tie,' I said.

'You can go on your own.'

'That would mean you'd miss an opportunity to sneer at my friends,' I said.

'Good point. I hadn't thought of that.'

'I'm sure they won't mind you as you are. I promise I won't tell them you're dressed like that because you thought they lived in a council flat.'

'No, I can tell them that myself,' said Elsie. 'Right. I've got time for a nice relaxing bath before I reapply my lipstick, and you've got time to write the first five hundred words of the next Master Thomas. Nothing swanky. Keep it simple. No metafiction. No foreshadowing of events via dubious analogies. And no flashbacks.'

Chapter Two

It must have been almost three months before that when I had run into Rob Muntham coming out of the village post office. I had literally bumped into a tall, slightly stooped, grey-haired figure, who was attempting to enter as I attempted to leave. I was just framing a muttered apology when the man addressed me.

'Ethelred?' he said.

I must have looked blank because he repeated himself.

'Ethelred Tressider, isn't it? You don't recognize me, do you? I'm Robert Muntham.'

'Rob Muntham?' I said. I had a horrible feeling that I had sounded as though I was correcting him on the subject of his own name, but at university he had never been called 'Robert'—he had been 'Rob' or, more usually, 'Shagger'. The new, fuller version of his name seemed to come with the gravitas that he had acquired from somewhere during the thirty-odd years since I had last seen him. And, thinking about it, he had also sobered up a bit since that last occasion, standing in the middle of the quad singing a song apparently addressed to a Zulu warrior.

He gave me a tight-lipped smile in response to my mode of address. 'These days I am, for my sins, *Sir* Robert Muntham.'

'Ah, yes,' I said. 'Congratulations. I read about it in the college magazine.'

'For services to banking,' he added.

'Ah, yes,' I said again. I wondered if he had really been given a knighthood for his sins. It seemed unlikely, even for a banker. Still, Sir Robert Muntham...

It's strange how some of one's contemporaries show wholly illusory promise, while others emerge unreasonably and gloriously triumphant. Shagger Muntham was unquestionably in the latter category. He captained the college rugby team and had narrowly missed a boxing blue. His capacity for beer qualified him as some sort of minor alcoholic deity. He knew all of the words to 'Eskimo Nell' and most of the words to 'The Harlot of Jerusalem'. These things were held, in the college, to be much to his credit. On the other hand, even his closest friends never claimed to know what subject he was reading. He was the only person I can recall being wildly congratulated on achieving a third-class degree. The party lasted several days and ended with him standing in the quad... No, I think I've mentioned that already.

Then, for a while, we heard nothing of him at all. Only later did his apotheosis become apparent. He had descended on the City when the main academic requirements were a pair of red braces and brash confidence. One he had already. The other he had bought, presumably, at a tailor's in Docklands. As time went by, we sometimes caught a brief mention of him in the national press. The college newsletter increasingly called upon him for short articles on life after university or to encourage us to give generously to some appeal for a new boathouse or scholarships for overseas students—each successive accompanying photograph showed him slightly plumper, slightly greyer, distinctly more pleased with himself. The articles on life after university at least showed no false modesty. If the Queen had been hoping to surprise Shagger, she would have needed to give him a lot more than a knighthood.

'Congratulations,' I said again. Then I added: 'Oddly enough, I get reminded of you quite often round here. There's a big house nearby called—'

'—Muntham Court,' he said.

'You know it?'

'Know it, seen it, bought it.'

'That's a—'

'—coincidence? Not really. The missus rather fancied being Lady Muntham of Muntham Court. So I got it to oblige. We'll keep the house in Chelsea too.'

'As one does,' I said.

'Yes, Ethelred,' he said, without his lip even inching towards a grin. 'As one does.'

I switched off the smile and tried to think who Lady Muntham might be. Could he still be with the girl he was going out with at university? 'So, you married Harriet?'

'Yes, that's right,' he said. 'Clever of you to remember. But she's not Lady Muntham. God forbid. Harriet and I parted company a while back. I later married Annabelle *en secondes noces*, as they say. I'm not sure which was more expensive: the divorce or the celebrity wedding that Annabelle wanted.'

'A cheap divorce then,' I said. But Shagger failed to find this amusing either.

'No, Ethelred,' he said. 'It wasn't a cheap divorce.'

His attention seemed to be focused for a moment on some distant object. Then, turning back to me, he said: 'Didn't you marry Geraldine? She was at that secretarial college.'

'Yes,' I said. 'But we also got divorced. It happens. She later went and lived with Rupert Mackinnon. You remember Rupert?' Rupert too had been a contemporary at college.

Shagger nodded. 'She got around a bit, your Geraldine,' he said. 'Still, I'm sure you discovered that.'

I shook my head. Other than her getting into bed with my former best friend—the sort of slip-up anyone might make—I had no reason to doubt Geraldine's fidelity.

'Got around? No, it was just Rupert,' I said.

Shagger's mouth started to form a lopsided smirk, as if I was attempting to be funny, but then a large green Jaguar drove past us doing about fifteen miles an hour. His face fell instantly. The car hesitated briefly at the crossroads before turning right at the Gun. The driver appeared to flash a quick glance in our direction, then the Jaguar shot forward. We heard it proceeding, rapidly but now out of sight, up School Hill and back towards the roundabout.

Shagger scowled after it. I assumed that, like many people these days, he disapproved of large, polluting cars.

'He looked lost,' I said.

'No, he knows exactly where he's going,' said Shagger.

I, in turn, started a polite smile to acknowledge what I assumed was an obscure joke on Shagger's part, but whatever he had meant by it, it was not a pleasantry. My grin faded without it having been registered, still less returned. Shagger seemed to be listening to the fading noise of the engine as the climate criminal progressed onto the ring road, merging with the late-afternoon traffic.

His momentary preoccupation at least gave me a chance to take in this man I had not seen for so many years—or at least, not in the flesh. Thinking back to the last photograph I had seen of him, though, I realized he had lost a little weight. The glossy self-satisfaction that had dissuaded me, and probably many others, from contributing to whichever good cause he happened to be promoting was less evident. And there was grey around his eyes, I noticed, as well as in his hair. Still, he looked prosperous enough. The tweed jacket was well cut, new and in all likelihood from Savile Row. The trousers were pressed to a military perfection. His brown brogues shone like old mahogany. He carried his tweed cap well for somebody who came from a generation that had largely abandoned headgear of any sort. One might have said that he was attempting to caricature the dress of the local squire if it were not for the fact that he had just become the local squire. My local squire. I wondered whether I could risk inviting a man with the biggest house in the village and a few million pounds' worth of real estate in Chelsea back to my own modest flat. Possibly not.

'So, do you live round here?' he asked.

I indicated Greypoint House on the opposite side of the irregular, though rather pretty, square that forms the centre of our village. Two ancient pubs, a post office, a quaint supermarket, a butcher's shop, an ex-farmhouse of uncertain age and my own humble residence, all masking the sea of comfortable modern bungalows that now makes up most of Findon. Shagger acknowledged it with a nod. 'Not a bad little place,' he said, taking in the grey, double-fronted Georgian facade, its bay windows, its lilac tree and its low flint garden wall. 'Writing is obviously reasonably profitable then?'

'My bit of it is those two windows up there,' I said. 'It's all flats now.'

'Such a shame,' he said. 'Shouldn't really be allowed to mess around with old houses like that.'

The last distant notes of the Jaguar's engine had long since faded away. I was about to touch my forelock and take my leave when Shagger suddenly said: 'Well, behind that bay window must be a very pleasant sitting room, and behind that sitting room there must be a well-stocked kitchen with a kettle and a jar of coffee. I suppose you've no plans to invite me back?'

Briefly I felt like Mole being addressed, and slightly patronized, by Ratty. I tried to remember whether I'd left a bucket of whitewash in the hallway...or was that Badger?

'Yes, do come back for a coffee,' I said. 'If you've nothing better to do.'

'What could I have better to do than have coffee with an old chum? Lead on, Macduff,' he said.

I wondered whether to correct his Shakespearean quotation, but, concluding that Shagger might not yet have heard of Shakespeare, I simply indicated the way. Shagger strode ahead, his hands behind his back, the well-loved squire walking at a measured pace and in very shiny shoes through his new village.

◄► ◄► ◄►

That was the first of a number of such meetings. Our relations with people often fall into patterns that are almost unique to them, without seeming in any way out of the ordinary. In Robert's case (I quickly ceased to think of him as

'Shagger') the pattern proved to be that he would drop in without warning, whenever he ventured into the village for a newspaper or some other minor purchase. He expected me to be at home, as indeed I usually was—we third-rate writers don't get out that much. Robert and I would have coffee and he would talk about our time at university or his time in the City. I was occasionally allowed to contribute to his narrative—for example to remind him how narrowly and unfairly he had missed a boxing blue or to tease him gently about his success with women or capacity for drinking beer. I often envied his gift of partial recall. Once when talking about academic matters he mentioned in passing that it was a shame he had missed getting a first—that he had also missed getting a second apparently troubled him less.

He would ask occasionally about my books, but was always satisfied with the briefest of answers. Often they were the same answers I had given him the previous week. We rarely trespassed very far into the present. Even the past seemed to stop short at the day he had left the bank.

'It was time to go, Ethelred,' he said, one day when our conversation had fleetingly edged up to that point and then backed abruptly away. 'You have to know when it's time to go. No point in lingering.' And the conversation had reverted to a rugby match against Teddy Hall in which Robert had (he reminded me) played a starring role.

But why it had been time to go and what would have happened had he lingered were topics that were always skilfully sidestepped.

'You're lucky to have this little place,' he said more than once. 'Everything you want to hand. No gardens requiring continuous maintenance by expensive staff. No dry rot hiding in the cellar. Just a snug little bolthole.'

'Bolthole from what, Robert?' I asked. 'This is what I have. This is it.'

'Capital little place, all the same,' he said, taking in most of the flat in a single glance.

Again, I felt I was being patronized, but perhaps justifiably so. I could, as Elsie had tactfully pointed out, scarcely claim even to be a second-rate crime writer. I had a bank balance that was entirely appropriate to my literary status. Robert had, for a time, run one of the biggest financial institutions in the City. He could afford to retire—grey-haired and with the beginnings of a stoop perhaps, but still a relatively young man. He was Sir Robert Muntham KCBE of Muntham Court. I wasn't.

Part of the pattern too was that his wife did not join him on these visits. It was several weeks before I met her. Annabelle proved to be some years younger than he was—an elegant and rather tense woman, who (I was later told) had had a reasonably successful career as a model before settling down and not having children. I'm not sure our first meeting was a success.

'This is Ethelred, one of my very oldest chums,' Robert had said, when the three of us happened to coincide outside the post office one morning.

'You live here—in Findon?' she asked, suggesting that Robert had not mentioned his chum much, if at all, on his return with *The Times* or a tube of toothpaste.

'I have a flat over there,' I said, anxious to avoid any repetition of the error that Robert had fallen into. 'It's just a couple of rooms up on the first floor.'

She looked from me to the flat and then back again. 'That must be very...' she said. But she was unable to come up with any advantages to living in a small flat just outside Worthing. 'So, what do you do, Alfred?' she asked.

'Ethelred,' I said. 'As for what I do, I am a writer.'

'I *thought* you said "Ethelred", but then I decided I must have misheard. Do you write under your own name—no, surely not?'

I told her the three names that I wrote under.

'I don't think I've read any of your books,' she said. It's a response I'm used to. Really, it doesn't bother me any more. 'What do you write?' she added.

'Crime mainly—as J. R. Elliot and Peter Fielding anyway. When I'm being Amanda Collins I write romantic fiction.'

She shook her head. She hadn't heard of any of me. 'So, do you write hard-boiled crime?'

'Not really. My victims die almost painlessly and usually with the minimum of blood to clean up afterwards.'

'Is that realistic?'

'No,' I said.

'Well, I must read one of your books anyway. Which do you recommend?'

I named a couple at random. Other than that the J. R. Elliot books are set in the fourteenth century and the Peter Fielding books in the present day, they're all much of a muchness.

'I hope you remember those titles, Robert,' she said to her husband.

Robert winked at me before saying: 'Of course, dearest.'

At that point Lady Muntham recalled that she needed to get some steak from the butcher but, before she set out on the fifty yards or so of road that separated us from Peckham's, she added: 'You must come and have dinner with us, Ethelred.'

I acknowledged, with a thin smile, a promise that I did not expect would ever be honoured. Then, a couple of weeks later a gilt-edged card arrived. When I next saw Robert, I apologized for the fact that I had invited my agent down to stay that weekend and so would be unable to attend.

━◄ ━◄ ━◄

Which was how I ended up sitting in my flat with Elsie discussing evening wear.

'Come on, Tressider,' she said. 'Or we're going to be late for Lord Snooty and his pals. I don't know what you were thinking about but you were miles away there. You've got to do five hundred words before dinner. No flashbacks.'

'I always end up writing flashbacks,' I said. 'It's the sort of writer I am.'

At Muntham Court

'Come closer to the fire, Master Thomas.'

'The fire? Thank you, my lady. You are kind. Very kind. Too kind.'

Yes, decidedly, just that little bit too kind, thought Master Thomas, inching closer as instructed, but no further than politeness dictated. The heat from this blaze was uncomfortable, even in January. Nevertheless, he rubbed his small, soft hands in front of it. Well-seasoned logs from the estate had had the snow dusted from them and had been piled by liveried serving men into the vast stone fireplace. The flames now leapt upwards into the cavernous, soot-crusted chimney, seemingly as eager to please Her Ladyship as everyone else who came in contact with her.

Clever things, these chimneys. Thomas, like most people, had grown up in a house where smoke escaped through a blackened hole in the roof, to the extent that it escaped at all. Now everyone was building houses with chimneys. That was modern times for you. And who knew what wonders the fifteenth century might bring?

'Sharing the fire with you makes it no less warm for me,' said the lady. 'And you have had a long and cold journey from London.'

'The radiance of your welcome warmed me the moment I stepped across your threshold, my lady. No fire needed. None at all. Not a single log. Scarcely even a twig.'

'Are you a flatterer, Master Thomas, because you are a poet or because you are a courtier?'

The problem, thought Master Thomas, was that he was unable to have a conversation with this lady without babbling like an inhabitant of the Bethlehem Hospital. Still, it was a good question: poet or courtier? Both would be better than the day job.

'I am a poor poet, Your Ladyship, and no courtier. I am just a humble customs officer, as Your Ladyship knows. And words that would acknowledge the name of flattery are clearly no flattery at all. So if I confess to being a flatterer, I am none.'

'But you are more than a humble customs officer if the King entrusts you with important messages for my husband.'

Thomas looked up from his contemplation of the fire and his calculation as to what it would cost to install a modest chimneypiece in his own small house at Blackfriars.

'Your husband thinks not. He wondered that the King had troubled me with a message of such insignificance.'

'I am sure that the King would not waste his servants' time.'

'That shows how little you know of kings, Your Ladyship, if you would pardon me for pointing out your good fortune. But your husband raised the same point. He thought that there must be more to it. He enquired whether the message might perhaps be in code.'

'And was it?'

'I can tell Your Ladyship no more than I could tell Sir Edmund. Messages in code are to be understood by the sender and the receiver. I am neither. I am merely a—'

'—humble clerk. Yes, I think you've said that already.'

'Humble customs officer, was what I was planning to say. Formerly apprentice to an apothecary. But "clerk" if you will. It is as Your Ladyship wishes.'

'And what did the message say?'

'I gave it to your husband sealed, just as it left the King.'

'The King had sealed it himself?'

'It bore the King's personal seal. The Signet.'

'And how does my husband intend to reply?'

'Sir Edmund will inform me when he returns from hunting,' said Thomas. 'I am to wait. I must confess that I had hoped he would return much earlier. I fear that the light is now fading. These January days are short.'

'You will stay the night, Master Thomas, and set out for London in the morning. A place can be found for you to sleep. You will be more comfortable here than in some miserable inn on the London road. However soon my husband returns, there is no question of your going anywhere this evening. I must in any case think of a suitable response to your other missive.'

'The poem from my master?'

'Indeed. Master Geoffrey Chaucer's poem.'

'I believe no reply is expected.'

'But of course a poem must be replied to! You know little of chivalry, Master Thomas.'

'That is true, my lady. Though I read romances avidly when I was young.'

'Arthur and Guinevere?'

'Roland and Charlemagne. Whatever I could get my hands on.'

'And did you dream of being a knight? Did you dream of carrying a sword?'

'My dagger is sword enough,' said Thomas, patting the ballock knife that hung from his belt. 'I am not entirely certain that I would know how to use it in a fight, but it would be unwise to travel the roads with no visible means of defence. A fly may be swatted with impunity, but the smallest wasp is accorded some respect. In any case, the dagger is useful for cutting up sausages.'

'You would use your Excalibur for cutting up sausages? Fie! I think those romances were wasted on you,' smiled the lady.

'I tell the stories to my children at bedtime,' said Thomas. 'Sometimes I do make Arthur cut up sausages with Excalibur. It is a fault with all my stories that I will sacrifice both character and plot to amuse my audience.'

The lady frowned. 'You have children? And a wife? But then...'

'I have a wife to whom I am devoted and three children, to whom we are both devoted in equal measure—Richard, Geoffrey and little Blanche. Blanche is the youngest—she is just walking. You appear perplexed, my lady. It is entirely natural that a man of my age would have a family.'

'No, of course. It was just...they must miss you when you are away.' The lady gave a tight-lipped smile. Thomas instinctively looked over his shoulder towards the door, then wondered why he had done it. The lady seemed ill at ease for no apparent reason. Perhaps she did not like children? There were no children in the house. If she were unable to bear children herself, it might be distasteful to her to discuss the children of others? But surely she herself had raised the subject?

'I am often away on the King's business,' said Thomas, breaking
the silence. 'The children are used to it. I have promised them a new
story when I return. As I ride, I make up stories. It passes the time. It
was a long journey down to Sussex, so I have thought of two so far.'

'Indeed,' said the lady, 'you must tell them to your children if...
when you return.'

'I shall do so,' said Thomas.

The conversation lapsed inexplicably. The lady twisted the bunch
of keys tied to her kirtle.

'They should not have sent you,' she exclaimed with a sudden
determination. 'Not you. It was wrong of them. Perhaps indeed you
should go now. I think that would be best.'

'I fear,' said Thomas with a shrug, 'that it is already too late.
I am, as it were, here. I shall have to accept your kind hospitality.
I hope, my lady, that you would not throw me out into the snow
merely because I have three children and place mirth before
gallantry. But I must in any case wait for Sir Edmund. Those are
my instructions.' He gave a slight bow. She did not smile in response.

'Yes, too late...' she repeated, though not to Master Thomas.

There was another pause, during which the fire crackled and
spat. A dog sleeping close to the hearth opened one eye, rolled over
and stretched out its legs. Then the thing that they seemed to have
been waiting for happened.

The outer door to the great hall was flung open and three
men strode into the room bringing winter with them. Thomas
felt the bitter rush of cold air and noticed white specks on their
cloaks—specks that were fading one by one as he watched, leaving
small damp patches. It must be snowing again outside, he thought.
Perhaps they were three of Sir Edmund's men who had ridden on
ahead to announce his arrival. They certainly seemed to think they
belonged here. He turned to the lady as if hoping for some sort of
introduction, but she stood mute and staring in their direction.
She wanted desperately to say something, but seemed to be waiting
for a cue.

The tallest of the three, a man with grizzled hair and a short
beard, advanced until he was just a yard or so away from the lady.

He carried a quiet authority—not one of Sir Edmund's men, then, but a knight himself, perhaps, with his own retainers.

'Lady Catherine...' he began.

'You bear bad news?' she gasped.

'I bear...yes, the news is bad. It is the worst. Please prepare yourself...'

'My husband...'

'Sir Edmund is dead,' said the man very quickly. 'He was...'

'By whom?' gasped Lady Catherine. Then, seeing the expression on the man's face, she suddenly fell silent.

'He was stabbed with a dagger,' the man continued very slowly and precisely. 'By an unknown assailant.'

'Who escaped...'

'Indeed...as you say...who escaped. But we have a description. A short man, with the appearance of a clerk, carrying a dagger and speaking in the manner of one from London.'

The three men and the lady turned as one to look at Thomas. The dog (who clearly knew whose side he was on) growled softly.

'I'm afraid,' said Thomas, 'that I haven't seen any other clerks from London near here.'

'Nor have I,' said the man. He turned to his two companions. 'Arrest this clerk,' he said.

Thomas blinked a couple of times. No, they were all still there. This was still happening. 'To what end?' he asked, as well as his dry mouth would allow.

'We think you may be able to help us with our inquiries.'

'About the stabbing? I met Sir Edmund only briefly. He was alive when I last saw him.'

'So you say.'

'I assure you that there's nothing I can remember that would be of any assistance to you gentlemen...'

'Perhaps we can jog your memory then,' said the man.

'I can't quite see how you would be able to do that.'

'Ever been tortured before?' asked the man.

'No,' said Thomas.

'Well, now's your chance.'

I reread what I had just written. I rarely begin a novel at chapter one and work methodically through a manuscript. Often I will write the ending quite early on and progress steadily towards it. Here I had obviously begun halfway through. I was not yet sure why Master Thomas had been dispatched to Sussex. Clearly he had been sent by his master, Geoffrey Chaucer, and clearly he had been dumped right in it. But why? And why had I chosen to set it at Muntham Court? Lady Catherine knew a great deal more than she had let on. Was she complicit in her husband's murder? If so, was she the instigator or somebody else's pawn...?

'Come on, Tressider, I said five hundred words, not half a novel,' said Elsie, looking round the door.

'It's only one thousand, seven hundred and fifty-one words—hardly half a novel even by my standards.'

'Whatever. Just save it and close the lid. The sooner we go to your snooty friends, the sooner we can piss off back home. I like the neck wear, by the way—I've never seen a bow tie at that angle before. Original.'

I closed the lid of my laptop as instructed and furtively straightened my tie.

'I'll get the car keys,' I said.

Chapter Three

Elsie had insisted that we drive.

'It's scarcely a ten-minute walk,' I'd pointed out, 'and it's a lovely summer evening.'

'I'm not walking up some muddy lane in high heels, thank you very much. You've been away from London too long, Tressider. You think mud is fine if it doesn't reach to the tops of your Hunters. We have something called pavements in London. Once you have them fitted in Sussex we'll walk as much as you like. Until then you get to drive me.'

Elsie discovered she had in fact left in my flat (to which she is a frequent visitor) something in black silk that would pass as an evening dress and that she imagined suited her short but well-rounded figure. She had also at some point in the past left a pair of black high-heeled shoes in my care. The heels increased her height by many inches, but not by enough of them to quite carry off the black silk item, which had been abandoned with me for good reason. I wondered whether to suggest she went as a Transylvanian fishwife after all, but decided not. Long experience had taught me just to tell Elsie that she looked great and to keep my fingers crossed for next time.

So, the wheels of my Mini crunched up the gravel drive, now in deep shadow from the two rows of ancient trees that flanked it, and performed a spacious arc in front of Muntham

Court. I applied the brake and went round to open Elsie's door.

Findon has a number of large houses. The undoubtedly quaint Findon Manor, the oldest of them, has long been a hotel. Findon Place is an impressive small Georgian mansion, carefully positioned to suggest that it owns the church. Findon Park is set in large grounds just outside the village. But Muntham Court eclipses them all. When it was rebuilt in the mid-nineteenth century, its owner had made concessions neither to economy nor to good taste. The house was vast and designed in equal measure for comfort and for putting visitors in their place. Nominally it was in the Jacobean style but the architect had been paid cash to lift features from any and every period. There were pilasters in profusion and ogees in abundance. Balustrades flowed and anything that could be ornamented was ornamented. Contemporaries might have claimed to despise it, but time had mellowed and softened everything. Few people ascended the drive and caught their first glimpse of the house between its neatly cut hedges without experiencing the intended sense of envy.

'I was expecting something bigger,' said Elsie noncommittally as she stepped from the car.

'It's stunning,' I said, still holding the door. 'It's like some fairy-tale castle out of the *Morte d'Arthur*. You would expect Sir Bedivere to come riding out of the shrubbery on his palfrey and greet a pale damsel on the lawn with a courtly bow.'

'Whatever you say, pet,' said Elsie. 'Anyway, it's good we've got here before too many people try parking their palfreys.'

'Why?'

'So we are well positioned to make a quick getaway if your friends turn out to be really boring.'

We were in fact one of two cars parked in front of the house—the other was a large green Jaguar. It looked familiar, but I didn't have a chance to comment on this to Elsie. As I locked the Mini, the front door of Muntham Court was thrown open and Lady Muntham walked towards us. She appeared every inch the gracious hostess in a midnight-blue dress that shimmered in the rays of a waning sun. Her blonde hair was tied back in a bun. The pearls that she wore round her neck were large but (in my view) very tasteful. She had perhaps applied a little too much make-up, but she had once been a model. Her smile lit up the garden.

'Ethelred,' said Lady Muntham, placing her hand on my arm. 'It's so sweet of you to come. And this must be Elise?'

'Elsie,' said Elsie.

'Elsie, of course. And you must call me Annabelle.'

'Yes, that's what I'd been planning to do,' said Elsie.

Annabelle led us through a hallway, paved with black and white tiles and containing an oak staircase that swept upwards into the mock-Tudor gloom. From there we proceeded, past a billiard room, into a conservatory that was, in its way, scarcely smaller or less grand than the hall. Its Victorian architect, having perhaps recently visited the Crystal Palace, had put together a vaulted structure of steel and glass. In its humid microclimate, stunted palms had clung on gamely through decades of neglect. Rattan-framed sofas added to the illusion that we had temporarily been transported to some distant and rather downmarket part of the Empire. Beyond the dusty glass panes a blood-red sun was beginning to set.

'Robert is delayed for a moment,' Annabelle said, pouring our drinks. She glanced towards the door, then added absent-mindedly: 'I think you said you would like a lemonade, Elise?'

'You are so very kind,' said 'Elise' in a strangely simpering tone that put me on my guard at once.

'And a whisky for you, Ethelred.'

I took the heavy lead crystal in my hand. The whisky seemed a long way down at the bottom, but it was a large glass.

'It's so airy in here,' I said, looking at the evening light reflected off the glossy palm fronds.

'It makes a change from the oak panelling in the rest of the house,' said Annabelle with a smile.

'You're not into oak panelling, then, Annabelle?' Elsie piped up from just behind my shoulder.

'It's all Grade One listed,' said Annabelle regretfully. 'There's not much we can do about it.'

'You could do white emulsion,' said Elsie. 'Or magnolia. You'd need more than one coat, of course. It's on special offer at B&Q at the moment.'

Annabelle gave me a tight-lipped scowl. Then she looked away and said: 'It really is too rude of Robert not to be here. I'm going to chase him out of wherever he is.'

She swished from the room, leaving Elsie and me alone.

'Could you get your eyes to stop following her every movement like some lovesick puppy?' said Elsie. 'Just for a moment, at least? And could you kindly kick her hard every time she calls me "Elise"?'

'I don't know what you mean,' I said.

'Yes, you do. Who does she remind you of?'

'Annabelle? She reminds me of nobody in particular.'

'I'll give you a clue: it's the unprincipled slapper you were formerly married to. Would you like to make a guess now?'

'Annabelle's not a bit like Geraldine.'

'She's a tad taller, I'll grant you. She's definitely not a real blonde and my hunch is those aren't the tits that God gave her. But I do know an unprincipled slapper when I see one. Steer clear of her unless you have authority from me in writing. In which lap-dancing establishment did your friend Shagger pick her up?'

'I don't know where Sir Robert and Lady Muntham met,' I said. 'By the way, *please* don't address him as Shagger and *please* don't suggest to anyone else they met in a lap-dancing club.'

Elsie smiled. She may have intended it as an enigmatic smile, but it failed to conceal the general shape of her plan.

'Whatever,' I said. There are some people you can't trust to behave themselves at dinner parties once they've had a few drinks. I didn't trust Elsie even on lemonade, but I also knew there was nothing I could do about it.

'The hall, the conservatory, the billiard room,' said Elsie contemplatively.

'What do you mean?' I asked.

'This isn't a dinner party—we're back playing *Cluedo*.'

'Only if one of us gets murdered,' I said with a confident smile. 'How likely do you think that is?'

'It's the host that gets murdered in *Cluedo*, so it's only Shagger who's got any worries. Do you think that's why he's not here? The former lap dancer's already bumped him off?'

'I am sure Robert will be with us soon,' I said. 'Anyway, if this was *Cluedo*, there should be a piece of lead piping on the floor over there. It's about half the size of the conservatory, if I remember the board correctly, so we wouldn't miss it.'

'What do you think a place like this costs?' asked Elsie, changing the subject.

'Millions to buy. Tens of thousands a year to run. Robert says they have a full-time gardener and an assistant, plus a housekeeper and a cleaner who comes in for a few hours every day. That's before you start repairing the roof or dealing with the death-watch beetle.'

'So, he must have a penny or two then, your banker friend?'

'I guess so.'

A noise behind us made us turn, but it was not Robert or Annabelle.

'The door was open, so we came in,' said the man. 'Annabelle said we'd be having drinks in the conservatory first, so we've been hunting for a room that looked like a conservatory or at least had drinks in it.'

'This will do, anyway,' said the woman, looking round the room.

'Closest we've got so far,' said the man.

They were both of middle height and nominally dressed for the occasion, he in a slightly scruffy white dinner jacket, she in a long red dress with a black stole draped loosely round her shoulders. Perhaps it was the newcomer's self-assurance, or perhaps it was the palm trees that surrounded us on all sides, but just for a moment I regretted that I had not thought of wearing a white dinner jacket myself.

Evening dress makes some people stiff and formal; the man seemed to wear his like an old pair of jeans and a sweater. He still had the air of a naughty schoolboy about him—a naughty schoolboy who has little fear of being caught. Since his hair was showing signs of grey, he'd probably been a naughty schoolboy for some years and was now fairly good at it. He went straight over to the well-stocked side table and uncorked a bottle of sherry. 'Will this one do?'

'No sign of champagne?' asked the woman.

'Wouldn't know where to start looking in this jungle. We don't know our way round here yet, do we, Fi? We'll know next time, if they ever invite us back.'

'Probably the champagne will be rubbish anyway. Do you remember the stuff they served up last time in Chelsea?'

'Spanish, wasn't it?'

'Bulgarian actually. Is that sherry medium dry?'

'It says medium dry on the bottle, but they always lie. Probably tastes like gripe water.'

'Any half-decent white wine?'

'None available to the general public. It's just the stuff Annabelle has set out on this table.'

'I'll risk the sherry then,' she said. I noticed that the black stole had a large cigarette burn in it. She could have turned the stole the other way, but she hadn't bothered.

The man poured a large sherry and gave it a quick and not altogether approving sniff before handing it on.

'You two OK for drinks?' he asked, as he returned to the whisky decanter. 'No waiting staff tonight it would seem. Sorry—we're Colin and Fiona McIntosh. Friends of the Munthams, but clearly not such close friends as to rate being met or greeted it would seem. We're used to it.'

'They'll be having their usual pre-dinner row,' said Fiona. She sipped the sherry and pulled a face. 'Better to get it over with beforehand. You'll find they're quite good hosts once they get to focus on you properly. Who are you, by the way? With the state of security here at the moment I guess there's a fifty-fifty chance you're axe-murders or something. Is that what you are?'

'He prefers poison,' said Elsie. 'Though he's used most methods at some stage.'

'I write crime novels,' I said quickly.

'Would I have heard of you?' asked Fiona.

'No,' I said. (Better to get that one over with too.)

I introduced myself and Elsie, and we all shook hands the necessary four times.

'You've known the Munthams for a while then?' I asked.

'Oh, yes,' said Fiona. 'In assorted configurations. It was Robert and Harriet, when we first met—and Miles and Annabelle, of course, as a separate but not too thriving operation.'

'Then it was Robert and Madge for a bit,' said Colin. 'Not sure what happened to Madge. Probably came to a bad end, like Jonah Jarvis.'

'That was when Annabelle was with—'

'Will? David? No, I can't remember either,' said Colin. 'Anyway, we have known them jointly and severally for a while.'

'But nothing changes,' said Fiona.

'No, nothing changes,' said Colin. 'Wouldn't be the first time Robert had invited us over and then failed to show up at all.'

As if on cue, Robert burst into the room to greet us, with Annabelle and another slightly dejected-looking guest in tow. Robert apologized profusely but said that he had been talking to Clive (the random dejected guest, I assumed) about business and had not noticed the time. Annabelle did not seem exactly happy, but there was clearly at least a temporary truce.

I looked at Elsie and realized, with a sinking heart, that she had probably not forgotten that she had been forbidden to address people as 'Shagger'.

Elsie held out her hand. She smiled sweetly. 'Good to meet you, Sh...ame we missed you when we arrived.'

'Yes, sorry about that,' said Robert. He seemed unaware that Elsie's stutter was a newly acquired disability.

'Well, Sh...all we get a chance to view this place later?'

'Yes, of course,' he said.

'Sh...uper!' said Elsie, giving up any pretence of subtlety. She gave me a grin. I glared at her but she had already lost interest in that particular game and was now engaged in a conversation with Colin and Fiona.

'So, what do *you* do?' I heard her say.

'I'm a doctor,' I heard Colin reply.

'I meant to say,' said Annabelle, touching my arm lightly. 'This is going to be something of a literary gathering. We have another writer coming this evening. Felicity Hooper. Do you know her?'

There is this charming belief that we writers all know each other—possibly through Society of Authors sherry parties or evenings of debauchery at Hay-on-Wye. I know a lot of crime writers, of course, but for a moment I couldn't quite place Felicity Hooper.

'What sort of thing does she write?' I asked.

'Family sagas,' said Annabelle.

'Ah, yes,' I said. 'Of course.' Not crime at all, and a lot more successful than I have ever been.

'Felicity Hooper?' asked Fiona, overhearing this last remark. 'Yes, that's right, family sagas with an uplifting theme: plucky heroine winning through in the foreground, God playing a minor supporting role in the background. As a man, He's lucky to get off that lightly. The men in her novels tend to be evil schemers or morons.'

'I know her. She sent a manuscript to me once,' said Elsie grimly.

'Not literary enough for you?' asked Fiona.

'Didn't think I'd make enough money,' said Elsie, reaching for a peanut from the small bowl on a side table. 'I was well wrong there. Though I also objected to being lectured to chapter by chapter on the need for courage and cheerful resourcefulness. Stuff that.'

At which point, I was introduced to Clive, and so I never learned the identity of the 'stuck-up, sanctimonious cow' whom Elsie was now discussing with Colin and Fiona. Still, once Elsie got going, it could have been almost anyone.

Clive seemed slightly distracted—irritated almost—by something that had happened earlier and asked what I did twice without apparently realizing it. The second time he registered my answer sufficiently to reply: 'I can't say I read a lot of crime myself.' Our conversation lapsed into silence several times, but this did not seem to trouble him very much. There were clearly other things on his mind—money perhaps. He had the air of having once been more prosperous than he was now. His dinner jacket was undoubtedly smarter than Colin McIntosh's, though it too could have benefited from a trip to the dry cleaners. The cuffs of his dress shirt were slightly frayed. He proved to be a former banking colleague of Robert's.

'It was pretty ungrateful of the bank to do that to him,' said Clive, suddenly breaking one of our conversational pauses.

'I thought Robert had just retired?' I asked. 'He said he didn't want to linger.'

'When they sack you, you get thirty minutes to fill your cardboard box and go,' said Clive. 'If you linger they call security.'

'Well, it doesn't look as though he needs to work,' I said, indicating the grandeur around us.

'I would have thought you needed to work all the more if you had a place like this to keep up,' said Clive. 'But the bank may have been more generous with the severance package than I thought. It wasn't that generous with me.'

'You left at the same time?'

'Pretty much. I'm a school bursar these days, which almost pays the bills. Maybe I should be thankful I'm not still a banker.'

I grimaced in return. That year bankers were being blamed for everything that was wrong with the economy, and their greed had become the yardstick by which all vices were measured. It was safer that year to admit to having the Black Death than to being a banker.

'Robert thought he knew of one or two good openings for me,' Clive continued. 'That's what we had been talking about.'

I was trying to think of anything encouraging to say, when all conversation in the room was brought to an abrupt halt.

'So, this is where you all are!' exclaimed an indignant voice from the doorway. A middle-aged lady in a rather old-fashioned frock of indeterminate colour stood on the threshold, her finger pointing accusingly at Robert—though we all immediately felt a strange sense of guilt.

'Felicity!' exclaimed Annabelle. 'How lovely to see you. But was there nobody to let you in?'

'*Anyone* can come *in*,' said Felicity. 'The place is wide open. But there is nobody to *tell you where to go*. You could wander the corridors here for ever. You really are the most inconsiderate host, Robert.'

Robert just grinned broadly and said: 'Gin and tonic?'

'A very large one might make up *a little* for what I have suffered. I hope the cooking tonight is going to be better than the butlering.'

'Not much Christian forgiveness there,' Elsie said in a whisper, though possibly not enough of a whisper because Felicity immediately looked in her direction.

Annabelle took charge of Felicity, as one does with a guest that one wishes to dispose of safely and quickly. With a firm hand on Felicity's upper arm, she headed determinedly in my direction. I found myself formally introduced to Felicity as briefly as could be decently done. Annabelle took Clive Brent and manhandled him away to be introduced, presumably, to more interesting people.

Felicity Hooper and I sized each other up for a moment. I decided her face was vaguely familiar, and for a moment there was a half-expectant look on her part—the look you give some-body who ought to recognize you, but hasn't. So perhaps we had coincided at one of the smaller literary festivals. Luton? I'd find out sooner or later.

She asked an opening question or two, which gave me no helpful clues, and I lied briefly about my sales figures.

'Well done you,' she said, her look telling me that she didn't believe a word of it.

Though I hadn't met her before (had I?) I knew roughly how her sales were. Occasionally she edged into the bestseller lists printed in the *Sunday Times*. She regularly appeared on the tables at the front of Waterstone's where her books were piled in drifts, ten deep. They were usually labelled 'three for two'. My own books slipped in modestly through the back door when nobody was looking, and found themselves obscure slots in the crime section, or (in the case of Amanda Collins) in the increas-ingly rare sections marked 'Romantic Fiction'.

'And yours?' I asked.

'Making the *Richard and Judy* list helped,' she said. 'Didn't they include one of yours a while back?'

'No,' I said.

'That's right,' she said. 'So they didn't.'

'I think that the Amanda Collins series isn't perhaps the sort of thing they go for—or the J. R. Elliot series for that matter.'

'Their list has been very well chosen lately.'

'Yes,' I said.

'Why don't you write under your own name?' demanded Felicity suddenly.

I didn't know—other than that I don't especially like my own name. The various names I had selected all seemed good choices at the time. I put this theory forward.

'And *Amanda Collins*?' she asked with raised eyebrows. 'You think you look like an Amanda?' She eyeballed me as though this question was more significant than it appeared at first sight.

'My photograph doesn't appear on the cover,' I said. 'So it doesn't really matter. Actually, I think that most of the people who write for that particular imprint do so under assumed names. We rarely choose to meet up with each other, so I can't be certain.'

This didn't seem to be the answer that Felicity was expecting, but our conversation was interrupted by the sound of wheels on the gravel outside. This time Robert sprang to attention and headed for the front door. He returned with a youngish couple, who seemed to complete the party because he said to Annabelle in passing: 'I've locked the front door.'

'A bit late for that,' said Felicity loudly.

'I agree,' said Elsie, who had materialized at my side. 'Half the villains in Sussex could have been in and out by now with the family silver. If this was *Cluedo*, we'd have all been murdered.'

'As you yourself said, only Dr Black is murdered in *Cluedo*,' I pointed out. 'And it's one of the guests that does it. The question is: which guest and with which weapon.'

'That's odd, when you think about it,' said Elsie. 'If they've found Dr Black's body, you'd think they'd at least be able to tell if he's been strangled, shot or stabbed, wouldn't you? Silly tossers.'

'It merely shows,' said Felicity, 'what a ridiculous genre crime is. It is exactly like *Cluedo*. Six or seven stock suspects, all with a motive and, strangely, an opportunity. Then you put them all together in a country house somewhere, with a convenient excuse as to why the police cannot investigate the murder themselves.'

'That may be a typical Agatha Christie plot,' I said, 'but you obviously haven't read—'

Felicity waved away Colin Dexter, Elmore Leonard, P. D. James, Ruth Rendell and indeed myself with a quick flick of her hand. 'You need to deal with real issues that confront real families,' she said. 'Or do you ever venture into the twenty-first century and mention problems like global warming?'

'Occasionally,' I said.

'No, he doesn't,' said Elsie loyally. She held out her hand to Felicity. 'Elsie Thirkettle. Literary agent. I turned down your first book.'

'We all make mistakes,' said Felicity.

'Maybe. Maybe not,' said Elsie.

From somewhere a long way off the noise of a gong resonated through the dimly lit corridors and rooms of Muntham Court. Each of us suspended the conversation that we were engaged in and proceeded, in carefully thought-out pairs, towards the dining room—another location on the *Cluedo* board, as it happens.

I found myself amongst more oak panelling and seated next to Annabelle at one end of the table. Elsie was at the far end, next to Robert. Half of the newly arrived couple was on my left. She was petite and dressed primly in a dark green, full-length dress with a high neckline. Somebody had spent a lot of time on her hair, which had been carefully and slightly conservatively styled. She had a nervous fragility about her, and occasionally she glanced towards her husband on the other side of the table.

'Is this your first visit to Muntham Court?' I asked, as soup was served by somebody who was, all too evidently, the assistant gardener in a borrowed black jacket and trousers of a slightly different colour—navy blue, possibly, though it was difficult to tell in that light.

'Oh, yes,' she said, flinching as generous quantities of soup were aimed more or less at her plate. 'Gerald and I live in Crawley. He's a solicitor there.'

'Are you a solicitor as well?'

She gave a tinkling laugh. 'Me? No, I'm not that clever. I used to be a secretary...in a bank, you know. In London. But since we had Scott, I haven't worked.'

I assumed Scott must be an infant of some description, which proved to be the case.

'He's almost eighteen months now,' she said, as if that was some sort of record for West Sussex.

I repeated his age with what I hoped was sufficient incredulity, and she nodded proudly. 'He's going to be very musical,' she said, 'and here's how we know why. It's terribly amusing.'

Surprisingly, it wasn't amusing, even when described at some length. While feigning complete attention, I surreptitiously took a small sip of the wine that had been poured into my glass earlier. Then I immediately took a second much larger sip and raised my eyebrows in surprise. Contrary to what the McIntoshes had predicted, the wine was excellent. The solicitor's wife beamed at me, assuming from my expression that she had finally found somebody who displayed an appropriate degree of reverence and awe for Scott's achievements. I ruthlessly used this brief pause in her monologue to turn back to Annabelle on my other side.

'It's an impressive place you have here,' I said.

'Next time you come, you must see the gardens,' she said, leaning towards me in a confidential manner. She was clearly unaware how low-cut her dress was. I tried to avoid admiring her cleavage too obviously.

'Yes,' I said. 'Are they very big?'

She leaned forward a little more. 'You'll have to explore them and find out.'

I caught a hint of expensive perfume and had a brief but disconcerting vision of a fly being led into the fragrant but deadly depths of a pitcher plant. 'I'd be delighted,' I said.

Then, disconcertingly, she added: 'John looks after them terribly well.'

'John?'

'The gardener. He looks after the gardens very well. Wonderful hands. You'd be amazed what he can do with them. Do you have green fingers, Ethelred?'

My eye caught Elsie's at the far end of the table.

'No,' I said quickly. 'I don't have any sort of fingers at all.'

I turned back to the lady on my left, who had been silently crumbling the remains of her bread roll. 'So, your son is going to be musical, is he? That's terribly interesting.'

◆ ◆ ◆

The detritus of the main course was being inexpertly removed from the table, when Robert Muntham got unsteadily to his feet and tapped a wine glass. We all turned from our respective conversations and looked towards him, perhaps with varying expectations as to what sort of entertainment we were to receive. Annabelle's face showed some surprise, as if a speech at this stage had not been planned. Scott's mother seemed mildly put out that her account of her son's development had been interrupted. Colin McIntosh was frowning and for a moment I wondered whether he would intervene and make his own announcement—then he sank back into his chair in a resigned way. But, for the most part, the guests showed nothing more than mild curiosity.

'Although Annabelle and I moved into Muntham Court some months ago,' Robert began, 'this is a kind of house-warming. It is the first time we have had a group of close friends sitting here in our modest little dining room. Nor are you a random selection. Each of you has a very special place in my life and I wanted each of you to be here for this very special evening—an evening that, I am confident in saying, none of you will forget.'

'Will there be fireworks?' called Clive, who had clearly relaxed a little under the influence of the wine.

There was a brief ripple of laughter—but there was still a strange tension in the air. It isn't just hindsight—even at that point I knew something wasn't quite as it should be. Something was about to go badly wrong.

'Fireworks?' asked Robert. 'Of a sort, maybe. For the moment, however, I merely wish to drink the health of everyone here round the table.'

He smiled at us with a sincerity that was almost malevolent, and then slowly raised his glass. 'To my chums!' We drank and for a moment that appeared to be that. Robert was swaying slightly on his feet and I thought he was about to sit down when he straightened himself and added: 'Yes, fireworks, Clive. Not a bad metaphor for life really. One glorious burst of colour, then you slip to the ground, burnt out and unnoticed. It's nothing at all, really. Nothing at all. Now if you will excuse me for a moment, I just need to go off into the next room.'

He bowed to us all, walked briskly to the door and vanished from sight.

I turned to Annabelle, hoping for some further explanation but she was already starting to address the room more generally. She looked round the table and gave a funny little laugh. 'Let me say, I have no idea at all what that was about. I would suggest that you talk amongst yourselves until Robert returns with whatever surprise he has cooked up—and for which I take no responsibility whatsoever.'

There was a burst of laughter—the sort of laughter that indicates relief rather than amusement—at this last remark, and the conversation started up again; but I noticed that Annabelle took little part in it and looked anxiously towards the door from time to time. Once she left and then returned a few minutes later, having presumably given instructions to the kitchen to delay the next course.

'Well,' she said, when a good quarter of an hour had elapsed without Robert reappearing. 'I have no idea what has happened to my husband, but rather than make you all sit here with no dessert, would anyone like a quick tour of the ground floor?'

Elsie, Fiona, Felicity and the lady on my left all immediately showed some enthusiasm for this.

'Very well,' said Annabelle, 'a tour for the ladies then.' She stood up suddenly, as though keen to begin. Colin had one hand on the wine bottle, a venerable magnum of red that had appeared on the table during the second course. He seemed to be turning it carefully so that Annabelle would not see the label. He hesitated and then shook his head in response to the question.

'What about Amanda?' said Felicity Hooper, turning to me. 'I think that Amanda here should certainly join the ladies.'

Since most of those present did not know all or any of my pen-names, this caused puzzled glances in my direction. I felt that I was being got at, but did my best to smile.

'Thanks, I'll stay here,' I said. 'The wine is very good.'

'But our little group of ladies would not be complete without you,' said Felicity.

'I'm fine,' I said in a way I still hoped showed as little irritation as possible. 'Thanks, Felicity, I'm very happy as I am.'

'Maybe the boys would like to come too?' Annabelle had paused halfway to the door. She was keen to be gone and wanted to cut through whatever Felicity's little game was and get on with things.

'Oh, all right,' said Colin with a yawn. 'Just to keep you company. We're not as nosy as you girls, but I suppose it would be good to stretch our legs.'

'So, the men will join us,' said Annabelle, her hand now on the door handle. 'Let's go then.'

'Except Ethelred, obviously,' said Felicity, 'since he has made it clear he prefers his wine to our company.'

'That wasn't what I meant, but never mind,' I said. I stretched across the table and poured myself a glass from the magnum. Though we had drunk a lot of it, the bottle still felt promisingly heavy.

'I think I'll stay too,' said Elsie.

'Whatever you wish,' said Annabelle, giving the door handle an impatient twist. 'The tour will commence straight away with whomsoever would like to join me.'

I heard her footsteps proceeding rapidly down the corridor. The other guests followed at their own pace in ones and twos, Colin and Fiona topping up their glasses before they went. Thus Elsie and I found ourselves alone in the cavernous dining room.

Elsie wandered round the table and flopped down next to me in Annabelle's chair.

'Is Felicity an old friend of yours?' she enquired.

'Friend? Apparently not,' I said. 'I've no idea what I've done to annoy her either. Go and join the rest if you want, I'm fine.'

'One house is much like another,' she said.

I drank my wine thoughtfully. I wasn't sure what it was, but it was remarkably good. I tried to remember if I had ever had better. Surely it deserved to have been decanted? Elsie looked out of the window at whatever could be seen in the fading light. I was suddenly aware that the summer was almost at an end. Colder days and darker evenings would soon be with us. For a while neither of us said anything. Somewhere a long way off we could hear a clock ticking. The quarter-hour chimed.

'Pretty quiet evening,' Elsie observed.

It was at that point that we heard feet approaching rapidly over a tiled floor. Annabelle burst into the room.

'Ethelred,' she said. 'Thank goodness you're still here. Come quickly! Something terrible has just happened...'

Chapter Four

So, it wasn't that dull an evening·after all—dagger in the ballroom was my best guess at that point, which shows how wrong even I can be sometimes.

Of course, there were things we should have spotted even at that stage, but Ethelred is not the most observant of people, as you will have already gathered from his narrative. Later—much later—back in his flat, I was able to fill him in on a number of things as I replayed the events of the evening.

Let's take you back an hour or two...

Ethelred kindly drove me to Muntham Court. I tried to dissuade him, but he insisted. He obviously didn't want me to ruin a perfectly good pair of Manolos just to get a breath of country air—Manolos being expensive and the other thing pretty widely available.

Chez Muntham proved to be one of these pseudo-olde-worlde joints that were put up by the Victorians and that nobody has had time to knock down yet. It had probably had a lucky escape in the fifties or early sixties, when people of taste went around with sledgehammers and wrecking balls. Muntham Court (I do wish to be fair as always) was reasonably big—but there wasn't much else to compensate for its being in the middle of nowhere. It was the sort of place you could get bored in pretty quickly—unless you happened to have the sort of gardener that they did. I caught a glimpse of him, wearing no shirt, but with much else to commend him, wheeling a barrow of garden stuff (don't expect me to be more specific) off into the distance. I wondered whether I could find an excuse to take a turn round the grounds later. I could always carry my shoes and/or get them covered with mud, if it was a good enough cause.

There was a large green car already parked in front of the house, but we appeared to be amongst the first to arrive. We were immediately greeted by some slapper in a blue dress, who had clearly never come across the expression 'mutton dressed as lamb'—though I thought I might usefully acquaint her with the phrase as the evening went by. She certainly didn't look like somebody who'd have a husband called 'Shagger.'

'Ethelred,' said Mrs Shagger, latching onto him as if he were a two-for-one offer at Lidl. 'It's so sweet of you to come. And this must be Elise?'

I am not, and have no plans to be, any type of Elise. I mentioned this in passing.

'Elsie, of course,' said the slapper. 'And you must call me Annabelle.'

She smiled in a way that threatened to crack her make-up, rock solid though it was, and we proceeded through a number of large and unnecessary rooms into a refuge for moth-eaten palm trees. It was set out for drinks, but we were the only drinkers so far. Well, it was still early doors.

'Now, Elise…'

'Elsie.'

'…a spot of champagne?'

'Lemonade,' I said. I do sometimes drink champagne, but not the cheap stuff I reckoned might be on offer.

'And you, Ethelred?'

The way he'd been looking at her since he came in, I would have thought anything served up in a doggy bowl would have been fine with Ethelred, as long as it came from her fair hands and was accompanied by a pat on the head and a scratch behind the ears.

'Whisky, please, Annabelle,' he simpered. There was a real and present danger that he was going to roll over on the floor to have his tummy tickled.

She used the drink order as an excuse to manhandle him again. 'You boys and your whisky,' she said, giving his arm an affectionate squeeze.

Drinks were served while Annabelle apologized for Shagger's absence and I offered a little helpful advice on interior decoration. She took it well, I thought. When she had gone, I offered Ethelred advice of a more general nature.

'Could you get your eyes to stop following her every movement like some lovesick puppy? Just for a moment, at least? And could you kindly kick her hard every time she calls me "Elise"?'

'I don't know what you mean,' he said.

'Yes, you do. Who does she remind you of?'

'Annabelle? She reminds me of nobody in particular.'

Of course, Ethelred's problem was that he'd been married to Geraldine for years, without discovering anything important about her—like the names and addresses of her various lovers, for example.

This took us onto the subject of Mr and Mrs Shagger (as Ethelred was keen I should not address them). I've given up trying to work out why people end up married to other people, other than to guess that it's done by some rather vindictive random number generator. Based on my other friends, they were no more unlikely a combination than most and, to be fair, at that point my knowledge of Shagger himself was limited to what Ethelred had told me. But why would any sensible man hitch up with a blatant gold-digger, ten years younger than himself, with long legs and a surgically enhanced chest? If I ever meet a sensible man, I'm going to ask him, but in the meantime it will have to remain a mystery.

It was round about that point that Colin and Fiona McIntosh arrived. I have to say that I took an instant liking to them. Neither of them looked as though they had spent more than five minutes getting ready for the evening's bash—including locating the dinner jacket at the bottom of the wardrobe and the dress trousers (for all I know) in the garden shed. They rubbished their hosts' champagne, confirming my suspicions, and then helped themselves to anything liquid they could find in the largest glasses on the premises. They were good people, though they too did not quite match my image of Sir Shagger Muntham, the eminent financier, and his circle.

Fortunately Shagger himself now made an appearance. My immediate impression was of somebody who had spent many years dining well and might now have an inkling that the bill was on its way. He was tall, a bit like Ethelred; but (though I wasn't planning to tell any crime writers this) he looked about ten years older than Ethelred, which didn't quite fit with their being drinking buddies at university. Either Shagger had been an old undergraduate, or he'd packed in a few extra years somehow since graduating. He also seemed to have lost weight, but not in a good way. His evening dress—smart enough in other respects, with impeccable creases in the trousers—just seemed a touch loose on him. His cheeks were just a trifle sunken. He was just a bit list-less. I don't know if you read much poetry but, frankly, if you had put him beside a lake from which the sedge had recently withered, he'd have been a dead ringer for Keats's palely loitering knight-at-arms—and that guy, as you'll be aware, was deeply in the shit. No, Shagger didn't look a well man. Maybe it was simply that Mrs Shagger had put him on a diet. I've sometimes thought I might like to lose the odd pound or two myself, but not at that sort of cost.

He had with him (other than his wife, who did not look happy) a rather hunky individual named Clive. Though his hair was distinctly thinning, he still had more than a little youthful charm. Clive remained somewhat in the background as we all introduced ourselves.

I remembered that I was not to address Sir Robert as 'Shagger'. 'Good to meet you,' I said. 'Shame we missed you when we arrived.'

'Yes, sorry about that,' said Shagger.

I asked whether we would get a chance to look round the joint later. Shagger thought we might, though he was not to know under what circumstances and roughly how dead he would be at the time.

I said I thought that would be super.

I turned to Colin and Fiona and established he was a doctor—Shagger's own doctor, as it happened.

'He doesn't look well to me,' I said.

Colin smiled, as if to say that wasn't something he could discuss with a total stranger, which (or are doctors taught how to double bluff?) probably meant it was pretty damned serious.

Fiona turned out to be a surgeon, making them one of these all-medical couples that you run into from time to time.

Then a familiar name was mentioned off to my right.

'Felicity Hooper?' asked Fiona, overhearing the same remark.

Ah, yes, I thought, Felicity Hooper—successful novelist but not represented by me in any way, shape or form. Years ago I had sent her a brief letter to let her know that, much though I loved the manuscript that she had chosen to share with me, I did not feel able to devote sufficient time at present to placing her novel and that possibly she might be better represented by some other etc. etc. etc. The reason I remembered Hooper was that she was one of those people who fail to spot an outright rejection and write back to explain why you and they are soulmates. It was on the fourth attempt that I finally shook her off, by which time I was explaining myself much more clearly. I'm told that one of her later books featured an obnoxious midget literary agent called Elise. Fair enough: it's a crap name, as I've already said.

The McIntoshes had never read any of Felicity Hooper's books. I proceeded to rubbish them, even though I'd only read the first half of the first one. As an agent you are permitted to do this.

I was just getting nicely into my stride when we were interrupted. 'So, this is where you all are!' exclaimed a frumpy individual standing by the door. Not everyone has my dress sense, of course, but this dame had either gone to her mother's wardrobe by mistake or thought that this was a fancy dress party. I sniffed the air but unexpectedly could not detect the odour of mothballs. I could have given her a few helpful tips on the fashion front. In spite of her blatant lack of dress sense the party seemed cowed rather than amused—possibly because it had taken no more than ten seconds for her to make it clear she looked down on everyone in the room. It was interesting to see how Mrs Shagger immediately sucked up to her. 'Felicity! How lovely to see you,' she said. (She did not speak for most of us in this respect.)

So, this was Felicity Hooper, then. The newcomer at this point launched into a general tirade about other people's bad manners, not greeting people at the door, lack of security, allowing terrorists to roam unchecked around the conservatory, hall and library, where we could all be murdered with daggers, ropes, lead piping etc.

Shagger shut her up with gin (it's not just babies you can feed it to) and her complaints were reduced by a few decibels. Annabelle then grabbed her firmly and disposed of her by introducing her to Ethelred—a mean trick, but I'd have done the same. I saw him grimace and heard him politely enquire after her sales figures.

'So, do you live round here?' I asked the McIntoshes, who had refilled their glasses fairly lavishly under cover of Hooper's entrance.

'No, we drove down from Clapham,' said Colin. 'This is our first visit to Findon. The invitation came a bit out of the blue, really. We were supposed to be at a College of Surgeons' dinner tonight, but we thought it would be more fun to see Robert pretending to be lord of the manor.'

'They fill your glass a bit more often at the RCS,' muttered Fiona.

'Say what you like about surgeons,' said Colin, 'but they do still know how to drink.'

'So did Robert before he married *her*,' said Fiona. 'I hope Robert's looking after the wine at dinner—both in terms of the quality and the quantity.'

'Do you think he's got any money left for wine after buying this place?' asked Colin.

It was at this point that the last couple arrived. In the ensuing introductions, and reshuffling of the pack of guests, I found myself back with Ethelred and La Hooper. She was complaining about crime in general.

'It merely shows,' she said, 'what a ridiculous genre crime is. It is exactly like *Cluedo*. Six or seven stock suspects, all with a motive and, strangely, an opportunity. Then you put them all together in a country house somewhere, with a convenient excuse as to why the police cannot investigate the murder themselves.'

That is, obviously, fair comment, but not the sort of thing you should say to a crime writer, unless you are their agent and contractually obliged to be ruthlessly honest. Hooper was being unpleasant on a purely amateur basis, which I rather resented. I suddenly realized who it would be good to see murdered tonight, though the chances of it actually happening were quite slim.

Ethelred in the meantime was defending crime writers in general. He wasn't making too good a job of it, so I introduced myself, just to see if La Hooper remembered me.

'Elsie Thirkettle. Literary agent. I turned down your first book. It was crap.' Well, that should give her a clue.

Then they did this gong thing to tell us dinner was ready in some remote corner of the house. And, each with our own thoughts on the evening so far, we all set off on our expedition to find the dining room.

><((º> ><((º> ><((º>

Annabelle had sat me next to Robert at one end of the table. Ethelred was at the far end, next to the gold-digger herself. 'I don't think we've been introduced yet,' I said to the man on my left, as soup was randomly allocated to guests by the village idiot in a borrowed jacket.

My neighbour was giving his full attention to protecting his trousers but he found time to reply: 'Gerald Smith. Blast.'

I offered him my napkin to mop up some of the soup that was now such a noticeable feature of his evening wear. He dabbed silently at his cuff for a bit and then glanced quickly up the table to check that the soup man was not on his way back. Gerald didn't look like somebody who could take a joke, especially one that entailed being served soup by a comedy waiter. So it wasn't really his sort of evening.

'I'm Robert's solicitor,' Gerald said eventually. 'And you are...'

'Elsie Thirkettle,' I said. 'Agent to the writer of fine but underrated literature seated at the other end of the table and currently talking to your wife.'

'She'll be filling him in on Scott, no doubt,' said Gerald, without enthusiasm.

'Sir Walter?'

'No, our son Scott. He's just eighteen months.'

'And doubtless has his father's nose, his mother's eyes and so on.' I'm not really into juveniles, but I know that this is what parents like to hear—doubtless it reassures the fathers no end.

'It would be surprising if he had,' said Gerald. 'He's adopted, you see. Jane wasn't able...we weren't able to have children of our own. So, in the end, we adopted. Scott.'

I nodded. I've never quite seen the point of children, so it is doubly a mystery to me why anyone should want to introduce a completely unrelated humanoid into their household to crap on the Axminster, but each to his (or her) own.

'That's good,' I said, trying to appear sincere.

'Yes,' he said. But he too didn't seem as sure as he should have been, and the conversation lapsed once again.

I checked out the other end of the table, where Ethelred was paying rather too much attention to his hostess's reconstructed frontage. She leaned forwards in a way that seemed to me to go beyond mere flirtation.

'Are they very big?' I heard Ethelred ask.

It seemed an unnecessary question.

'Bloody good wine,' I heard Colin say.

I turned to see Shagger putting a finger to his lips. Annabelle presumably was unaware of this particular extravagance. Shagger noticed my glance and gave me a wink before calling the village idiot over for a whispered conversation.

Reluctantly I turned my attention back to Gerald. 'Is Jane a solicitor too?'

'No, she's a full-time mother,' he said. Again, did I detect a lack of enthusiasm for this career choice? 'She used to work in a bank.'

'Like Robert?'

'Same bank. She used to be Robert's secretary.'

'I see,' I said.

I finally caught Ethelred's eye and he turned immediately to the less dangerous charms of Jane Smith.

'We've got a very good gardener, here,' said Shagger, over to my right, as though he had suddenly been reminded of the fact. 'Acres of gardens of course. You need somebody full-time. He's called John O'Brian. I don't know where Annabelle found him, but she reckons he's very good.'

'Is that the guy I saw earlier?' I asked. 'Lots of muscle, not much shirt, good firm bum?'

'Yes,' said Shagger. Like Gerald Smith, he seemed to harbour some secret sorrow this evening. 'Yes, that's the chappie.'

'Do you do much gardening yourself?'

'No, I leave that to John. Annabelle spends a certain amount of time overseeing John's work. She has a lot of fun in the garden, she tells me. Are you all right?'

Some of my soup had gone down the wrong way. Gerald patted me on the back.

'No, I'm fine,' I said, but changed the subject away from gardening to avoid any repeat performance. Obviously, if I employed somebody like John O'Brian, I wouldn't have wasted him on mulching the rose bushes either, but I suspected Annabelle might be in breach of the Working Time Directive.

I looked across the table at Clive Brent, who in turn was casting furtive glances in Annabelle's direction. She caught his eye once and then frowned and turned away. What was that all about? Robert was fortunately now deep in conversation with

Fiona McIntosh, but the air, frankly, was getting electric with intrigue and suppressed desire.

✦ ✦ ✦

We were well into the various courses when Robert stood up and tapped a glass for silence.

I don't know what sort of speech the others were expecting. Most of the party was, by this stage, fairly drunk, the wine having flowed more freely than Colin had predicted. There had been a brief and almost imperceptible contretemps between Mr and Mrs Shagger, when the village idiot had produced a big, cobwebby bottle of red and Mrs S had waved him away, only for Mr S to wave him back again. This obviously confused the village idiot, who had stood there, not unlike Balaam's Ass, until Shagger took the heavy bottle from him by force and went round the table pouring drinks. Mrs S ostentatiously declined. Anyway, having stuck to lemonade, I was probably the only member of the party who was entirely sober when Robert scraped back his chair and began to address us.

He explained that he and the gold-digger intended this as some sort of house-warming and that we were a specially selected group of chums. I wondered briefly whether Shagger had slept with all the women and his wife with all the men—but that would have ruled me (and Ethelred) out, so possibly not. I got the impression he might be drunk enough not to hold back on little details of that sort, so I continued to listen with interest.

'Will there be fireworks?' asked Clive.

'Fireworks? Of a sort, maybe. For the moment, however, I merely wish to drink the health of everyone here round the table.'

So, nine of us drank each other's health in wine, one in lemonade. Robert burbled on a bit longer and then, quite abruptly, took his leave.

I'd had a chance to watch Annabelle's face during all of this, and it had changed from mild puzzlement to genuine concern. Whatever Robert had in mind, she had not been let in on it. On the other hand he might have just gone to the loo. It was reaching the stage in the evening when a number of bladders were realizing that they were not as young as they once had been.

We talked amongst ourselves for a bit. Annabelle left and came back. Felicity was the next to depart, and returned complaining that the facilities were almost impossible to find. Gerald and Jane made a family outing of the same trip, which also took some time. They came back separately, having mislaid each other in the labyrinthine corridors of Muntham Court. In the meantime Fiona McIntosh had also excused herself.

A good fifteen, maybe twenty, minutes had elapsed when Mrs Shagger's patience finally wore out and she suggested that, since Robert had deserted us, we should take the opportunity of touring the ground floor with her to admire the various treasures, and so on and so forth, that Muntham Court had to offer.

Everyone decided to go except Ethelred, who seemed to have had a row of some sort with Felicity Hooper. So I stayed back with him and the others departed. Annabelle went with the Smiths and Felicity Hooper, then Clive Brent drifted out on his own, followed by the McIntoshes, each clutching a glass.

Ethelred was morose and untalkative. I was wondering whether I shouldn't after all go for a wander round, when I noticed John O'Brian, wheeling his now-empty barrow in the very last of the fading light, back to wherever barrows get put when darkness falls. He disappeared round a hedge and was, sadly, lost to sight.

I was just wondering how soon I could get Ethelred to drive me home, when Annabelle returned and announced Shagger had kicked the bucket.

◄ ◄ ◄

Fair enough. It was only later that things started to get *really* interesting.

Chapter Five

So, then there was one.

Annabelle had whisked Ethelred off with her, leaving me alone at the table. Since all the action was clearly going on elsewhere, I wandered out into the corridor.

The weird thing was that people were obviously rushing around in a blind panic elsewhere, but here all was silence and calm. I could hear the ticking of a large clock somewhere nearby, but that was all. I decided to go left, but all of the oak panelling looked much the same. I wasn't sure if I was heading for the front door or the kitchen. Like I say, it was a reasonably big house.

Then I turned a corner and collided with Clive Brent, who was hurrying in the opposite direction.

'Do you know where the others are?' I asked.

'Others?' he said.

'The other guests. You all cleared off, then Annabelle came back saying something had happened to Robert.'

'Robert?'

He wasn't really being much use. I wondered if I should give him a good shake and start again. It works with Ethelred sometimes.

'Haven't you been with the others?' I asked.

He gave me a guilty look. 'No—I sort of lost them,' he said. 'I was…looking around.'

Then I heard a voice in the distance yelling: 'Robert!'

'Let's go that way,' I said, pointing in the direction of the distance. Another couple of turns of the corridor took us to a little gaggle of people in evening dress, standing on what was clearly the wrong side of an oak door. They looked worried.

'Robert!' Colin was calling through the keyhole.

'Has he moved?' asked Gerald.

This seemed to be an ongoing conversation, because Colin just shook his head briefly. 'All just as before. Maybe...how much had he had to drink?'

'What's Annabelle doing?' asked Felicity in an irritated manner. 'Surely she's got round to the window by now? It's ridiculous that a key can't be found.'

'I should have gone with her,' said Colin. 'I said that at the time.'

'She's got Ethelred with her,' I said.

They all turned and looked at me at this point. Felicity said: 'Fat lot of good he'll be.'

'You should have gone with Annabelle,' said Fiona.

'I said that at the time,' said Colin.

'Did you?' said Fiona.

'Did I what?' asked Colin.

Yes, in a crisis, this was precisely the conversation we were having. We were, frankly, a total shower and (with one exception) all drunk enough to believe that we alone had the solution.

'Somebody should phone for an ambulance now,' said Felicity. 'This is getting ridiculous.'

'There's a doctor here already,' said Fiona, slurring her words only slightly. 'Two actually.'

'No, somebody phone,' said Colin, still kneeling by the door. 'He must have had a heart attack or something. And if Annabelle doesn't appear in a moment, I'm breaking the door down.'

'That's a pretty solid door,' said Clive, studying it for the first time.

'There must be something we could use as a battering ram,' said Colin. 'Somebody should go and look for an oak bench.'

That Muntham Court might contain an oak bench was a reasonable theory, but nobody seemed capable of carrying out the necessary empirical research. Gerald glanced around vaguely as though a bench might suddenly appear. If Robert wanted manly action, he had wined and dined us a little too well.

'How long have you been here?' I asked.

'Just arrived,' said Colin. 'We sort of got lost. But Annabelle and the others must have been here for five minutes or so.'

'We were being shown round,' said Jane, slightly diffidently. 'We got lost, too, then we found Annabelle here outside the library. She tried the door, but it was locked, so we knocked, obviously. When nobody opened it, we looked through the keyhole. Robert's in there, but slumped over his desk. Annabelle said that the quickest thing was to break in through one of the windows.'

'Is anyone calling an ambulance?' asked Colin.

'I'm onto it,' said Fiona, tapping numbers into her mobile. 'Damn—this is a whole lot easier when you're sober,' she added. She tried 999 again, but this time very slowly.

'Let's smash the door down then,' said Clive, with a confidence that marked him out as the drunkest of the party. The oak bench had not appeared, but he was still up for it—a shoulder charge against a solid oak door obviously seemed to Clive both prudent and likely to be effective.

It was perhaps as well that, at that very moment, we heard the sound of breaking glass somewhere inside the room.

'That could be the cavalry arriving,' said Clive, with more than a trace of disappointment in his voice. The chance to kick a door in comes rarely to most people.

'I can see two figures at the window,' said Colin, who had refused to give up his vantage point by the keyhole. 'One of them has got the window open and is climbing in—that's Ethelred. Good man. Now Annabelle's in.'

'Ambulance on its way,' said Fiona, snapping her phone closed, 'but it's likely to be ten minutes or so.'

'Excellent work all round,' said Colin.

'What on earth are they doing?' asked Felicity. 'They need to get this door open *fast*.'

'Annabelle's over by the desk with Robert,' Colin reported. 'Can't see what she's doing exactly. Ethelred's heading this way.'

And finally, after the metallic rasping noise of bolts being pulled back, the door opened. We all pushed past Ethelred and stood in a sort of loose circle round the desk looking at Robert.

Then we all rather wished we hadn't. Colin and Fiona asked us all to give them space while they tried resuscitation, and we were happy to give it to them. But they didn't look that hopeful.

Strangled. With the rope. In the library.

Chapter Six

It all happened so quickly.

When Annabelle hurried me out of the dining room, leaving Elsie behind, I was not quite sure where we were going—only that we needed to get there fast.

I was led at a brisk trot out of the front door and round the side of the house. It was now almost dark and I stumbled once or twice on the uneven surface. There were rose bushes under the windows, which snagged my trousers at least once as we squeezed between them—but there was no time to check for possible damage. We stopped on the soft earth, by a tall, well-lit window. The interior of the library could be seen clearly—the book-lined walls, the armchairs, the large antique globe and, in the centre of it all, Robert slumped, face down, on his desk, as though he had pitched forward in the middle of writing something.

I tried pushing the window, but it wouldn't budge. It had been securely fastened from inside.

'We'll have to break the glass,' said Annabelle. She handed me a large flint; this was, in her view, quite clearly Men's Work.

It was an iron casement window with leaded panes. That we should not break windows is something so firmly instilled in us from childhood that I paused for a moment, flint in hand, before striking the centre of the pane closest to the latch. I felt a brief moment of exhilaration as I heard the glass fracture and fall inwards. I knocked away some of the jagged fragments still clinging to the lead beading, then gingerly put my fingers through, opened the window and hauled myself in.

'Give me a hand,' ordered Annabelle. 'I can hardly be expected to climb up there in this dress unaided.' I quickly apologized and pulled her in after me.

We stood for a moment by the window, my hand still holding Annabelle's. Robert had not stirred at all. In the still-ness of the library, there was no sound of breathing, no rhythmic movement of Robert's back as his lungs drew breath. It was not looking good. We glanced at each other, then at Robert, lying face down, a whisky glass beside him, his favourite pen neatly capped and lying beside the blotter on the vast mahogany desk. There was something odd about his neck, but I couldn't immediately see what. While I was still wondering what to do, Annabelle took charge.

'Let Colin in,' she said, relinquishing my hand and heading towards Robert.

The door was not in fact locked, but was bolted at the top and bottom. The bolts were stiff and it took me a few seconds to push them back. Once I did, and the door had swung open, the rest of the dinner party surged past me. At the same moment I heard Annabelle behind me give a gasp and turned to see her, white-faced, looking helplessly in my direction. I looked again at Robert and now saw what had been odd about his neck. A thin cord had been wound several times around it and then tight-ened by means of a pencil, inserted into the cord and twisted. Fortunately at this point Colin and Fiona took over. Fiona untied the ligature and together they lowered Robert to the floor. Colin checked Robert's pulse, then listened to his chest.

'No signs of life at all,' he muttered. 'How long since we called for the ambulance?'

'Two or three minutes,' said Fiona.

'How long do you think he's been lying here?'

'Ten minutes? Could be twenty—absolute max.' They looked at each other doubtfully.

'If it's twenty...shit...OK, we'll try CPR anyway,' said Colin.

But even before the ambulance arrived, it was clear that this was going to be a murder inquiry. If any guests had plans to go home early, they were going to have to cancel them.

>+< >+< >+<

The police interviewed us one by one. While awaiting our turn, I sat in one corner of the conservatory with Elsie. She had consented on this occasion to drink brandy.

'How's Lady Muntham taking it?' she asked. That she did not call her Mrs Shagger spoke volumes. We were all in a state of shock.

'Clive Brent and the McIntoshes are looking after her,' I said. 'I think Colin's given her a sedative.'

Elsie nodded. 'It's all a bit of a puzzle though, isn't it?'

'That's what I was thinking. The door was very firmly bolted. I had to break a window to get in. It would have been easy enough for a murderer to get into Muntham Court—doors have been wide open most of the evening. Somebody could have hidden until Robert went to the library and then gone in after him. But how did they lock everything up afterwards? It's a classic puzzle—a man dead in a locked room.'

'And the answer is?'

'Suicide or a very ingenious murderer,' I said.

'Not suicide,' said Elsie. 'You can't strangle yourself. You'd pass out before you could do any permanent damage. It has to be murder and it has to be one of the guests. I reckon there must have been fifteen to twenty minutes between Robert leaving the room and our finding the body. During that time Annabelle, the Hooper woman and the Smiths left the room for five minutes or so. I think Fiona McIntosh did as well. Clive Brent claims he got lost during the tour. Then both McIntoshes were out of sight of the main party for a while.'

'I'd be careful what you say to the police,' I said. 'I think you'll find they'd prefer you to stick to the facts. All we know is that Robert was found strangled in a locked room. And, as for it being one of the guests, it would have been very easy for anybody to break in while we were at dinner...'

By the time the police got to me, they had already put together an account of the evening and I could add almost nothing to what they knew. Early on, we had all agreed, it would have been straightforward for an intruder to enter Muntham Court and hide in the library or close by. Doors and windows had been left open with staggering generosity. Robert's speech, with hindsight, was regarded by everyone as a little odd, but nobody could put their finger on why. The time between Robert leaving the room and the discovery of the body was adequate for a killer to strike. Meanwhile, all of the guests had been out of sight of the others at least briefly. In addition to the guests, there had been two members of staff at Muntham Court that evening. Diana Michie, the housekeeper, had been in the kitchen. The idiot boy proved to be called Dave Peart. He was precisely what he had appeared to be—the assistant gardener, pressed into service as a kitchen assistant and waiter. The gardener himself, John O'Brian, had been working late, but had not been seen inside the house by anyone— when the police arrived he had already gone home, apparently unaware that anything unusual had happened. Gillian Maggs, the cleaner, had finished her work that afternoon and had left hours before the guests arrived. That might have given the police some sort of shortlist but, bearing in mind the general level of security at Muntham Court, half the population of Sussex (East and West) had had the opportunity to murder Robert. The problem was how any of them—guests, staff or casual intruders—could have got out of a room that had clearly been locked from the inside.

◆ ◆ ◆

I suppose it must have been around three o'clock when I decided that nobody could reasonably object if I stretched my legs in the garden, and I opened the front door to be surprised (as one always is slightly surprised) by the bracing chill of a late-summer night. It brought back memories of other times when I had been awake at this hour at this time of year—usually early-morning journeys to the airport with Geraldine, driving down to Gatwick to board charter flights leaving for Alicante or Goa or wherever she had decided we should go that year. The clean freshness of the air and the silence recalled past nights, past relationships, past departures. At the moment, however, nobody was going anywhere. My car was still parked for the quick getaway that Elsie had planned, should the evening prove dull. The once-clear path was however now blocked by a police car and a van, beside which there were, for some reason, two portable floodlights, their dormant cables coiled round their bases. There was also a pile of what appeared to be plastic sheeting. I wondered if I should take notes for my next book. Probably not. These things were easy enough to make up.

The official investigation was still proceeding somewhere inside Muntham Court, and I could be doing no possible harm admiring the stars from where I was, but a vague feeling that I should not be there made me wander round to the side of the house. It would be good to sit on a bench for a few minutes, away from other people, to gather my thoughts. A bench was there, but somebody else had had much the same idea. A hatless policeman was already lounging on it, the red tip of an illicit smoke glowing in the dark. On hearing my approach he started to his feet, his cupped hand poised to lob the offending butt into the bushes. He saw me and dropped back onto his seat, the cigarette still in place. He should probably have looked the guiltier of the two of us—nobody had actually told me that I couldn't leave the house, but he was almost certainly forbidden to smoke on duty. He simply smiled, however, and nodded.

'Nice evening, Joe,' I said.

'Almost morning, Ethelred,' he replied.

We had met before. A little late in my career as an author of police procedurals I had taken to consulting my local police station on points of detail. He had recently briefed me, over coffee, about scene-of-crime investigations. The plume of smoke that he calmly exhaled suggested that he thought I owed him one—at the very least that I would not dare mention this to his inspector.

'Did you know Mr Muntham well?' he asked me.

'Sir Robert Muntham,' I said. 'I'd known him a long time. I'm not sure I knew him well.'

'Very sad, anyway. I mean, sad that he decided to kill himself. It's a bit like that Simon and Garfunkel song. You know the one...'

'"Richard Cory"?' I looked at the policeman. I hadn't got him down as a Simon and Garfunkel fan. I adjusted his age upwards a few years. 'Interestingly, the song was based on an earlier poem by Edwin Arlington Robinson.'

'Who?' he said.

Well, *I* had thought that it was interesting anyway.

'It's odd though,' he continued. 'Mr Muntham had everything, didn't he? Money, a title, this place...And yet he chose to end it all.'

'Are you saying it must have been suicide?' I asked. 'Is that what Lady Muntham has been told?'

'Of course, the investigations aren't complete. You obviously shouldn't repeat what I've just said...'

'No,' I said.

He turned away and deftly flicked the remains of the cigarette onto the lawn, where it remained glowing for another minute or so. We watched it until the last small dot of red faded to nothing.

'I'd probably best be getting back,' he said at length. 'Good to see you again, Ethelred.'

'Good to see you, Joe,' I said.

◄══ ◄══ ◄══

The first hint of dawn was already in the sky when we were finally told we might leave. Felicity Hooper, the McIntoshes and the Smiths elected to stay on in various corners of

Muntham Court. Elsie consented to walk back, in the light of the amount of brandy we had both consumed. Clive Brent came to her rescue, however, and offered us both a lift back into the village. He proved to be the owner of the green Jaguar. We sank back gratefully into the deep leather upholstery, and nobody mentioned carbon emissions.

Elsie insisted on a cup of hot chocolate before wandering off to occupy my bed. Just as the village was waking up and going about its business, I finally fell asleep on the sofa.

I seemed to have dozed only for a few minutes when I opened my eyes and saw Elsie sitting in front of me, drinking coffee.

'I thought you were awake,' she said cheerfully.

'You've just woken me,' I said.

'I was right then.' She took a big slurp of coffee.

'Don't you need to sleep?' I asked.

'No,' she said. 'The post has arrived. It looked interesting.'

'I doubt that. It will just be bills and junk mail,' I said, sitting up and taking the bundle from her. 'You could have opened any of it, if you were curious—just so long as it prevented your waking me up.'

'I'm glad you said that,' she said, producing an opened envelope. 'You might like to read this one yourself then. It's from your dead mate, Shagger. And he's asking for your help.'

Chapter Seven

D*ear Ethelred,*
Without beating about the bush too much, there are two possibilities.
If nothing out of the ordinary has happened in the past few days, then
destroy this letter and forget you ever received it. If conversely you
have noticed anything untoward (and you'll know if you have) then
a second message awaits you and I will sadly not be able to deliver it
personally. You will find it in my library at Muntham Court, in the
middle right-hand drawer of my desk amongst the stock of envelopes.
It's not addressed to you but you'll recognize it when you see it.

    I am also enclosing a letter to be posted to my solicitor, Gerald
Smith—again only under the circumstances I describe. You can
read it if you wish, but it will look better if you just passed it on
unopened. It's not urgent, but he needs to have it if things go as I
envisage. Sorry to be a bit cryptic. I need to cover all eventualities,
and this currently seems the best way to do it.

    Your old chum
    Shagger

'I suppose,' said Elsie, who had been rereading the letter over my
shoulder, 'you could say that this untoward thing had happened—
from Shagger's point of view it's all gone as untoward as it possibly
could. Hence, we need to retrieve this message from the library. It
would seem Shagger knew somebody was about to bump him off

in an ingenious manner and wanted us to know who it was going to be. That's kind of him, of course, but it all looks a bit tortuous.'

'You could say that,' I said.

'I just did say that,' said Elsie.

I reread the note. It certainly appeared to run contrary to the police theory of suicide—or at least to the police theory as expounded by Joe the previous evening. Perhaps his views were over-influenced by sixties folk-rock.

'I can't just waltz in and ransack the library,' I said, returning to the matter in hand.

'We won't have to. Those instructions are pretty specific. It shouldn't take us that long.'

'Us?' I said.

'You'll obviously need me there,' said Elsie.

I declined to comment on that but did ask where the enclosed letter was. Elsie produced that from the bundle. 'You didn't open that too?' I asked.

'No, I only open *your* mail,' she said, virtuously.

I took the letter and put it in my dressing-gown pocket.

'But you *are* going to open it?' she asked anxiously. 'Shagger more or less says you can.'

'He says he'd prefer me not to.'

'But he says you can if your agent wants to see it.'

'That is not my reading of Robert's letter.'

'Ethelred, could you stop behaving like a total pillock and *open the letter?*'

'No,' I said.

Elsie was clearly beginning to regret her earlier good behaviour.

'In future, I'm going to have all your post steamed open while you sleep,' said the recently virtuous Elsie.

'But, sadly, this time you didn't,' I said.

Elsie sipped her coffee, casting only the occasional glance towards my dressing-gown pocket, then said: 'Anyway, it looks as though Shagger knew who his killer was going to be.'

'Well, he was pretty certain he wasn't going to be around to deliver the message in person.'

'We need to find this second message,' said Elsie thoughtfully.

'And give it to the police,' I said.

'If he'd wanted to alert the police,' said Elsie, 'he'd have written to the police himself. Their contact details are in the phone book. Their cars have blue flashing lights. They are deliberately easy to locate. This is something he wants only *us* to know about—'

'—only *me* to know about,' I corrected her.

Elsie shrugged. 'Same thing,' she said. 'Writers and agents are, legally, a single entity.'

Elsie often used the word 'legally' to cover what would otherwise be quite large gaps in her arguments. This appeared to be a case in point. There was, however, a stronger reason for her not to join me in ransacking the library.

'Don't you have to get back to London?' I asked. 'You said you didn't have time to stay for the Findon Sheep Fair.'

'Most things, Ethelred, take priority over a sheep fair, whatever that is. My return to London will have to be delayed while we ponder this question: How do we get into Shagger's library without exciting attention—particularly the attention of whoever bumped him off?'

The phone rang.

'Ethelred,' said Annabelle, as soon as I had picked up the receiver, 'you have to come over at once. I need you here.'

'I'll be with you in fifteen minutes,' I said.

I put the phone down. Elsie was looking at me pointedly.

'What?' I said.

'Let's hope she gives you a nice dog biscuit when you get there,' she said.

>-< >-< >-<

Although I pointed out to Elsie that, my car still being at Muntham Court, we would have to walk there through the rural mud and mire, she made light of difficulties.

'Yeah, I can manage in these shoes. The road wasn't that bad after all.'

'I think there may have been rain overnight.'

'It should have washed some of the mud away then,' said Elsie.

✦ ✦ ✦

Annabelle was only slightly perturbed to see Elsie.

'Ah, Elise...so very sweet of you to come too. While I'm talking to Ethelred perhaps you would like to—'

'—talk to me too?' suggested Elsie.

'Why not?' Annabelle said, weakly. Things were obviously very bad indeed.

She took us into the conservatory, and sat us down in wicker chairs amongst the spreading palms. The sun was already warm on the large glass panes and the air felt steamy. Perhaps Annabelle thought it was somewhere we would not be disturbed. People were probably breakfasting or indeed (if they had nobody to awaken them) sleeping in one of the house's many bedrooms. I envied them.

'I've just had a call from the police,' she said, with a grimace.

I nodded.

'They think it was suicide,' she whispered.

'Isn't it a little early...' I began, though after last night's conversation, I was not entirely surprised.

'They are saying that it would have been impossible for anyone to have killed Robert and then got out of the room, bolting the door and locking the windows after them. Of course, there'll have to be an inquest, but they've clearly already made up their minds. All the inquest will hear is that anything other than suicide would have been physically impossible.'

'Perhaps it was suicide,' I said. 'After all, who could possibly have wanted to see Robert dead? Certainly none of the guests.'

'Perhaps not one of the guests,' she conceded, 'but an intruder on the other hand...Robert was very careless about security. I was always talking to him about it. But do men listen?'

'No,' said Elsie.

'Have the police looked for signs of an intruder?' I asked.

'They *say* they have. They tramped round the garden at first light, making a mess everywhere, I've no doubt. They've had people in funny boiler suits taking fingerprints and swabs and things in the library. But they'd made up their minds from the start.'

'The police are occasionally right,' I said.

'But it *can't* be suicide,' said Annabelle. 'He wasn't depressed. He wasn't even unhappy, was he? We'd only just got married— well, eighteen months ago. We'd bought this lovely new house. He had me...He wouldn't have killed himself—I know he wouldn't. Ethelred, you saw a lot of him—he talked to you—he wasn't unhappy, was he?'

'No,' I said. Actually, he'd often seemed pretty miserable, but no more so than dozens of other people who were still out there, alive and getting on with their day. Still, what was I to tell Robert's widow? Should I say that he seemed to spend as much time as possible finding plausible ways to delay his return to Muntham Court—even if that meant visiting me?

'I'm not sure how I can help,' I said.

'You're a crime writer,' she said. 'You know all about clues and things. Amateur detectives always manage to spot things the police miss.'

'Not in real life,' I said.

'So, it's all rubbish in your books then?'

'Pretty much,' volunteered Elsie. 'Still, I think we could help you check for clues. Let's start with the library.'

Annabelle looked at her curiously. She seemed naturally suspicious of Elsie's plan and in any case, as it transpired, had a plan of her own. 'Thank you, Elise,' she said after a long pause. 'It would be very useful indeed if *Ethelred* checked the library. There may be...something...that we haven't spotted. I think, however, we might get you to start with the garden.'

Thus it was that I found myself in the library alone.

I have to admit that being alone anywhere in that cavernous, gothic house was slightly spooky. As I entered the library I was sure that I felt the temperature drop a couple of degrees. When I had last been in this room, after all, my friend Robert had been stretched out over that desk with a thin rope wound round his throat.

I searched for any feasible exit, other than the door through which I had just entered or the window by which I had got in last night. I went over and peered up the chimney, but it was of the narrow domestic variety—practical Victorian rather than capacious and romantic Jacobean—and not designed for rapid exits from murder scenes. The chairs were large and comfortable, but not big enough to conceal an assassin of any size. The globe, which I had noticed from outside the room, was a remarkable piece of Victorian artisanship. I checked the outlines of long-dissolved countries—Austria-Hungary, the Ottoman Empire, French West Africa. It had probably come with the house. It didn't seem the sort of thing you would own unless you already possessed a vast library to go with it. I tapped the oak panelling that gave the room its rather gloomy and melancholy character. Most of it sounded hollow, as I guess most panelling does, but my researches revealed nothing of interest. I gave up tapping halfway round and looked again at the window catches to see if there was any way they could be made to fall into place after somebody had made their exit—a piece of thread, say, tied to the catch. The catches were, however, all quite stiff and there was no sign of thread still attached to any of them. There genuinely seemed to be no way in or out of the library other than the obvious ones.

Duty, as it were, done I sat down at Robert's desk in Robert's chair and started opening drawers.

He had said the middle right. It proved, reassuringly, to be full of envelopes and other stationery—all heavy and cream-coloured. I riffled through them all, expecting to find a note tucked between two envelopes, but there was nothing. Robert hadn't wanted anyone to find this by chance. I started again, looking carefully inside each envelope. About halfway through, I found a sheet of plain white A5, folded once and placed in one of the thick, creamy envelopes. As Robert had said, it was not addressed to me, but this was clearly it.

The contents were not remotely what I expected.

What you must seek is not so very far
From Andes hills or Afric slopes, a jar
Will grant the seekers everything they crave
You shall receive where formerly you gave

This was clearly Robert trying to be clever, and succeeding in being incomprehensible. True, anyone stumbling on this by accident would assume he had just copied out a few lines of rather bad poetry from somewhere, if they bothered to assume anything at all about it. And knowing I was looking for clues as to the whereabouts of something, it meant more to me—but unfortunately not as much more as I would have liked. I searched the room again, this time looking for a hiding place for the third clue rather than an exit. I spent some time prodding the globe—especially around South America and the African Rift Valley—but without revealing any secret compartments. I checked the atlas on the bookshelves, being careful to ensure that no slip of paper had been hidden between the African or South American pages. I scoured the room for a tobacco jar, or any other sort of jar, in which further clues might have been placed. The key message was clear—it was not sending me to Africa or South America but was saying that there was a further clue 'not so very far' away—somewhere in the room, or maybe elsewhere in the house, and that it was related in some way to those continents. But where was it? Was Robert just cleverer, after all, than I was? Or was the whole thing in some way a big joke?

I looked again at the desk itself. It was very tidy—Robert's pen still lay parallel to the edge of the desk on the leather-bound blotter, just as he had left it. There were a few books piled on the other side—none were about Africa or South America, but I did go back to the bookshelves and check *Out of Africa* and a couple of books by Sir Richard Burton.

After half an hour or so, I gave up and went to find Elsie and Annabelle.

I had expected to find them in the garden. What I had not expected was the look of triumph on Elsie's face.

Chapter Eight

Playing girl-detectives can be fun, so long as you don't have to play under the direction of some snotty cow, to a set of rules that she is clearly making up as she goes along. Still, anything that gave Ethelred a chance to check out the library uninterrupted...

The slapper and I divided up the garden between us and I wandered up and down, not really knowing what I was looking for, but safe in the knowledge that the police would have already found it if it had been there.

We met again in the middle of the lawn at the extremities of our respective traverses.

'Anything?' I asked.

'Nothing over here,' she said. 'Was there anything in the rose bed under the library window?'

'It looked as if the police had been all over it,' I said. 'Big footprints everywhere. And those roses have vicious thorns. I left it out.'

'Maybe it would be worth double-checking,' said my new playmate.

'OK,' I said. Anything to give Ethelred another few minutes of uninterrupted snooping. As I approached the flower bed I could see him through the library window, tapping the panelling. That wasn't going to get him very far—didn't he know what a drawer looked like? Back to the job in hand anyway.

Working your way between the rose bushes was a real nuisance. They were waist high (on me anyway) and seemed determined to snag everything. Then I got lucky.

On a thorn, at about knee height, was a small scrap of cloth. I knelt down and checked it out. It was navy blue wool. A big enough chunk that you'd have thought its loss had been noticed. And it didn't look as though it had been there that long. I called Annabelle over.

'This could be really important evidence,' she said, frowning. 'We need to photograph it and then remove it with tweezers and put it in a clear bag.'

'Or call the police?' I said.

'No, let's bag the son of a bitch up,' she said.

'OK,' I said. It was her game of amateur detectives, after all.

I went off to the kitchen to find something suitable. When I returned, she was photographing the cloth in situ with her camera. She was taking her game seriously.

'Of course,' I said, tweaking the scrap off the thorn with finger and thumb (no tweezers being immediately available),'this could be from some copper's uniform. You said they were rampant in the roses.'

'No, it's got a red pinstripe running through it,' said Annabelle. 'This isn't a chunk of police trousers.'

I looked more closely. There was a just-discernible hint of a thin red stripe. Annabelle had good eyes.

'The kid who was waiting table last night was wearing blue trousers,' I said. 'I'm sure he was.'

'Was he?' Annabelle looked deeply shocked for a moment and then said: 'No, they were plain blue—I'm sure of it. No red stripe'

'It's not much of a stripe,' I said, looking closer. To be quite honest I'd have missed it, if Annabelle hadn't seen it and pointed it out. It was subtle. Classy even. The cloth had felt soft to the touch too—it must have been an expensive suit that had been ruined in the bushes.

'I'm certain,' said Annabelle. 'None of the guests or staff was wearing anything at all like this.'

I held up the clear bag and squinted at it. 'Odd thing to wear for a murder—navy blue pinstripe.'

'Why?' asked Annabelle.

'Well, you'd think a murderer would wear serviceable black jeans and a black sweater—mask optional. Or they might wear old brown trousers and a green top to look like a walker who had just strayed off the South Downs Way and onto the Muntham estate. Blue pinstripe isn't quite right for casing a joint in the country. You look out of place. People would just say: "What's that merchant banker doing casing the joint?" They'd be onto him like a shot.'

'Let's check round the rhododendron bushes over there,' said Annabelle tetchily.

'Whatever you say,' I replied.

This was less productive from my point of view, but Annabelle quickly called me over.

'Look!' she said triumphantly.

On the ground were a couple of cigarette ends—filter-tips, smoked almost down to the last scrap of tobacco.

'The murderer,' she said, 'must have stood here, smoking, and watching the library window for a chance to break in.'

Even if she was allowed to make up the rules of the game, that seemed to be stretching the evidence to its absolute limits. Still...

'Shall I bag those too?' I asked.

'Absolutely.'

I guessed we were playing at being SOCOs—I'd have to check with Ethelred. I studied the ciggies briefly once they were in the bag. They looked pretty ordinary. They had no lipstick on them, suggesting a man, or maybe a woman who was not wearing lipstick at that precise moment. That ruled out a few people, but not enough to make an arrest.

'What about the gardeners?' I asked.

'Neither of them smokes,' she said. 'At least, I don't think they do.'

'Robert?'

'I didn't allow it.'

'OK, so we're after a chain-smoking merchant banker with a tolerant wife,' I said. 'Sorry,' I added, as Annabelle's look told me I was not taking this as seriously as I should.

Nevertheless, it was something to go on. Somebody had been tiptoeing through the roses not that long ago and somebody had stopped for a couple of crafty cigs in a spot with a good view of the library. And the police had missed both, which was sort of careless of them.

So, when I met up with Ethelred I was feeling quite smug.

My new best friend, Annabelle, went off to make us some coffee and I had a chance to compare notes with Ethelred in the conservatory.

'My professional view is that it's a poem,' I said, handing the sheet of A5 back to him. 'I don't handle poetry. The royalties are rubbish.'

'Robert is trying to tell us something in a deliberately cryptic way. He wanted me to take action only if he was dead. So he tells me that the instructions are here at Muntham Court. If he had still been alive, he could have destroyed this link in the chain and retrieved the letter to his lawyer from me, unopened. Neither I nor anyone else...' he looked pointedly at me at this juncture, '...would have been able to take it any further. Likewise, if anyone had stumbled on this without reading the letter he sent me, they too would have been none the wiser. Somewhere, there's a third note. My guess is that you need all three to make any sense of it and that it would be possible to put all three together only if Robert was dead.'

'One small objection,' I said. 'Why not just write to you and say: "X is going to bump me off—destroy this letter if they don't get round to it"? Or why not just take you aside last night and tell you? How difficult would that have been?'

'I don't know,' he said. He opened the paper up again. 'What does he mean by "not so very far"? What sort of jar gives you everything you crave?'

'A jar full of chocolates. Creamy ones with a fondant centre. Apricot or orange.' I was pretty confident on that one.

'Possibly,' he said. 'I'm not sure Robert necessarily shared your tastes in everything. One of the problems with bad poetry, of course, is that the meaning often gets distorted to suit the metre and the rhyme. "Afric" is clearly only there because it scans better than "African". We could analyse a given word to death, only to discover it was just there for the rhyme.'

Annabelle returned at this point with three steaming mugs on a tray. Ethelred quickly trousered the verse.

'The McIntoshes and Smiths are still here,' she said. 'Ethelred, you should talk to them before they leave. Clive is coming back later today. I'll try to get John O'Brian to come in too.'

Ethelred looked a bit uncertain. We'd got a couple of possible clues but interviewing all the suspects was clearly a complete waste of time.

'Please, Ethelred,' she said. 'I'm depending on you.'

I swallowed my coffee quickly so that I wouldn't spit it all over everyone when Ethelred replied. I braced myself for a really creepy response.

'Of course, Annabelle,' he said. 'I'll do anything I can for you.'

I thought she was going to give him a good scratch under the chin, but she just said: 'You've no idea how grateful I am.'

So was he. Even if she'd entered him for Crufts he couldn't have wagged his dear little tail any harder.

Bless.

Chapter Nine

Elsie was taken away, protesting ineffectually, to conduct further outdoor investigations, and the McIntoshes came to talk to me amongst the palms.

'I'm happy to tell you all we know if that's what Annabelle wants,' said Colin. 'We've obviously already given the police exactly the same information.' He looked impressively rakish, still in last night's dress shirt and trousers, though with no tie or jacket. He hadn't troubled to shave, which also suited him in a funny sort of way. Fiona looked much fresher, possibly having drunk slightly less. She sat alert and ready for anything I might throw at her.

'We were with you pretty much from when we arrived,' said Colin in answer to my initial question. 'We stayed a few minutes longer than we should while we refilled our glasses— I don't get to drink Lafite very often and I'm not sure when I shall again. Anyway, in the process we lost visual contact with the main party touring the house. We wandered round a bit and explored upstairs, thinking they might have gone there.'

'Didn't see a soul until we ran into Elsie,' said Fiona. 'Then we joined the others outside the library. Other than a bit of attempted resuscitation, that was our evening pretty much.'

'Needless to say, neither of *us* had any reason for wanting to see Robert dead,' said Colin. 'Just in case that was your next question.'

'And it could have been suicide?' I asked.

'Oh, yes,' said Colin. 'No doubt about that. He could have wound the rope tightly round his neck and then used the pencil to tighten it. But equally somebody else could have done it that way. I can't help you much with the exact time of death. We all know it was somewhere in the twenty minutes before we found him—probably earlier rather than later. We don't know how long it took him to die, of course, but it was probably fairly quick—well, that's what we've told Annabelle anyway. For all I know it actually was.'

'So it could have been murder?'

'Only if you can get your murderer in and out of the locked room. The other big objection is that there was no evidence of a struggle.'

'And Robert was quite a strong man,' I said.

They looked at each other.

'I'll tell you what I had to tell the police about that too,' said Colin. 'It will all have to come out now anyway, so I can't see the harm. No, he was not a strong man in any sense. Robert was dying. He had pancreatic cancer. The prognosis is rarely good, but, by the time they found it, there was very little that could be done—and nothing that Robert was willing to have done to him. He probably had six months at the most—say one or two with a reasonable quality of life, and no quality of anything thereafter. He'd come up to London the day before the party, and we'd talked through the results of the latest tests, though he'd known for some time that it was hopeless. We'd discussed it again briefly yesterday evening—at least, he took me to one side during drinks and asked me if there couldn't be anything they'd missed. Of course, I said that you could never be certain — but frankly we both knew the score. The funny thing is that he took it all very well. It was almost as though it was a relief for him to know for certain.'

'So, not suicidal?'

'He didn't seem depressed, if that's what you mean. He was actually strangely cheerful.'

'I see,' I said. 'And did Annabelle know?'

Colin shrugged. 'I assume Robert would have told Annabelle. I never discussed it with her myself.'

'How were things between Annabelle and Robert?' I asked.

'Yesterday? No better, no worse than usual,' said Colin. 'You'll gather they'd both been round the block a few times. It was his second marriage—her third. Always focuses the mind a bit, I think. They seemed determined to make it work. There were differences between them. She was a bit more careful with money than he was—at least over some things. She didn't stint much on his cash buying this place. Or buying frocks. But she didn't like to see him wasting it.'

'On decent wine for his friends, for example,' said Fiona. 'God knows how Robert sneaked those bottles into the dining room last night. Annabelle would have gone spare if she'd had the slightest idea what the wine must have cost. They had plenty of other topics for rows of course—it wasn't just money—but they always seemed to make it up. A bit like us, really.'

'Nothing like us,' said Colin. 'If you were like Annabelle, I'd poison you at the first chance.'

'Not that we're suggesting Annabelle had anything to do with Robert's death,' said Fiona.

'On the other hand, if it had been Annabelle strangled...' Colin looked out of the conservatory towards the garden. 'You have to admit, Robert would have been a suspect.'

'But it wasn't Annabelle,' said Fiona. 'It was Robert.'

'Poor sod,' said Colin. 'First the bank...now this.'

🐟 🐟 🐟

Gerald Smith arrived in the conservatory dressed in a blue striped shirt and pale blue jeans. I realized that I had had little contact with him the previous evening, but was now able to study him properly. Even in jeans nobody would have mistaken him for anything except a lawyer. There was caution behind the friendly smile.

'We'd arranged to stay overnight rather than drive back to Crawley,' he said rather apologetically, 'even before…what happened…so I brought a change of clothes with me.'

It was not an unreasonable thing to have done, but he seemed the sort of person who probably apologized a lot and rarely meant it. So I simply nodded.

'Jane's still asleep,' he said. 'I'm assuming I can tell you anything you need to know. I didn't want to disturb her. It was a tough evening for her and she needs some rest.'

'Tough for all of us,' I said.

'Well, yes, but tougher for her having worked with Robert so long.'

'How long?'

'Almost ten years, I suppose, by the time she left the bank.'

'You weren't out of each other's sight all evening?'

'No—not really. What I saw, she saw, and vice versa.'

'You left the dining room for ten minutes or so, shortly after Robert went out?'

'Closer to five, I would guess. It took a minute or two to find the loo. OK, maybe seven or eight minutes in total.'

'And you saw nothing suspicious while you were in the corridor—nobody around who shouldn't have been there?'

'Absolutely not. We'd have told the police straight away.'

'Yes, of course. And you were both with Annabelle during the tour?'

'Yes…'

'You don't sound certain.'

'We left the dining room with her and then took a look at the billiard room, I think it was. Annabelle was in a hurry to move on. Felicity insisted on inspecting some object in a glass case in there. We went over to look at it too and Annabelle was gone when we'd finished. We found her a bit later, outside the library. She looked really worried.'

'How much later?'

'I don't know. The object in the case proved to be some Russian icon. It didn't look that interesting to me, but Felicity proceeded to give us quite a lecture on Russian Orthodox church history. So I guess it was five or ten minutes later we caught up with Annabelle.'

'And you told the police this?'

'Yes. Between you and me, I don't think they were that interested in who was where. They asked me several times whether Robert had any reason to commit suicide.'

'And did he?'

Gerald said nothing for a moment, then replied: 'No. Not really. There was the business of his leaving the bank, of course.'

'He said he resigned.'

'I represented him in what might have been a case of wrongful dismissal if the bank hadn't settled. Actually, they'd have been better going to court. Robert didn't have much of a case. You remember Nick Leeson?'

'The guy who brought down Barings?'

'That's the one. Robert had allowed somebody much the same freedom to trade with much the same effect, except the bank woke up to it a bit earlier and didn't quite go under. Still, they lost a packet. The bank wanted to sack them both. I ensured Robert left on reasonable terms.'

'And the other guy—the trader?'

'Sacked. Full stop. No money, no references. But I wasn't representing him.' Gerald smiled. He clearly thought he was a pretty clever operator, and maybe he was. 'No, I'd have said they were equally culpable, but he wasn't as well looked after. I'm surprised in the end he bore so few grudges against Robert.'

'And the terms on which Robert left would have been enough to maintain this place?' I asked.

'I'm good,' smirked Gerald, 'but I'm not that good. No, I guess Robert had invested better on his own behalf than he did for the bank. I hope so, for Annabelle's sake.'

Then I remembered something.

'Robert gave me a letter to pass on to you,' I said. 'If I'd realized you would still be here, I might have brought it with me. But I've posted it, unopened, as Robert requested. I don't know what it is, but apparently it's not urgent.'

'How very mysterious. Still, if it's not urgent…'

'It should be with you on Monday.'

'We're going away for a couple of days anyway. I'll look at it when I return to the office.'

Then another thought occurred to me.

'By the way,' I said. 'Who was the guy fired with Robert? The one who bore surprisingly few grudges under the circumstances?'

'I thought everyone knew that,' said Gerald. 'It was in the papers. He was quite famous for a few days. It was Clive Brent.'

◄ ◄ ◄

I had arranged to meet up with Annabelle and Elsie in the library. Elsie appeared, hot and distinctly put out after fruitlessly traipsing round the remoter parts of the garden for clues. She seemed to feel she had been sent on a wild goose chase and that she deserved better after her blue serge discovery.

Annabelle asked me what I had found out and I told her briefly that neither the McIntoshes nor Gerald Smith had had much information of note. I did say that the McIntoshes, in their medical capacity, had not ruled out suicide and that I'd been told Clive had left the bank at the same time as Robert.

'Could Clive have harboured any sort of grudge?' I asked.

'Of course not,' said Annabelle. 'Robert saw Clive as being one of his closest chums. Robert was trying to find Clive a job, for goodness' sake. Why would Clive want to kill him now?'

'I just thought I would ask,' I said. 'Maybe, Annabelle, the police are right. After all, how could anyone have got out of this room after killing Robert?'

'You discovered nothing earlier?'

'Not a thing,' I said.

She sighed—but really, I had done all I could.

'Let's try to reconstruct the scene,' said Annabelle, as though we were having difficulty learning something quite simple. 'Elise—you sit at the desk.'

'Can't I be the murderer?' asked Elsie.

'No, dear, you're going to be murdered,' said Annabelle. 'And very soon. Now, Ethelred—you stand over there to the left of the fireplace—by that panelling. A little bit further back—yes, just there.'

'I'm not sure...' I said. Whichever way a killer might have entered, it would not have been from the fireplace.

She looked critically from me to Elsie and back again. I couldn't see this was getting us anywhere. Then I must have leaned on something because Annabelle suddenly said: 'Wait a moment! The panelling—it moved.'

I looked. There was a series of oak Tudor roses carved the length of the room. The one closest to me looked a little more worn than the rest—sort of smoothed. Otherwise it was just a regular bit of carving.

'What did I touch? This?' I still wasn't sure I had made contact with anything. I could have done no more than brush against it.

'Press it again,' said Annabelle. 'Press it again—harder this time.'

I pressed harder. Then suddenly part of the panelling gaped. Annabelle was by my side in a moment, sliding the whole panel back to reveal an opening, slightly smaller than a standard door, but allowing access to anyone willing to stoop a little and step into the darkness.

'It's a secret passage!' she said.

'So it is,' I said. I looked through the opening into the gloom. 'I wonder where it goes?'

Annabelle produced a torch from the desk drawer and shone it experimentally into the aperture.

'It goes some way,' I said, over Annabelle's shoulder.

'Come on, Ethelred,' said Annabelle. 'The two of us should check this out together.'

'Or better still, all three of us,' said Elsie.

And so, one by one, all three of us stepped through the opening into a stone-floored passageway.

✦ ✦ ✦

The torchlight showed that the walls on either side were rough, unpolished oak panels. The ceiling was low enough that my hair brushed it once or twice, but not so low that it felt claustrophobic. In a couple of places there were brackets for candles, but there were also electric light fittings—black bakelite, maybe dating back eighty years or so to a time that I still think of as 'early this century'.

We followed the passage for a short distance before reaching a dead end. A quick investigation with the torch revealed a wooden lever, and pulling on the lever opened another panel. We found ourselves in the billiard room, blinking in the sunlight that was streaming through the windows.

Of course, the passage, like everything else at Muntham Court, was a piece of Victorian whimsy. Just as the architect had added Jacobean strapwork to the exterior, he had thought fit to provide a secret passage for the amusement of his client and perhaps of his client's guests. It was a neat nineteenth-century rationalization of the cramped and twisting secret passages of more ancient buildings. The candles, and later the electric light, would have permitted an entertaining, but completely comfortable, transfer between two of the male strongholds of the house. Its later neglect, demonstrated by the antiquity of the electrical wiring, suggested that the house's more recent owners had had no use for it.

'A way in *and* out,' said Annabelle thoughtfully. 'You realize what this means?'

Elsie said nothing but took the torch from Annabelle and retraced her steps, vanishing for a moment round the corner. She quickly returned.

'Not a way in,' she said. 'There must have been a lever, like at this end, but it has broken off at some stage. Can't get the panel to budge. You can get out of the library this way, but not in—or at least you can get in only if whoever is in the library opens the panel for you.'

'This is important,' I said. 'We need to tell the police.'

'Yes,' said Annabelle. 'We shall tell the police…when we need to. But we don't want them taking over things just yet—they haven't exactly been Sherlock Holmes. Let's gather all the information we can first. You still need to talk to the others.'

'I don't think I'll find out much more…' I said.

'Of course you will,' said Annabelle. 'You were so clever finding this passage. You can do anything.'

And she gave me a little kiss on the cheek.

Chapter Ten

'So,' I said to Ethelred, once we were alone together. 'Let me reconstruct things for you.'

'We've just done that,' he said, a slight note of irritation in his voice. 'Annabelle made you sit there, then I—'

'Not the murder. I mean the little farce that has just been enacted for our benefit.'

'But—'

'Oh, come on. Ethelred, *wonderful* Ethelred, just go and stand by that random bit of panelling for no reason at all.'

'Annabelle doesn't speak like that,' said Ethelred. 'You make her sound whiny and high pitched...'

'It's close enough for our purposes,' I pointed out. 'I don't claim to be Rory Bremner. Now, *wonderful* Ethelred, why don't you press the random bit of panelling? No, press the totally random bit of panelling harder. Well, I'm amazed! A secret passage in my own sweet little house! And I never suspected. Who would have believed it?'

'She *doesn't* talk like that,' said Ethelred. 'If Annabelle says she didn't know about the passage...What?'

'Let's begin with the killer's footprints on the dusty floor of the passageway,' I said.

'I didn't see any...'

'Exactly. And why didn't you see any?'

'I don't know,' he said.

'There were no dusty footprints because there was no dust. The passage was as clean as a whistle.'

'That's why then,' said Ethelred. 'What? Why do you keep looking at me like that?'

'You're a man, aren't you?'

'When I last checked, yes—though I am a paid-up member of Mystery Women.'

'Joining a club devoted to the promotion of female crime writers doesn't make you any less obtuse, unfortunately. If you were a woman in fact rather than in fiction you would know about dust and its funny little ways. Some women, not me obviously, dust things daily, because if you turn your back on dust, even for a moment, it sneaks into the room and quietly takes up residence on all horizontal surfaces. A lost passageway should be very dusty and full of cobwebs, not swept so you can eat your dinner off it. That passageway had not been lost for very long at all.'

'Maybe the people who lived here before didn't tell Annabelle...'

'If you were selling a house, would you fail to mention to possible purchasers an interesting little feature like a secret passageway?'

'No, but...'

'Annabelle knew very well that secret passage was there. But for some reason she wanted it to stay a secret for just a bit longer. Now, conversely, she wants people to know about it. Why?'

'Or, alternatively, she really didn't know, but just happened to ask me to...*What*?'

'You'd believe anything she told you, wouldn't you?'

'I need to get on with interviewing people,' he said, switching the subject with no great subtlety. I let it go. We both knew deep down that she was an unprincipled slapper. Soon Ethelred would be forced to admit it to himself or, alternatively, I would have to draw him a picture. One or the other. We could see how things progressed.

'Who do we talk to next?' I asked.

'I talk to John O'Brian,' he said. 'Just me. I'm sure you'd be happier staying here.'

I weighed up the options: sit on my own in a deserted library full of old dusty books or interrogate a young, muscular hunk of a gardener. It was a tough call.

◄ ◄ ◄

'So, John,' I said, 'how long have you worked for Lady Muntham?'

John O'Brian swallowed hard and blinked a couple of times in a rather endearing sort of way before replying. He was an outdoors sort of guy and looked uncomfortable indoors, perched on the chintz seat cover in clean, neatly pressed clothes. He had the type of chin that looks good with a day's stubble on it and the type of body that looks good with as little on as possible. I wondered if I could ask him a question that would involve him having to take off his shirt. Difficult, but not necessarily impossible.

'I've worked here since the Munthams moved in,' he said, swallowing hard. 'They sacked the old gardener and Lady Muntham recruited me. She needed somebody younger who could be a bit more active in the garden.'

Which was clearly what she got. 'And you worked quite closely with Lady Muntham?' I asked.

'She's a keen gardener herself. She likes to get out in the fresh air.' He was looking at the floor as if he had developed a sudden interest in faded, moth-eaten carpets.

'And she would be out in the garden how often?' I asked.

'Most days, I suppose.'

'So, you'd work side by side, as it were? On hot days, possibly without your shirt on?'

'I'm not sure,' interrupted Ethelred, 'that this is terribly relevant. We know that Mr O'Brian works here. It's what happened yesterday that we need to concentrate on.'

'So, John, what happened yesterday?' I asked, with a sideways glance at Ethelred. I reckoned I could raise the shirt question again later.

'Like I've already told the police,' said O'Brian, looking up and meeting my eye for the first time. They were nice eyes, now I had their full attention. Baby blue. 'Like I told the police, I started work at nine as usual. Lady Muntham wanted things looking right for the guests, so I said I'd keep working until all of the jobs were done. I raked the gravel. I mowed the lawns and did some weeding and some trimming. When I was done, there was a load of weeds and cuttings and stuff to take to the heap at the back of the house, then there was the tools to clean and put away, so I kept going until it was almost dark, then I had a wash and went home. This morning, Lady Muntham phoned me and told me that Sir Robert had sadly passed away and that the police were likely to want to ask me some questions.'

'And that was the first you knew of Sir Robert's death?' asked Ethelred.

'Yes. It was a bit of a shock, that,' said O'Brian. 'I can't rightly get my head round it.'

'And you saw nothing odd that evening?'

'There were the guests arriving, but I didn't pay much attention. I'd tidied up at the front of the house already.'

'You saw nobody round the back of the house, near the library?' O'Brian paused and looked at me and then back at Ethelred and then back at me.

'Maybe,' he said.

'Maybe?'

'You'll have spoken to Mr Brent already?'

'No, he's arriving later.'

O'Brian paused again.

'I did think I saw a fellow in the shrubbery round the back,' he said at last.

'One of the guests?' asked Ethelred.

'I don't think so.'

'What did he look like?'

'He was wearing this dark blue suit,' said O'Brian, frowning.

'Not a dinner jacket?'

'No, a lounge suit. It was blue. Dark blue.'

'In the fading light you could confuse the two.'

'I'm sure it was dark blue,' insisted O'Brian with a touch of annoyance. 'Maybe with a faint red stripe.'

'How tall was he?'

O'Brian clasped his hands together and looked into the distance. 'How tall? I couldn't say exactly...'

'Quite tall? Short? Average?'

'I'd say...average,' said O'Brian.

'What colour hair?'

Again, a fairly simple question seemed to trouble him. 'Difficult to tell—it was getting dark, you see, Mr Tressider,' he said eventually.

'Blond? Brown? Black?' asked Ethelred.

'Brown...brown-ish...maybe blackish brown.'

'Sure about that?'

'Absolutely.'

'What was the man doing?'

'Like I said, just loitering, smoking a cigarette. Filter-tip.'

'No, I don't think you did say that,' said Ethelred, making some notes. 'Did he stay long?'

'I just sort of glimpsed him,' said O'Brian. 'Just for an instant. Then he was gone.'

'Did you challenge him? He was, after all, in the Munthams' garden.'

'I thought he was maybe a guest.'

'But you just said that you don't think he was a guest.'

'I thought *at the time* that he was a guest. Later, after...when I thought a bit more, I decided he couldn't have been.'

'On what basis?'

'All of the gentlemen were wearing dinner jackets. So the man couldn't have been a guest.'

'What time was this roughly?'

'I'm not sure. Round about the time the guests were arriving—could be a bit later.'

'What did you do next?'

'I was taking the last load of cuttings to the heap, so I just carried on. Then, like I say, I had a wash and went home.'

'So, not long before Sir Robert was found dead?'

'Yes, I suppose so.' O'Brian looked worried again. Each question seemed to be making him more uncomfortable.

'An hour or so before his death, let's say?'

'You'll have to ask Mr Brent.'

'Did he see him too?'

'What?' For a moment O'Brian looked like a cat that had dodged round a corner to avoid a playful terrier and walked into a group of Dobermanns with time on their hands. He certainly wasn't enjoying being interviewed.

'Did Clive Brent see him too?' repeated Ethelred patiently. He looked up from his notebook in his usual vague manner that might have been masking a razor-sharp intellect, or more likely just meant that he was working on his shopping list.

'Somebody said Mr Brent had seen him,' O'Brian said.

'Who said that?'

'I don't remember.'

'It doesn't matter. I'll ask Mr Brent when I see him. For the moment let's just say it was after the guests had arrived?'

'Yes, after the guests had arrived, certainly.'

'Thank you,' said Ethelred, nose now back in his notebook, amending his shopping list.

'If there's anything more...' said O'Brian, though he clearly hoped there wasn't.

'You've been very helpful,' said Ethelred, closing the note-book.

'Very helpful,' I said.

I wondered if O'Brian knew what a crap performance he had just given. Probably not, because he smiled at both of us as if a great weight had just been lifted from his shoulders, and walked quickly out of the room.

✦ ✦ ✦

'So, Clive,' said Ethelred, 'thank you for coming back. It means I can talk to pretty much everyone today.'

'I wanted to check how Annabelle was anyway,' said Clive Brent.

Today, he was dressed in jeans and a red polo shirt with short sleeves. The first thing that struck me, sitting demurely in the background as Ethelred fired off the questions, was his strange resemblance to John O'Brian. OK, one was the hired help and the other a high-powered banker, but they both had the same sort of rugged, muscled charm. The bare arms were powerful. The eyes in both cases were blue—steely blue in this case.

'Yes, of course,' said Ethelred, in reverential tones. 'We need to rally round. Annabelle's being terribly brave, of course, but it's hit her very hard.'

'You've spoken to most of the others—John O'Brian and the rest?'

'Yes, I've spoken to John O'Brian and the McIntoshes and Gerald Smith.'

'What did O'Brian have to say?'

'He was helpful,' said Ethelred.

Brent shrugged. 'He's always hanging around this place. I don't think he has a home to go to.'

'He works here,' said Ethelred, 'and Annabelle asked him to come in today.'

Clive Brent nodded briefly at these self-evident facts and looked at his watch.'OK, well, perhaps you could ask me whatever you need to ask me?'

'Very well. You've known Robert and Annabelle some time?'

'Yes. I've been a colleague of Robert's since—oh, since way back. He was already working for the bank when I joined. For a while he was in Germany and I was in London, then he was in London and I was in Singapore, but we kept meeting up—the way you do. Towards the end we worked very closely together.'

'He was your line manager.'

'If you want to put it like that. He always said to regard him as a chum rather than as a boss.'

'But he was the boss nevertheless?'

'Obviously.' Brent glanced at his watch again. It was a smart watch.

And you left the bank together?' asked Ethelred.

'Obviously.'

'Obviously?'

'I'd assumed he'd told you, though there isn't much to tell. The bank was pushing us to make the biggest profits we could. As long as the money came in, frankly nobody seemed to care much what risks we took. That's how things were in those days. When we came unstuck on that gamble on the Singapore dollar, it shouldn't have surprised them. We'd have made it up the following year, but they were pleased to discover they had grounds for sacking us. It was a stitch-up, but it had all become very public and everyone was trying to save their own skin. The chairman and directors were good at that.'

'Still, Robert stood by you? Took the blame?'

Brent laughed. 'Is that what he told you?'

'He didn't really tell me anything.'

'My dear chum Robert wriggled and squirmed and tried to dump one hundred per cent of the blame on me. Only when it was clear that that wouldn't wash and that he was going to get sacked anyway did he do the noble thing, including making a token request that I should keep my job. Of course, I didn't keep it.'

'He was trying to find you another job?'

'So he said. It was a bit vague. Now he's gone, I don't even know which bank he'd been talking to on my behalf. It was only to please Annabelle anyway.'

'To please Annabelle?'

'I mean, in the sense that she reckoned I'd been badly treated. She was very...well, supportive.'

Ethelred nodded thoughtfully, but seemed less pleased than he might have been by Annabelle's thoughtfulness.

'You were the first to arrive yesterday evening?'

'Yes, Robert wanted to talk about these contacts of his. In the end we talked a lot about golf and the weather. Finally he patted me on the knee and told me that he hoped to hear something soon about a job. Then Annabelle pitched up and said the other guests were here. Complete waste of time.'

'And you were with the other guests the whole time until after Robert was found dead?'

'Yes,' he said. 'The whole time.'

'No, you weren't,' I said.

They both turned to look at me.

'We met in the corridor, Clive,' I said. 'You were on your own.'

'Oh, yes, that's right,' said Brent. 'I was taking a squint at a painting—it looked like a Constable—and then realized that the others had gone on. I was only away from them for a couple of minutes'

'A couple of minutes?' I said.

'Yes,' said Brent indignantly. 'A couple of minutes at the most.'

'And you saw nothing untoward before Robert's death—no sign of any intruders, for example?' asked Ethelred.

Brent's eyes narrowed a shade. For a moment I thought he was going to pass on that one. He took a breath. 'I thought I saw somebody in the garden,' he said.

'One of the guests?'

'No,' said Brent. 'Somebody wearing a navy blue pinstriped suit.'

'That must have seemed very odd,' said Ethelred, frowning and flicking back through his shopping list.

'Odd? Yes, I suppose it was.'

'Did you tell anyone?'

'I didn't think it was important,' said Brent. 'I just caught a glimpse of him. I can't even be sure...'

'Old, young?'

'Youngish,' said Brent slowly. 'Yes, perhaps thirty.'

'How tall?'

'Quite tall.'

'As tall as I am?'

'Possibly a bit shorter than you are. Say five ten, five eleven?'

'What colour hair?'

'I didn't really see,' said Brent.

'Didn't see his hair?'

'No.'

'Wearing a hat then, maybe?' asked Ethelred.

Brent thought about this for a while.

'A hat?'

'You weren't sure about his hair. Neither was O'Brian.'

'Really? What did he say?'

'Just that he'd seen somebody similar.'

'With a hat?'

Ethelred said nothing.

'Yes, a hat,' said Brent, at last. 'I'm pretty sure he had a hat.'

'What sort?' asked Ethelred. 'Panama? Trilby? Cap? Beanie?'

'Perhaps a beanie?' Brent said cautiously. He didn't sound at all sure.

'A blue pinstriped suit and a beanie?' I interjected. 'That must have looked pretty weird on a summer's evening in the middle of the country.'

'Yes,' said Brent. 'That was...that was what made me suspicious.'

'But you didn't tell anyone?' asked Ethelred.

'No. I've told nobody except you.'

'Not even the police?'

'I didn't remember him until this morning.'

'How did you see him? Were you out in the garden?' asked Ethelred, his pen now scribbling away.

'No,' said Brent quickly, trying to read the notes upside down. 'I saw him through a window.'

'And where was he when you saw him?'

'In the rhododendrons,' said Brent. 'He was smoking.'

'You are certain of that?'

'Absolutely. I saw him flick the butt onto the ground.' He thought for a moment and then added: 'Filter-tip.'

'Well, we can get him for littering, if nothing else,' I said.

Neither of the men found this amusing.

'You'll need to tell the police all this,' said Ethelred.

Brent sighed. 'Do you think so?'

'Of course.'

'I don't see that this intruder can have any relevance. I'm not even sure why Annabelle...'

'Not sure why Annabelle what?' asked Ethelred.

'...Why she wants you to question us all.'

'She just wants to be sure the police missed nothing'

Brent shrugged. 'I can't see this is necessary.'

'She doesn't like to think it was suicide...that Robert was that unhappy...he'd just remarried, after all.'

Brent made a face. 'Why does Annabelle think everything is about her? I'm guessing Robert was a pretty sick man?'

'But with months to live—months he could have shared with her,' said Ethelred, who was clearly under the delusion sharing time with Annabelle was in some way desirable.

'It was a sham of a marriage,' said Brent with some vehemence.

'I don't think Annabelle saw it that way,' said Ethelred.

Brent laughed. 'No?'

'No,' said Ethelred firmly. 'She loved him.'

'How many people have you questioned this morning?'

Ethelred listed the names.

'And that is still your view?' asked Clive Brent.

'It's the one thing that I am certain of,' said Ethelred.

'It looks as though Annabelle made a good choice of detectives then,' said Brent. 'Anything else?' he added, looking round the room.

'I've got all I need for the moment,' said Ethelred. 'Thanks.'

✦ ✦ ✦

'Well, that was interesting,' I said.

'Interesting?'

'Seeing how many lies could be packed into forty-five minutes,' I said.

Ethelred looked at his notes. 'Such as?'

'Well,' I said. 'Let's begin with this intruder. O'Brian says that the light was bad and that he scarcely got a glimpse of him—in fact, come to think of it, they both said that. Anyway, in spite of it being almost dark, O'Brian is certain that the man was wearing a blue suit with a red pinstripe—whereas I could see the red stripe in the material only when it was close up and in good light. Brent confirms the blue pinstripe suit but is vague about most other things, except that the guy was wearing a beanie—something O'Brian would surely have spotted and commented on? And why is O'Brian so sure that the man in the blue suit wasn't a guest? He was out in the garden and says he didn't pay much attention to people arriving. How does he *know* all the male guests were in dinner jackets? Brent says he told nobody about the man in the suit, but O'Brian clearly knew Brent had also seen him. Oh, and both can spot that a cigarette has a filter tip at some distance in fading light.'

'Anything else?'

'There's something else I can't quite put my finger on, but I think that both were lying all the way through.'

'Clive Brent was certainly wrong about Annabelle,' said Ethelred. 'She was devoted to Robert—and he to her.'

'Well,' I said, 'you're the one who's been married. But if that was connubial devotion, I think I might just stay single.'

Unless John O'Brian was available, of course. He was a liar, but he was a hot liar. And possibly stupid enough to commit murder for that special lady in his life.

Chapter Eleven

Elsie had wandered off, leaving me alone in the conservatory. Like Elsie, I felt there was something a little queer about the last two interviews that I couldn't quite put my finger on. Nothing to worry about—just something that wasn't quite right. I was therefore rereading my notes when Jane Smith appeared. She was still wearing her evening dress and looked tired.

'I thought you wanted to talk to us all,' she said. She sounded defiant and slightly pathetic at the same time, almost like a child justly fearing some punishment but building themselves up to a self-righteous denial.

'Gerald came and saw me earlier,' I said. 'I think he didn't want to disturb you.'

'He should have brought me along. You said you wanted to speak to all of us.'

I hadn't really made a public pronouncement on the subject, so Annabelle or one of the guests must have told her that. 'Why don't you sit down?' I said.

She sank into the chair opposite me and moodily toyed with an imaginary speck of dirt on her sleeve.

'Does Gerald think I have nothing to say in my own right?' she demanded.

That seemed likely on the face of it. He was that type.

'Do you have anything to add to what he told me?' I asked.

'How should *I* know? I don't even know what he *said*.'

For a moment I thought she was going to stamp her little foot, but she chose this point to burst into tears. I stood by nervously as I usually do under these circumstances. I half held my hand out to her but then, on further consideration, withdrew it. 'I'm sure...' I began. I fumbled in my pocket as a preliminary to offering her a handkerchief that was almost certainly not there. Still, it gave me something to do—something that wouldn't make things worse. Not making it worse is often as much as you can hope for.

'Why,' I said cautiously, 'don't I just tell you what Gerald said?' I looked at her and decided that I hadn't put my foot in it yet.

Breathing a quick sigh of relief, I got her to sit down and gave her a quick summary of what I had written in my notebook.

'That isn't all,' she said, the sobs slowly subsiding and the initial defiance reasserting itself. 'That isn't everything he told you. It *can't* be.'

I checked my notes again. 'It's pretty much all.'

'What did Gerald say about Robert and me?'

'Just that you had worked for him.'

'Nothing more?'

'Is there anything more?'

She looked at me, trying to read my expression.

'Oh, not really,' she said eventually. 'But didn't he say that I was more than Robert's secretary?'

I wondered for a moment whether she meant some higher position in the bank—or perhaps that she had some glorified title such as Senior Executive Assistant—but then I realized...

'Yes, we had a relationship,' she said, looking away. 'That's what they call it, isn't it? A relationship. Before Gerald came on the scene, of course, or Annabelle for that matter. We...we slept together. It all lasted about a year. In a way it was rather sordid, but in a way it was rather wonderful—do you know what I mean? Then that silicon-enhanced bitch Annabelle came along...somebody told me last night that the two of them had met in a lap-dancing club, which wouldn't surprise me...and, well, the rest is history, as they say.'

'And Gerald knows about you and Robert?'

She looked at me again and gave me a brief smile. 'Yes. I told him soon after we started going out together.'

'But it all happened before you had even met Gerald?'

'Before we started going out properly, yes.'

I pulled a face, but it didn't sound that bad. Some husbands and wives have a bit of a thing about their spouse's ex-boyfriends and girlfriends, but Gerald hadn't mentioned any of this to me. I caught no hint of jealousy. If it was all some time ago, it didn't seem very relevant to anything. Perhaps it still meant something to Jane though?

'You don't suspect Gerald of murder?' she said suddenly.

'Are you suggesting that your fling with Robert, years ago, could be a motive?'

'No, of course not. It would have to be more than that, wouldn't it? More than just that I had once slept with Robert?'

I thought she had implied she had slept with him a lot more than once. Still, I felt I could set her mind at rest.

'It would need to be a lot more than that, surely?'

There was a long pause.

'Yes, of course. It's silly of me even to think it,' she said.

'And he had no opportunity,' I said.

'No. I was with him the whole evening.'

'There you are. You know that it couldn't be him.'

'I've wasted your time,' she said, standing up. 'I am really, really sorry.'

'It's OK,' I said.

'Sorry,' she said. She stifled a final sniffle, gave me a brave smile and clutching her handbag to her body, she walked primly from the room.

After she had gone I wondered what had troubled me about *that* conversation. Yet again, I felt that I had been told only part of a story, and that the most significant part had been held back.

✦ ✦ ✦

My interview with Dave Peart was necessarily brief.

'Am I getting paid for my time here or what?' he demanded. 'My dad says Saturday should be time and a half. All day.'

'I don't know,' I said. 'You'll have to ask Lady Muntham.'

'If it's down to Her Ladyship, I know the answer to that one then. Tight cow.'

He folded his arms and looked at me defiantly.

'Maybe you could just tell me briefly what you were doing yesterday?'

'Already told the bloody police, ain't I?'

'Yes, you've told the police,' I said, 'but it would help if you also told me.'

'Huh! I don't have to tell you nothing, mister.' He made a noise halfway between a laugh and a snort and looked fairly pleased with himself until he noticed the resultant snot on his shirtfront. 'Bugger.'

'Quite right,' I said, trying to ignore what he was doing with his thumbnail. 'You don't have to tell me about anything that you noticed. But I suppose you're not really the observant type?'

'Didn't say that,' he said, rubbing off the last of the yellow mucus with the tip of his forefinger. With a well-practised flick, he launched it towards a distant part of the floor.

'So what did you do and what did you see?'

He sighed, as though I had tricked him, then he said: 'In the morning, up till dinner-time, I helped John in the garden, see? We was weeding and pruning mostly. Then I helped a bit in the kitchen and with laying the table. I got sent home at tea-time to change—I borrowed a jacket from Dan—he's my brother— but the trousers didn't fit, so I took my dad's, 'cause he only wears his suit for weddings and when he's up before the magistrate, and I reckoned he wouldn't miss them. Didn't look too bad in that get-up. Proper little waiter, I was. So, like you know, I served the soup, then the main course and it was all rush, rush, rush—a bit like those cooking programmes on the telly, but without so much bad language. I did pretty well, though I say it myself. Might go in for waitering full-time—it's got to pay better than this job anyway. Well, Her Ladyship doesn't ring for the dessert, does she? Didn't exactly bother us if it got cold. Unappreciative toffee-nosed whatsits, as Mrs Michie called them. So we waited and we chatted and we waited a bit more. After a while Mrs Michie says: "I wonder what's keeping them?" Later on the police turned up. Didn't get home until almost two in the morning, did I?'

'Did you see any sign of an intruder?'

'I was running around the place so fast I wouldn't have noticed a dozen intruders.' He laughed but this time wisely decided against a derisive snort.

'Did you see anyone wandering around the garden in a blue suit?'

'I ain't never seen nobody wander round the garden in no blue suit.'

A quadruple negation seemed conclusive, so I moved on.

'You really saw nothing all day?' I asked.

'Wouldn't say that.'

'Wouldn't you?'

'All right—I really will tell you something, Mr Amateur Detective. Mrs Michie sent me out in the afternoon to get some carrots from the kitchen garden. OK? John was in the green-house with Her Ladyship. They'd have had more privacy in the potting shed if they were planning to get up to that sort of thing—but the greenhouse being glass, it didn't leave much to the imagination. They didn't notice me pulling carrots ten feet away from them. I bet *he* got time and a half.'

'Did Lady Muntham and Mr O'Brian often...'

'As often as they could. But don't take my word for it. Ask anyone in the village pretty well.'

'And did Sir Robert know?'

'Can't say, rightly. Don't see how he couldn't. But then I don't see how John didn't know about that Brent fellow—took him a while to twig to that one.'

'Clive Brent?'

'That's the one. Big green Jaguar. He parks it on the bypass sometimes and walks up. Thinks nobody won't notice.'

'I see,' I said.

Dave Peart laughed. 'You wouldn't credit what goes on at this place,' he said. 'You would *not* credit it.'

⊷ ⊷ ⊷

'Young Dave Peart,' said Mrs Michie, wiping her large red hands on a tea cloth, 'has a vivid imagination. It comes of those magazines he's always reading—I know where he keeps them in the potting shed, under the growbags. He thinks those bags are too heavy for me to lift, but they're not. Sex. That's all that boy can think of. I wouldn't set too much store by what Dave Peart tells you.'

'There's nothing going on between Lady Muntham and John O'Brian then?'

'Nothing that I know of.' Her face, perhaps through long and careful practice, was completely expressionless. She pushed a strand of greying hair behind her ear and stared at me with her unyielding, almost colourless eyes. It was my move.

'And Clive Brent?' I asked.

'He's a slippery customer, that Mr Brent.'

'Meaning?'

'Acts like he's got some sort of hold on this family. Marches in. Demands to see him. Demands to see her. He's just the bursar of that school down the road. And only part-time.'

I paused, my pen hovering above the paper, then wrote nothing.

'So, yesterday, you started work at nine?' I asked.

'Worked nine in the morning until ten at night, with scarcely a break. That's not even legal, that's not. Then I had to hang around answering questions from the police.'

'Were you in the kitchen all that time?'

'Pretty much. I had Gill Maggs—she comes in from Findon Valley—to help me in the morning, then Dave Peart in the afternoon, not that he's much use to anyone, even when his mind's partly on the task at hand. It would have been good to have Gill back in the evening, but Her Ladyship wouldn't hear of it—this is costing enough without that, she said. So it was just me slaving away in the kitchen and the boy spilling soup over people in the dining room.'

'The food was lovely,' I said, perhaps a little too late.

'Was it now?' she said. 'Well, that's good to know.'

'I really enjoyed the...' I began. Then I realized that I couldn't remember a thing we had eaten. 'The...starter,' I concluded lamely.

She looked me straight in the eye and said nothing.

'Did you notice anything odd during the afternoon or evening?' I continued. My pen was still poised above the blank page.

'There was nothing to notice, not in the kitchen. Where I was all day. Cooking. The *starter* and everything. It was soup, by the way, in case you were still wondering what you'd been eating.'

'It was delicious,' I said, though I could remember only how it was served, not which variety it was. Better to move the conversation on. 'You didn't see any sign of a man wearing a blue pinstriped suit—maybe with some sort of woolly hat? Standing over by the shrubbery.'

'With a woolly *hat*?'

'Yes,' I said.

'In the middle of summer?'

'A couple of people say they saw him.'

'After how many glasses of wine would that have been?'

'John O'Brian reckons he caught a glimpse of him.'

Mrs Michie pulled a face. She seemed more inclined to believe John O'Brian's word than most other people's, but she was still doubtful. 'He said nothing to me. When did John see him?'

'Just before he went home, I think.'

She made the same face again, just in case I hadn't fully appreciated it the first time, and shook her head. 'He popped in to say goodnight, but he didn't say anything to me.'

'Maybe he didn't think it was important.'

'An intruder in the garden? Not important? How do you make that out then?'

'He thought at first it might be a guest.'

'Not in a woolly hat.'

'I suppose not,' I said.

'Funny John never mentioned that to me.'

'Do you think I'll be able to speak to Gillian Maggs?' I asked.

'She won't be in until Monday. Gill was gone by lunchtime, though. She couldn't have seen anything.'

'Do you have her phone number by any chance?'

Mrs Michie eyed me up briefly. 'Her Ladyship'll have that, I reckon. Is it really worth bothering Gill?'

'Probably not,' I said. 'Probably not.'

Chapter Twelve

As my old dad always used to say: 'If you want to catch a villain, you've got to think like a villain.' Of course, as a fruit and veg stallholder, he was rarely called upon by the Essex Constabulary to catch villains, so that was one bit of advice I always took with a pinch of salt. Still, some things were true even though my old dad said them, and I tried to get myself into the mind of a murderer as I sat in the library and worked through the series of events.

There were plenty of ways into the library before it was locked—Muntham Court that evening had not been exactly Fort Knox. The problem with Shagger's death being murder had been getting the killer out of the locked room again. It was a shame that the solution to such a classic problem was anything as naff as a secret passage, but it did mean that a killer could have made their escape and even hidden in the passage until things had quietened down. But, it would have been no casual intruder, because locating the opening mechanism had not been that easy—even for somebody of Ethelred's mighty intellect, aided by the helpful and knowledgeable hints of the owner of the house. So, it had to be somebody who already knew the house well and who knew that Shagger would take a break halfway through dinner and head for the library...

It was the last bit that puzzled me. Why would anyone expect a host to abandon his guests and then sit around in the library, obligingly waiting to be murdered? Unless, of course, they had actually arranged to meet Shagger at some appointed hour or after some agreed signal—that made a lot more sense. Prior to his departure, Shagger had stood up, spouted a load of crap and then cleared off. But surely, if you wanted to slip away for a few minutes without arousing suspicion couldn't you just say you needed to speak to the cook or fetch more wine?

I went over to the relevant piece of woodwork and pressed, just as Ethelred had done. Various Victorian cogs and pulleys whirred away efficiently behind the panelling and the outline of the entrance appeared. Like the lack of dust, the lack of noise was telling. This was a well-maintained Victorian mechanism—not some long-unused and rusty piece of ironwork. I ran my hand over the panelling. It felt good to the touch. It was well-polished oak that would yield plenty of fingerprints—mine for the most part, I realized, though possibly still with odd traces of the murderer's.

Time to go through a few drawers.

Most of what was in Shagger's desk was of minimal interest. Ethelred hopefully still had the poem safely stuffed in his pocket, and would remember to take it out before he sent the trousers to the cleaners. The middle drawer was now just a receptacle for high-class stationery. Then, nestling at the bottom of the lowest drawer I found something really interesting. Had Shagger been hiding this from his wife? And why? I flicked through it and it proved quite rewarding. I tried cramming the whole thing into my handbag but it was a bit of a tight fit, so I tore out the relevant pages and stuffed them well down amongst the many useful things that my bag usually contains. Back to the secret passage then.

Taking a torch with me, I pushed the panelling to one side as before and stepped into the gloom. I pulled the panel closed behind me. It clicked into place. It felt sort of cosy once you were inside. The sounds from the house were muffled. I tiptoed along the stone floor as I reckoned the killer must have done. I found the lever at the far end. Another well-maintained piece of machinery opened the panelling for me. I was in the billiard room. I pushed the woodwork closed. I had travelled from the library to the billiard room in total secrecy and in about thirty seconds. Had I bolted the library door, there would now be no way back in, other than breaking a window or finally locating that elusive oak bench. I checked the billiard-room windows— they were fastened but not locked. I gave one a push—it had a rubbish catch and swung open with minimal pressure. If I could have been arsed, I could have completed my reconstruction by jumping out of the window onto the lawn and making a break for the shrubbery.

Instead, I walked round by the corridor (which I noticed took slightly longer) and back in through the library door. In my absence somebody had been sitting in my chair, and it wasn't Goldilocks.

Ethelred and a badly dressed woman looked up at me from where they were seated. She already looked cross but I reckoned I could wind her annoyance up a notch or two.

'No, Ethelred,' Felicity Hooper said, looking in my direction. 'This really is the last straw. I'm willing to talk to you, but I am not being interrogated by some panel of…of…Well, I'm not. That's all there is to it.'

'Elsie's just passing by,' said Ethelred with more hope than genuine conviction.

'What gave you that idea?' I asked.

'I'm going back to London,' said La Hooper, getting up.

Fine by me.

'Look, Felicity,' said Ethelred, 'you've kindly stayed on to help us. It would make no sense at all going back home now without telling us what you saw. I am sure that Elsie wouldn't mind leaving…' Again, the beseeching look in my direction. 'Alternatively, of course, I don't see the harm in Elsie staying and…' He turned to the stony-faced Hooper woman.

Poor Ethelred. I wasn't sure which of us was the rock and which of us was the hard place, but I had no doubt as to who was between the two.

'Perhaps…' he began, looking at each of us in turn.

'Oh, very well,' muttered the Hooper woman. 'Let's just get this out of the way, shall we? What can I tell you that the others haven't?'

'How long have you known Robert?' Ethelred asked quickly, before she could change her mind.

'What's that got to do with the price of fish?' demanded Hooper. But I thought that I detected just a hint of a blush on her unmade-up cheek.

'I'm just trying to get some background,' said Ethelred. 'Robert told us that we were not just some random group of people. What connected us may be important.'

'I'd known him a very long time, as you are well aware.'

Ethelred looked puzzled.

'We did meet occasionally in Oxford,' said Hooper.

'Who—you and Robert?'

'Robert and I, you and Robert, all three of us.'

'You were at Oxford? Which college were you at?' asked Ethelred, still groping his way towards an identification.

'I wasn't at any college. I was training as a physio at the Radcliffe.'

'Ah, yes…' said Ethelred.

'All right, since you obviously *don't* remember me, Felicity Hooper isn't my real name any more than Amanda Collins is yours.'

'So, at Oxford I would have known you as…'

'Amanda Collins.'

Ethelred's mouth looked as if it was saying 'oh', but no sound emerged.

'I went out with Robert in his first year,' she continued. 'Not for that long, perhaps, but long enough that I do remember meeting you from time to time.'

'I always wondered,' said Ethelred, 'where I got that name from.'

'You got it from me,' said Felicity Hooper.

'How funny,' said Ethelred.

'Amusing? For whom?' demanded Hooper.

'Well, I mean—'

'When I started writing fiction, Ethelred, I had planned to write under my own name. My publisher informed me, however, that this would be inadvisable since there was already an established writer called Amanda Collins and it would be unwise to allow the public to confuse my work with the drivel that the other Collins was chucking out twice a year. I'd worked out that Collins was just a nom de plume for some third-rate hack. When I found that the third-rate hack was you, I saw it as a strange sort of compliment, I suppose, but since you clearly don't even remember me, I no longer have even that small crumb of comfort.'

'No, of course I remember you,' said Ethelred, but not in a way that would have convinced even the most charitable of former acquaintances.

'Whatever,' said Hooper. 'I went out with Robert for two terms, actually. He was known as "Shagger" then—a nickname not bestowed lightly or without mature consideration.'

'He was good then?' I enquired.

'He was *crap*,' said Hooper with a sudden vehemence. 'He earned the name by dint of quantity rather than quality. Of course, I was a virgin when I first encountered him. I had nothing to compare him with. The first time, you have no idea whether you're getting the proper service or not, do you? You just decide that sex isn't everything it's cracked up to be—if you run into somebody like Shagger Muntham.'

'So,' said Ethelred, 'he was your first...'

'Absolutely. It was his first time too.'

'Really?' asked Ethelred.

'I certainly hope so,' said Hooper. 'Otherwise some poor girl got him when he was even less clued-up. It doesn't really bear thinking about. Shagger's theory on most things, which he extended to sex, was that if he was having a good time everybody else was having a good time.'

'And you put up with that for two terms?' I asked. I was beginning to see her plucky little heroines in context.

'Well, from late Michaelmas term until midway through Hilary,' said Hooper.

'When you dumped him?' I asked.

'When it all just drifted to a conclusion,' said Hooper without bitterness. 'I could put up with the bad sex. It was the fact that he was always covered in mud and drunk that really wore me down. I qualified and moved to London shortly after. Didn't see him again for years—not until about twelve months ago, actually, when he wrote to me to say how much he'd enjoyed one of my books.'

'Did you know any of the other guests last night?' asked Ethelred.

'Well, *you*,' said Hooper pointedly. 'And *you*,' she added, looking briefly in my direction.

'None of the others?'

'I'm not a lawyer, banker or doctor. I had no reason to have met them.'

'You left the room briefly during dinner...'

'To go to the loo. Do you want me to spell it out for you?'

'No,' said Ethelred, wisely.

'I didn't murder Robert,' said La Hooper. 'I didn't need to murder Robert. But I did need a pee badly.'

'Can you think of any reason why anyone would wish to murder him?'

'Where do you want me to start? He cost a lot of people a lot of money towards the end of his banking career; some might feel a little aggrieved. There must be plenty of his ex-girlfriends out there. And their husbands. But above all—and you must have noticed this, Ethelred—Robert's great talent was making people feel insignificant. He was a patronizing shit, to put it another way. He had the ability to be charming, but most of the time chose not to be. That can be quite a put-down. It can get up people's noses. You can get killed for very much less.'

◄ ◄ ◄

'I'm not sure we're making much progress.

'On the contrary, I think you've done very well,' said Annabelle, reaching out to touch Ethelred's arm.

Ethelred tugged at an ear (his own) and looked doubtful. 'The only new lead is this man in a blue suit, seen in the garden.'

'And the piece of blue fabric found by Elsie,' said Annabelle. 'And the cigarette butts.'

'And the secret passage,' I added.

'Exactly,' said Annabelle, guiltily avoiding my penetrating gaze. 'And the secret passage'.

'Up to a point,' said Ethelred. 'We've found a secret passage but there's no evidence it was used by anyone to get into or out of the library. Then, as I say, a couple of people think they saw somebody suspicious—possibly wearing a beanie. In the end it doesn't amount to much.'

'A beanie?' asked Annabelle.

'Clive thought so.'

'We're all tired,' said Annabelle, 'and we're all naturally upset. Let's call it a day and come back to it fresh tomorrow.'

'Maybe I should speak to Gillian Maggs,' said Ethelred.

'Why?' asked Annabelle.

'She may have seen something earlier that day.'

'Oh, I doubt it. She was in the kitchen most of the time.'

'Still, I think I should just have a word with her. Mrs Michie said you would have the number.'

'Did she? Yes, I must have it somewhere, I suppose. I'll look it out for you tomorrow.'

'I could phone her today.'

'No, take a break. You can catch the end of the Sheep Fair. Elsie would enjoy that.'

Ah yes, the Sheep Fair. I had forgotten that.

'Would I?' I said.

'Everyone goes to the Sheep Fair,' said Annabelle.

* * *

Ethelred drove me back into the village, but not before he and Annabelle had had a short conversation out of my hearing. The truest thing that Annabelle had said that day was that we were all tired. Maybe I would be able to think more clearly tomorrow. After the Sheep Fair.

Chapter Thirteen

I cannot pretend our visit to Findon Sheep Fair was a great success.

'So where exactly are the sheep?' demanded Elsie.

'There aren't any,' I said. 'It's still called the Sheep Fair, but there aren't any sheep these days.'

'Doesn't the Trade Descriptions Act apply in Sussex?'

'Wouldn't you like to go on one of the nice merry-go-rounds?'

'No, I want to look at sheep, just like you promised.'

'Wouldn't you like to purchase some charming examples of rural arts and crafts?'

'Are they mainly made of wood and bits of old wool? Are they all coloured beige or grey?'

'I expect so.'

'You really know how to treat a girl right, don't you?'

It was a warm early September afternoon. It had rained on and off for days, but now the sun shone on the 'Sheep' Fair. Local families, less concerned than Elsie about accurate nomenclature, had blocked Nepcote Lane with a crawling line of saloon cars and estates that stretched back to the centre of Findon village.

On foot, we had overtaken the whole queue in five minutes or so. Now those at the front were being ushered efficiently into an adjacent field, and we were proceeding through the madding crowds of Nepcote Green. Elsie was good at negotiating throngs of this sort. Her technique had little to do with dodging and weaving and more to do with making it clear to oncoming traffic that it was entirely their problem. By sticking in her slipstream, I too made good progress. The ground was soft but not yet soft enough to be called muddy. The late summer sward was flattened and trampled dark green underfoot. The smell of crushed grass hung in the air. Inside the booths and marquees it intensified and mixed with mildew, sweat and the aroma of country crafts (two parts leather, one part lavender, one part pure nostalgia). It was what people were breathing, at that very moment, at country fairs up and down the land.

'Do you want to try fishing for things at that stall over there?'

I indicated a round edifice painted bright yellow and red at which one or two children were trying to capture plastic ducks with short, hooked rods.

'What do I get if I hook one?' asked Elsie.

'If it's a prize-winning duck, then one of the things on the shelf there,' I said.

Elsie eyed up the cuddly toys, the blow-up mallets and other enticements.

'Which have an average value of what?'

'A fiver, maybe.'

'A fiver, absolute max. And with what chance of winning?'

'Elsie, this is just for fun.'

'You can't afford fun, Tressider, unless you deliver that manuscript to me PDQ. Any progress yet?'

'Lots,' I said.

'Do try to be more convincing when you lie,' said Elsie. 'Fiction is supposed to be what you're good at.'

My gaze drifted back over the green to where Dave Peart was engaged in duck fishing. He had already won a giant inflatable mallet. I wondered briefly what people did with them, other than carry them around fairgrounds looking slightly embarrassed. Perhaps at another stall you could win inflatable nails.

'That'll be useful,' said Elsie, watching as Peart was presented with a second, identical, inflatable. 'Does everyone in the village come to this, then?'

'Most people,' I said. 'Look, there's Mrs Michie over there, selling cakes.'

'As in "chocolate cake"?' asked Elsie.

I was about to reply, but my agent had already gone.

⋨ ⋨ ⋨

'I know Sir Robert's dead,' said Mrs Michie, a little defensively, 'but I didn't want to let the Women's Institute down. Always have a stall here every year.'

I nodded. It was unreasonable to expect the entire Muntham household to go into full mourning, and Dave Peart could in any case be seen trying to win a coconut, impeded only slightly by the two mallets he was trying to control. Possibly other members of the Muntham Court staff were there too.

'I suppose,' I said to Mrs Michie, as Elsie calculated the calorific content of the various cakes in front of her, 'I suppose you haven't seen Gillian Maggs here?'

Mrs Michie had been rearranging what seemed to me to be a perfectly well-ordered display of cakes on the table in front of her. She paused at this point and stood up straight, her hands on her hips. 'What if I have?'

'I was just wondering,' I said. 'I need to talk to her.'

'I know,' said Mrs Michie. 'You said. You're doing quite a lot of talking, aren't you? If Gill's here, I expect she'll be here to enjoy herself, not to answer questions.'

'Well, yes, of course, but...'

'It's all a waste of your time, anyway. If there was something to find, the police would have found it. And I doubt you'll get much out of Her Ladyship's friends either.'

'Won't I?'

'They'll stick together as per usual. That's what they're good at. Anyway, there's nothing Gill Maggs will be able to tell you.'

'I'll bear that in mind.'

'You do that.'

'But if you did see her, could you say I was looking for her?'

'If I see her. That'll be three pounds fifty.'

'Cheap at any price.' Elsie counted out the money and her chosen cake was put into an old Tesco bag.

'I can't help feeling,' I said to Elsie as we walked away, 'that Mrs Michie doesn't want us to talk to Gillian Maggs.'

'Not necessarily,' said Elsie, looking down into the bag with affection. 'You see, Mrs Michie still divides the world into "us" and "them". Because you can employ the subjunctive—or at least you have some idea of its possible uses—and because you get invited to dinner at Muntham Court, you are "them". Gillian Maggs, Dave Peart and John O'Brian are, however, "us". If there's any conflict of interest, it's no contest which side she'll be on.'

'So, because I'm a writer, I'm "them"?'

'Not *just* because you're a writer,' said Elsie, 'though it doesn't help your case.'

'I'm sure I used to be "us",' I said.

'Maybe a long time ago,' said Elsie, patting my arm. 'A very long time ago.'

'Shall we just go back to the flat?' I asked.

'You should probably get on with some work. We need to keep your publisher happy. Just remember that writers are to publishers what sheep are to shepherds. Viewed collectively, you're essential—in fact they'd look a bit silly without you. Individually, however, you are all just so many mutton chops and a woolly hat.'

'You are a great comfort.'

'That's my job. So, how's the book going?'

'Master Thomas is in Sussex. He's been stitched up by somebody.'

'An evil woman?'

'I'm not sure. I'd been thinking that Lady Catherine was behind it all, but I'm beginning to feel she is innocent.'

'I bet she's not. Where is Master Thomas now?'

'He's about to be dragged off to some dungeon and be tortured.'

'Why?'

'He doesn't know. He's been duped.'

'Silly tosser,' said Elsie.

✦ ✦ ✦

At Bramber

Thomas had, in the course of his work, been granted the opportunity to visit several castles and inspect the different parts of them, including (though purely in passing, and as briefly as he decently could) the dungeon. Dungeons were, in his view, not happy places. They lacked most of the things that made life comfortable. What little they possessed was designed for the most part to make life distinctly unpleasant. Their long-term residents had appeared despondent, even those who were unchained. Staying out of dungeons seemed a good rule to follow. Unfortunately, he had just broken that rule.

Thomas had been permitted to ride his own horse to Bramber Castle, though what had happened to the animal since he had dismounted in the courtyard, he had little idea. He had also been deprived of his sausage-cutting Excalibur. Introductions had been made during the journey to the extent that he knew that he had been detained by the Sheriff of Sussex and two of his men, but all three seemed to feel that they could wait until they were in the dungeon to get better acquainted with Thomas. And even then, they were happy to prevaricate until the following day. Maybe their chambers elsewhere in the castle were drier and warmer and maybe they were not awoken from time to time by rats running across their faces. It was only a guess on Thomas's part.

Now Thomas was seated on a low three-legged stool and the three men were standing facing him. It was perhaps morning or perhaps early afternoon of the day after his arrest. It was difficult to say down here. Possibly at some stage he would be able to ask.

'Master Thomas,' said the Sheriff, 'you are aware of the seriousness of your position?'

'I am aware that I am under arrest. That is sometimes serious.'

'You do not ask by what authority?'

'You are armed and I am not. That is usually authority enough. I am curious to know the charges. But only if it is agreeable to you gentlemen to tell me.'

'You will be charged with the murder of Sir Edmund de Muntham.'

'Thank you. I am very obliged to you for clearing up that small matter. The only thing I am still unsure of is why you should think I might wish to murder Sir Edmund.'

'You covet his wife.'

'I already have one wife. I really have no need for another. I am told that Mohammedans are permitted several wives, but they clearly have a stronger constitution than we Christians.'

'You wrote Lady Catherine de Muntham a poem.'

'I would not presume to do any such thing. She is a great lady and I am merely a humble—'

'—clerk—yes, we know.'

'—customs officer, I was going to say.'

'You lie, Master Thomas. We have seen the poem. Lady Catherine gave us the manuscript that you brought with you from London.'

'Yes, of course. But I merely copied it out, with one or two minor improvements of my own. My master, Geoffrey Chaucer—a far superior poet, as he frequently tells me—wrote the verses and asked me to make a facsimile of them and give it to her...'

The Sheriff held up a gloved palm, its fingers spread. Thomas noticed that the leather was soft, but already darkened and marked from handling the reins and the sword. 'You came to Findon to murder Sir Edmund out of jealousy. You detained him with a letter *that purported to come from the King, but that was in fact some piece of nonsense that you concocted.'*

'No, I must assure you, it is genuine.'

'The message asked him to watch for smugglers, did it not?'

'Yes, as I recall.'

'Is it likely that the King would trouble Sir Edmund in this way? You detained him, I say, with this pretended message from the King, while his men rode off onto the downs to hunt. You followed Sir Edmund and overtook him.'

'Overtook him? On my horse? You do Sir Edmund, and his horse, a grave injustice.'

'You found another pretext to approach him, then stabbed him through the heart with your dagger and returned to Muntham Court, feigning to await his return. Though offered the hospitality of Lady Catherine, you declined it and showed every sign of being anxious to flee from the county before your crime was discovered.'

'No, it was Lady Catherine who urged me to leave, while I said that—'

'You lie, Master Thomas, and you lie badly.'

'I lie badly—you are quite right, I really must learn how to lie better. In the meantime I have little choice but to tell you the truth.'

'There are ways of ensuring that men are truthful.'

'Yes, I believe you mentioned that. Yesterday, or the day before, depending on how long I have been here.'

'You have, I assume, been shown the instruments of torture?'

'Somebody kindly offered to do so, but I told him not to trouble himself. I am an officer of the crown. I am broadly aware of the range of instruments available to you. I have no wish to be better acquainted with them.'

'Then, Master Thomas, you would do well to tell us the truth now rather than later.'

'As I say…I have told you all that I know.'

'You do not seem to appreciate the seriousness of your position. I am not sure whether you are brave or stupid.'

'Not brave, unfortunately. But hopefully not stupid either. I have no more wish to be tortured than anyone else. If you gentlemen

intended to harm me, however, then I think you would have already done so. My horse could, after all, have stumbled in the icy road and thrown me, breaking my neck. These things happen. You had no need to bring me here to kill me.'

'We have not brought you here to kill you, clerk—we have brought you here to discover the truth.'

'But you are intelligent gentlemen. I doubt that you really believe that a clerk, particularly a clerk with so little interest in tales of chivalry, would single-handedly overcome a battle-hardened soldier like Sir Edmund. Nor do I think you believe that Lady Catherine would have the slightest interest in me. Though, I must confess, I find my face pleasing enough, few ladies share that view. Torturing me would be unlikely to reveal anything that you did not know and returning me to my master the King in an imperfect state might be inconvenient for you.'

'Might it?' asked the Sheriff, with a raised eyebrow.

'Yes, I really think it might. If I were guilty of treason it would be another matter, of course.'

'You mean,' said the Sheriff, permitting himself the briefest of smiles, 'that an innocent man has nothing to fear?'

'Dear me, no. I am not so naïve as to think that,' said Thomas. 'So, let me ask you a question that I have frequently found useful under circumstances such as these: what is it precisely that I can do for you good gentlemen?'

'You can tell us the truth, you insolent quill-driver,' growled one of the flanking men at arms, but he was promptly silenced by the chief questioner.

'How helpful were you offering to be?' asked the Sheriff.

'As helpful as I need to be to get out of here without being tortured.'

The Sheriff considered this.

'We know,' he said very carefully, 'that Sir Edmund was murdered by a man dressed as a clerk. We have a witness, who is willing to swear to this.'

'How fortunate,' said Thomas, nervously rubbing his hands together. 'How fortunate.'

'As long as there is only one witness, of course, there is always some room for doubt,' continued the Sheriff. 'Our witness is a man of impeccable honesty, family, integrity, appearance, smell and so on and so forth, but that may not stop some people questioning the accuracy of his statement. In view of the frequency with which he has given evidence for the Crown in court, you would think that people would trust him, but we live in a sadly cynical world. And it is important that this matter is cleared up as soon as possible. We would not wish, for example, for suspicion to fall on some innocent party because of doubts about the identification of the killer. That would, to use your own expression, be inconvenient. We would not want that. I am sure you would not want that.'

'Indeed not,' said Thomas, rubbing his hands now with some speed. 'I most certainly would not want that.'

'Of course, there would be no such doubts if we had apprehended this criminal clerk. Or, now I think about it, if we had a second witness of equally impeccable character, who was willing to swear that he too had seen this person.'

'Seen them in the act of murdering Sir Edmund?'

'Not necessarily, if the witness felt unable to recall such an event. It might be sufficient that the reliable witness had seen a clerk, of medium height, dressed in a black gown and a grey hood, loitering in the woods above Muntham Court late in the forenoon.'

'Just so. Could it be that the reliable witness had seen this clerk, with an ink-black robe and a hood the colour of summer thunderclouds, half-concealed amongst the trees, clutching a gleaming and deadly blade? And that the witness overheard the clerk muttering terrible threats against Sir Edmund?'

'I think the reliable witness would be wise to stick to a simple and unembroidered statement.'

'Strangely,' said Master Thomas, 'I think I could have seen somebody dressed exactly in the manner you describe, while I was speaking to Sir Edmund. He was half-concealed in the bushes a little way ahead of us, and vanished off before we had finished our conversation.'

'You presumably thought little of it at the time, and therefore had no need to warn Sir Edmund? You returned to Muntham Court immediately?'

'Exactly.'

'I have taken the words out of your mouth?'

'No, quite the reverse, I assure you,' said Thomas.

'I shall have a statement drawn up for you to sign,' said the Sheriff. 'You saw a clerk with a grey hood.'

'I'd prefer a hood the colour of thunderclouds on a summer's day.'

'Grey,' said the Sheriff. 'You could of course stay here until we have some summer thunderclouds to compare the hood with—or we could just say it was grey. As the other witness did.'

'On reflection, I remember it as merely grey. And while I am waiting for this document to be drawn up, perhaps I might have some breakfast if it is breakfast-time, or dinner if it is dinner-time?'

'You may have both,' said the Sheriff, generously.

Chapter Fourteen

'How's it going?' asked Elsie.

I shut the top of my computer immediately.

'Fine,' I said. 'Just fine.' It's a thing I have. You don't say any more than you have to about any work in progress. It was certainly much too soon to share it with Elsie.

'Has Master Thomas been tortured yet?'

'As much as he needs to be.'

'I'm sure I could give you a hand,' she said. 'I'm good at plots.'

'I can manage on my own. Thanks.'

Some time before we had written a book jointly. It was an experience I wanted to forget.

'I've been thinking about this suspect,' said Elsie, changing tack, as she so often did.

'Which one?'

'The guy with the blue suit and beanie.'

'Two witnesses saw him,' I said.

'Two witnesses *say* they saw him.'

'I can't see that John O'Brian and Clive Brent would concoct a story together.'

'Not when they are rivals for the attention of Mrs Shagger. Don't pull that face—you know as well as I do that she was sleeping with one or both. But I agree—they don't seem to be likely conspirators. So maybe there really was somebody wearing a blue suit in the grounds that evening. Of course, it doesn't make him the murderer.'

'It would be good,' I said, 'just to have some sort of independent corroboration that there was such a person.'

My mobile rang. It was Annabelle.

'Ethelred,' she said. 'I've got some really good news. We've found the beanie.'

The light was beginning to fade by the time we got back to Muntham Court. Annabelle and Dave Peart were waiting for us in the garden.

'He found it in the shrubbery,' said Annabelle. 'Didn't you?'

Dave Peart, to whom this last remark had been addressed, gave an embarrassed shrug. 'Yeah,' he said eventually.

'It was very clever of him,' she added.

I took the beanie from Annabelle. It was made of black wool and looked pretty new—the sort of anonymous headgear you can pick up in any market for a fiver or so. It felt warm in my hand.

'Show Mr Tressider where you found it,' said Annabelle.

Dave Peart gave another shrug and set off across the lawn towards the shrubbery. We went several yards into the mass of overgrown bushes before he pointed to a spot on the ground, just short of the garden wall.

'There,' he said. 'On top of them leaves there, just by the old wall, isn't it?'

'Right,' I said.

'Well, aren't you going to examine the spot or nothing?'

'There doesn't seem a lot to examine,' I said. 'Just leaves.'

'Thought you was some sort of detective.'

'I'm some sort of crime writer,' I said.

I knelt down and immediately regretted it as I felt the damp start to seep into the knees of my trousers. I gave the leaves a cursory inspection. I got up again.

'The garden wall would be easy to climb,' I said. 'It would seem likely that the intruder dropped the beanie here as he was going over the wall, or maybe as he was looking for the easiest place to climb it.'

The spot was well hidden from the house, as it was from the rest of the garden. This would be a good place to slip over the wall—a good place to vanish afterwards. I had no intention of climbing over it myself, but, placing my hands on the smooth flints that topped it and one shoe in a convenient gap lower down, I pulled myself up far enough to see what was on the other side. A muddy footpath hugged it for twenty or thirty yards, coming from (as far as I could tell) the main road and veering away upwards and onto the downs in the other direction.

'I'll give you a leg up if you want,' offered Dave from behind me.

'That won't be necessary,' I said, dropping back down. 'Where does that path go?'

'Storrington, I'd say. Can't think why anyone would go there that way, though, when there's a perfectly good road. Unless they was poaching or something.'

'It would take you there through the woods,' I said. 'You could slip away unnoticed.'

'Who's going to notice you on the road anyway?' asked Dave. 'You drive past some geezer walking along the grass verge. You don't see his face or nothing. Or he could leave his car in the village—round the side of Winton's store. No point in slogging over the downs to ruddy Storrington. It'd take you the better part of an hour.'

'What does it matter whether he went to Storrington or to Worthing or to anywhere else?' interrupted Annabelle. 'The point is that we have two reliable witnesses who saw the man, and now this evidence that he really was here. Ethelred, we should phone the police now and tell them what you have discovered. They can take over from here.'

'Whatever you wish—' I began to say.

'We haven't talked to Gillian Maggs,' said Elsie.

'True but—' I said.

'I am sure that she saw nothing,' said Annabelle.

'Not much effort to give her a call,' said Elsie. 'Probably still time to do it tonight.'

'She goes to bed very early,' said Annabelle.

'We could call her early tomorrow then,' said Elsie.

They stood facing each other. Neither appeared to be blinking.

'I'll ring her myself,' said Annabelle, 'and ask her to phone you tomorrow.'

'So, we'll delay going to the police?' I asked.

'Entirely as you wish, Ethelred,' said Annabelle. She turned sharply on her heel and strode off towards the house.

'There's gratitude,' said Elsie.

'She must be very tired,' I pointed out.

'Very. Nice beanie though,' she added, pointing to the object that I still held in my hand. 'That would keep you warm and dry.'

'Yes,' I said.

Elsie gave me one of her despairing looks.

'What?' I said.

'Time for us to go home,' she said.

'Don't you need to get back to London?'

'Thought I might stay another day,' she said. 'The weather's improving now.'

'Yes,' I said.

And she gave me another despairing look.

The Holy Sister

Thomas made the return journey to Muntham Court without an escort and with the bare minimum of instructions. More snow had fallen while he had been at the castle, but now the sun shone from an ice-blue sky. His horse's hooves crunched through the snow, following a long, snaking trail left by an earlier traveller—a traveller who hopefully knew roughly where he was going. At Washington he asked for further directions. By late afternoon he was back at Findon.

'My lady has gone to Chichester on urgent business,' said a servant. 'But we have another guest, caught in last night's storm and happily still with us—a holy sister, from a convent near London. She is warming herself by the fire. If you would like to join her, I will bring you some mulled wine.'

Thomas had rarely felt comfortable around holiness. To attend the occasional Mass was a necessity, but he was as happy avoiding priests as not. A nun or an abbess, or whatever she was, was likely to be dull company for a long winter evening. Thomas had not examined the state of his soul recently, but he was fairly sure that it was in good order and did not require maintenance at present. Still, it would be impolite not to greet the lady in a suitably decorous manner and perhaps ask for her blessing.

She proved to be a small, rather rotund figure dressed in a pale grey habit and white wimple. Tucked into her girdle was a rosary made of green beads. Attached to the beads was a gold brooch, consisting of a crowned letter A and some words that Thomas could not make out. So intent was she on what she was eating, she did not notice Thomas until he was a few feet away.

'God be with you, Mother,' he began.

The Prioress looked up. 'Tell you what,' she said, 'these honey cakes are the pilgrim's pyjamas and no mistake. They say too many honey cakes make you fat, but with my build you can carry a few extra pounds without it showing. Also the order makes you wear dresses that look like an old sack, so there's no point in maintaining a size VIII figure underneath it. Are you Master Thomas, by any chance?'

'Yes,' said Thomas.

'Lady Catherine asked me to pray for you,' she said, stuffing the last few crumbs into her mouth. 'St Peter's pastries!—I knew I'd forgotten to do something. Sorry about that. Still, no harm done by the look of things.'

'I have been locked in a dungeon and threatened with torture,' said Thomas. 'A prayer would have been good.'

'Let's say I owe you a couple of Hail Marys then,' said the Prioress, wiping her lips with the back of her hand. 'Now where's that dolted daffe with the wine?'

And Thomas was sent to look for the dolted daffe.

'So, run that past me again,' said the Prioress.

She and Thomas were sitting by the dying embers of the fire in Lady Muntham's private quarters. The dregs of the pitcher of mulled wine were now only just warm.

'As I said, my master, Geoffrey Chaucer, requested that I should take a message to Sir Edmund and a poem to his wife.'

'Did that strike you as odd?'

'No, I am often sent on errands of one sort or another.'

'To Sussex in the middle of winter?'

'Rarely, I grant you…'

'Go on.'

'I reached here yesterday morning. I found Sir Edmund about to set off hunting. I explained that I had a message for him, with the King's seal upon it. He took it, broke the seal and read it.'

'Then?'

'Then he asked me what the message meant.'

'And?'

'I was unable to explain. There was very little to it. Just a request to watch the coast and guard against those who would bring goods into the realm without paying the necessary duties.'

'Not the most urgent of messages?'

'Arguably not.'

'Might have waited until the spring?'

'The collection of the correct duties on wine, spices and so on and so forth is of course of the utmost importance…but, yes, I would have said it could have waited until the snow had melted.'

'What was the exact wording of this important message?'

'I don't remember. Sir Edmund read it, then gave me the parchment to read myself, then I…then I tucked it inside my robe… and here it is!' Thomas drew the folded sheet from inside his robe, where it had sat for a day and a night and a day.

' "The King sends greetings to his trusty servant Sir Edmund de Muntham," ' read the Prioress, who seemed to have acquired the parchment. ' "I require you to watch well our coast of Sussex as you do value your life and chattels, and to bring to justice those that land wine or other goods without the payment of such taxes as are due unto our Royal Person." Not much there. What did you say the Sheriff thought of the letter?'

'He thought that it must be a piece of nonsense that I had concocted.'

'But just you and Sir Edmund read the letter?'

'That's right.'

'So how did the Sheriff know what was in it?'

'I'm not sure.'

'And the poem. You wrote that yourself?'

'No, it was Master Geoffrey Chaucer. A great poet.'

'So you didn't know what that said either?'

'Yes, I read it. In fact, I tidied it up a bit as I copied it out. I can still remember the poem, if you'd like to hear it.'

'Try me,' said the Prioress, though not in the manner of one who expects a pleasant treat.

Master Thomas coughed and began to recite.

'Your bright eyes twain will slay me suddenly
I may the beauty of them not sustain
For they do pierce straight through my poor
    heart keen

Unless your word will heal (and hastily)
My heart's cruel wound, while yet it is still green.
Your bright eyes twain will slay me suddenly

I may the beauty of them not sustain.

Upon my oath I say (and faithfully)
That of my life and death you are the queen

And with my death shall truth at last be seen:
Your bright eyes twain did slay me suddenly
I could the beauty of them not sustain
And they did pierce straight through my poor
    heart keen.'

'St Oswald's oatmeal!' exclaimed the holy sister. 'What tedious
nonsense! Some poor pathetic male whingeing about being treated
badly by his mistress. He's probably only after one thing, and it
isn't either of her eyes. It's enough to make you become a nun, except
I am one already. You men are a bigger help to religion than you
sometimes imagine.'

'As you know,' said Master Thomas, 'the convention of courtly
love is that the lover can expect nothing except perhaps one brief
smile that is recompense for many years of pain and devoted service.'

'And marriage?'

'Well, obviously he can get married—to anybody except the lady
in question, who must remain unattainable.'

'And that's it?'

'Yes.'

'It doesn't sound much fun for anyone.'

'Not much.'

'Hold on, here's a thought. What if the hidden message was not
in the sealed document for Sir Edmund, but in the poem?'

'It could have been. I hadn't thought of that. I guess it could
have been an acrostic. Or maybe the message might be hidden in a
few key words. The problem with that, of course, is that I changed
some of it…I cut a few lines that didn't really seem necessary, for
example.'

'But Chaucer knew you had made changes?'

'No, not really.'

'So a coded message saying: "This is to warn you that a man
is coming to kill your husband," could have got changed during

your redrafting to one saying: "This man is coming to kill your husband."'

'*That seems a little far-fetched.*'

'*You're right. Trying to send concealed messages in a poem is a really bad idea. Who would have wanted Sir Edmund dead?*'

'*Well, the Duke of Gloucester, allegedly. And maybe the Duke of Lancaster. Possibly Simon de Burley too. The court's a hotbed of intrigue these days.*'

'*Tricky. Perhaps the more important question then is: Who set you up?*'

'*No, the only important question now is: Can I get out of here and safely back to London?*'

'*But a murder has been committed.*'

'*So it would seem.*'

'*And the Sheriff seems intent on a cover-up.*'

'*Yes, I would have thought that was likely.*'

'*In which case, the culprit may go free and some poor innocent man will be hanged.*'

'*The former certainly—though not necessarily the latter. I'll need to ask for directions to Horsham. I can pick up the London road from there.*'

'*And you are planning to let him get away with it?*'

'*Put simply, yes, I am planning to do just that.*'

'*Call yourself a man?*'

'*My wife asks me the same question from time to time. Since she implies she already knows the answer, I rarely trouble her with a response.*'

The Prioress fixed Thomas with a stare. '*Has it occurred to you that Lady Catherine may be in danger?*'

'*Is she?*'

'*By St Stephen's sausages, I fear she is! So, Master Thomas, don't you think you should do something about it?*'

'*Such as?*'

'*We'll find out what is going on and bring the murderer to justice.*'

'*But how?*'

'*Let's go back to the beginning. How exactly did all this start?*'

I scrolled back to the opening of the chapter and reread it. The Prioress was worryingly familiar. Whoever it was, however, she was not Chaucer's Prioress. I took down my copy of Chaucer from the shelf. If this was Chaucer's Prioress, then her greatest oath ought to be 'by St Loy'—these food-related expletives were innocent enough, but incongruous coming from one who was (surely?) committed to frugality and abstinence. She should also 'let no morsel from hir lippes falle', rather than spray honey cake in all directions. On the other hand, she definitely resembled somebody I knew.

'I hope you're keeping it simple,' said Elsie. 'No meta-fictional cleverness?'

'Heaven forefend,' I said.

'And no poxy flashbacks.'

'Maybe just the odd one,' I said. 'I need to know how the story starts.'

The Flower of Cities All

It was, thought Master Thomas, merely a question of whether the soot fell faster than the snow or vice versa. A snowfall overnight, when the fires were dead or smouldering, caused the early-morning city to appear briefly as a bride—robed in virginal white, though a little frostier than a husband might wish. But, if the snow fell during the day, it was at once mixed with bituminous smuts and was grey, even before the carts had rolled through it and the chamber pots had been emptied on top of it, and the stray dogs had pissed in whatever remained. It wasn't a good plan to slip in the snow in London, because a lot of what was on the ground hadn't exactly come out of the sky.

Thomas extracted his foot from the icy puddle into which he had plunged it. Below the grey ice, the water was yellow. Unless there was a good fire at the Customs Office (which was unlikely) that foot would be wet all day. Still, at least the other one was more or less dry. It was, as Master Thomas always liked to point out, important to look on the bright side.

And, to be entirely fair, the sun had just broken through both the cloud and the smoke to reveal an improbably blue sky, visible in thin strips above the narrow lanes of old London. He was fortunate to live in this great city, so large and populous that it could be smelt two miles away, and bound by walls so strong that only treachery (usually available at a price) could cause the city to fall to any of its many enemies. Londoners were proud people, suspicious of foreigners, of the nobility, of the King and, with good reason, of each other. They were proud of their stinking city on its stinking river, proud of its growing wealth. Thomas's job, in the Customs Office for the Port of London, was to grab as much of that wealth for the King as he reasonably could. In return for which, the King looked after his servants as well as might be expected.

'There is,' said Geoffrey Chaucer, Thomas's superior and as close to the King as Thomas usually got, 'no earthly need for a fire in your room. The snow is almost melting and the fire in my own room will in any case send forth some warmth into yours. I shall have more sea coals placed on my fire.'

'Thank you,' said Thomas. 'You are very kind.'

'Don't mention it,' said Chaucer. 'In any case, you will not be in the office long today.'

'Indeed, indeed,' said Thomas, rubbing his hands together—a nervous habit he had developed, but a useful one in an office with only indirect access to heating.

'Do you know Sussex?' asked Chaucer.

'Sussex? Sussex?' said Thomas. He had also developed a habit of repeating his words in a jocular tone, a mannerism that was beginning to irritate even himself. He rattled off his minimal knowledge of the southern counties. 'Sussex. The seat of the Lord Bishop of Chichester. The site of some noble castles—Arundel, Lewes

*and so on. And some notable ports—Winchelsea, Rye, Shoreham—
none of which are the responsibility of this office. Good sheep country,
as I have heard. Fine sheep country. Quite exceptional—'*

*Chaucer held up his hand. 'Excellent, Master Thomas. You are
the very man for the job, then.'*

*'Am I? Am I?' He was going to need to watch this repetition
thing. 'What job would that be then?'*

*'To take an important message on behalf of the King to Sir
Edmund de Muntham.'*

'Who is where...?'

'Findon.'

'And that is near...?'

*'Nowhere, really. But it is in Sussex and since you know Sussex
so well, you are clearly the right person to entrust with such an
important mission.'*

*'I understand. I un...So, when the snow clears, and the weather
is a little less harsh and the roads a little more passable, you wish me
to go to Sussex?'*

'No. As I said, you will not be long in the office today.'

'You want me to go today?'

'Yes.'

'In the snow?'

'Yes.'

'Along dangerous and largely impassable roads?'

'Yes.'

*'On which I might die of cold or be bludgeoned to death by
robbers?'*

'Yes.'

*'I suppose I couldn't wait until the young sun has run half his
course into the Ram?' said Thomas.*

'What?' said Chaucer.

'It's a poetic way of denoting April,' said Thomas.

*'Is it?' said Chaucer, scribbling something quickly onto a sheet of
parchment and then folding it over. 'Well, the answer's "no" anyway.
I need you to go immediately. Go home and pack and I'll have the
letter waiting for you when you return. Then piss off to Sussex.*

Oh, and copy out this poem first—I want you to give it to Lady Catherine de Muntham when you see her.'

'Gone to his dinner,' said Master Richard, Thomas's fellow clerk, when he eventually returned, a small leather satchel over his shoulder and both feet now soaking. 'The Comptroller left this for you, though—letter for some geezer in Sussex.'

Thomas took the single sheet of folded parchment secured with its wax seal and weighed it in his hand.

'At first sight, a pretty insubstantial thing to justify a man catching his death of cold on the road, isn't it?' said Master Thomas.

'What business has the Port of London with Sussex anyway?' asked Richard. 'Sounds like a job for one of the Clerks of the Signet. I'd tell that fat windbag you won't go. Not your responsibility, Master Thomas. I'd tell him: "Stuff your letter where the friars go when they die."'

'You mean up the Devil's arse?'

'Precisely.'

'No. He'd only use the metaphor in one of his poems.' Thomas looked again at the slim missive in his hand.

'Tell him you're sick,' suggested Richard.

'But I'm not. The King is sending some customs-related message to Sir Edmund de Muntham. I suppose it must be important.'

'Sir Edmund de Muntham?' asked Richard.

'That's right.'

'The same Sir Edmund de Muntham who narrowly avoided losing his head for treason?'

'There's probably only one of them.'

'The same Sir Edmund de Muntham who had to run off to his estates in Sussex to avoid a good kicking from the Duke of Gloucester's supporters?'

'That's right.'

'The same Sir Edmund de Muntham who has fallen foul of every faction at court?'

'As I say—'

'The same Sir Edmund de Muntham that it would be very risky going anywhere near, unless you wanted a good kicking too?'

'The King's messenger enjoys a certain degree of protection...'

'Only if you can point out that's who you are before you lose consciousness. You wouldn't be the first King's messenger to be beaten to death—though with luck you might be the last.'

'That would be lucky?'

'For the rest of us, yes.'

'But why should anyone know I am carrying a letter for Sir Edmund?'

'Thomas, this is the King's court that we're talking about here. Everyone will know you are carrying a letter for Sir Edmund.'

'Good point,' said Thomas, rubbing his hands together. 'Good poi...I'd better get started then.'

Chapter Fifteen

Elsie had, for reasons she chose not to explain, gone out for a walk in the rain. I was sitting in front of my computer, nominally writing a novel but in practice mainly watching the rain run down the window.

I had written the first chapter of the Master Thomas novel and the plot was becoming a little clearer in my head—though it might require some redrafting of Thomas's arrest. Sir Edmund had made enemies, one of whom had followed him to Sussex and killed him—at least, that seemed likely. I needed to research this a bit more and work out which faction he might have belonged to, but there were plenty to choose from. The Merciless Parliament of 1388 would convict almost the entire court of treason, including (interestingly) a colleague of Chaucer's and Master Thomas's named Nicholas Brembre. Of obscure origins and staggeringly rich, Brembre was eventually hanged. He would be a good historical character to introduce. The fact that he was a financier would make his grisly end quite popular. But Brembre was a loyal supporter of the King. Did that mean that both the King and the Duke of Gloucester wanted Sir Edmund dead? And to which faction, if any, did the Sheriff owe his loyalty?

I was so taken up with this problem that it took me a moment to realize that the noise in the background was the phone ringing. I answered it.

'It's Jane,' said the caller.

'Yes...' I said.

'Gerald is in the swimming pool, but he could be back any moment.'

It seemed odd that Gerald should be swimming in the rain, though it can be raining hard in Findon but sunny in Horsham. Then I remembered that they had been about to go off on a short holiday somewhere.

'You're phoning from the hotel?' I asked.

'Yes, from our room.'

'Right.'

'Look—there's something you need to know. It's about Clive Brent. It was Robert's fault that he was fired.'

'I think Gerald told me that,' I said.

'Yes, but you don't know the whole story. Nobody really does except Gerald—and Clive up to a point. And Gerald would have given you the official version. This derivatives thing that almost brought the bank down was Robert's idea. Clive was just on the fringes of it all. When the balloon went up, Robert told Clive he'd be fine. But then...'

'But then?'

'Robert dumped him right in it to save his own skin. Made out that it was Clive acting on his own. He said he would do the decent thing and resign, because he should have watched Clive more closely. Going like that took the pressure off the other directors. That's why Robert got a reasonable settlement from the bank when he left and Clive got nothing.'

'Does Clive know all this?' I asked.

'I guess he must have worked it out.'

I tried to remember what Clive had told me himself. 'And you're saying if he had worked it out...' I said.

'It would be a good motive for murder, wouldn't it? If the police should be investigating anyone, it's him.'

'You could tell the police,' I said.

'No, I can't—and I don't want Gerald to know that I've told you.'

'Well…' I started to say, but the line went dead. Bad reception in Antibes or the arrival of a damp husband. It was not clear which.

I returned to the matter in hand. I was just wondering whether to make Alexander Neville (archbishop and traitor, 1340-92) the villain of the piece when the phone went again. Gerald Smith had clearly gone straight off to have a shower, giving Jane a second shot at implicating Clive Brent. But that was not who it was.

'Clive Brent here,' said the caller.

'Good to hear from you,' I said.

'Is it? Look, there's something you need to know about John O'Brian.'

'Fire away.'

'You know he's been having an affair with Annabelle?'

'Just a rumour. I don't believe it.'

'No, it's absolutely true, I assure you. And I think he's been blackmailing her.'

'Surely not?'

'Take a look at their bank account. He must be the best-paid gardener in Sussex. If the police should be investigating anyone it's him.'

'But if he was blackmailing the Munthams, why should he want to kill Robert?'

'Look, Ethelred, there was something very funny going on there.'

'I'll check it out,' I said.

'Don't tell Annabelle I said any of this.'

'No, of course not.'

The phone rang again almost as soon as I had put it down.

'Jane's gone for a walk,' said the caller. 'I haven't got long though.'

'Hi, Gerald,' I said.

'Look, there's something you need to know about Felicity Hooper.'

'Tell me about it.'

'You know she had a fling with Robert at Oxford?'

'Yes, she told me.'

'Did she say anything about an abortion?'

'No.'

'Robert phoned me about a year or so ago. He mentioned in passing that he'd met Hooper again, then right out of the blue he asks what his position would be if somebody that he had known years before tried to sue him for distress caused by an abortion she had had to have. I asked him to be more specific, but he said he was just curious to know in theory what might happen.'

'And?'

'I said if it was a long time ago, then the courts would probably rule it out for that reason alone, but it was a bit outside my area of expertise; I offered to get a colleague to advise him. He said thanks and he'd get back to me if he needed further advice.'

'And?'

'That's it really. It sounds as if he got Hooper pregnant and she had an abortion. Years later she contacted him again and made some sort of threat.'

'Or maybe it really was a theoretical question?'

A snort of derision came down the line. 'Robert only asked my legal opinion if he really needed it. He was in trouble. I'm sure of it.'

'So, your answer reassured him?'

'Must have done—he never mentioned it again.'

'Strange—when you said so little, I mean.'

'That's true. He seemed very tense at the beginning of the conversation, but quite chatty when we had finished.'

'And that was the whole conversation?'

'Well, it was a year or more ago, but, yes, that was pretty much all of it—other than the chatty bit at the very end.'

'But do you think it has any bearing on the murder?'

'Absolutely. Hooper has a clear motive. If the police should be investigating anyone it's her.'

'But it was a very long time ago—why should she want to kill Robert now?'

'Look, Ethelred, there was something very funny going on there.'

'I'll check it out,' I said.

'Don't tell Jane I said any of this.'

I was becoming confused about what I could tell to whom, but I just said: 'No, of course not. I hope you enjoyed your swim.'

'Yes, it was great,' he said.

It was only as I put the phone down that I remembered that it was Jane who had told me about the swimming pool. Gerald was going to find that last remark of mine very odd if he gave it any thought.

I needed a break to clear my head, but I was not about to get one. Elsie strode into the room, dripping wet, clutching an equally wet black beanie. She held it out triumphantly.

'How dry is that now?' she demanded.

So, there it was. My agent had finally flipped. It had to happen sooner or later.

Chapter Sixteen

I really object to the way it rains in the country.

London rain comes more or less straight down, observing the laws of gravity. It's wet, but it's well-behaved. Country rain comes at you from all angles.

It hadn't even been raining that much when I went out—just enough to prove my point. There was something I needed to check out. It involved creeping up a gravel drive, but I figured nobody was going to be out in the garden when it was pissing down. So even when the rain got heavier, I counted it as a blessing of sorts.

It was on the journey back that I realized that I should have got Ethelred to drive me, but then it wouldn't have been my discovery. Even now, he didn't quite seem to get the point, any more than he had in the garden the day before.

'No,' I said in reply to his question. 'I don't want a quiet lie-down and I don't want a cup of strong sweet tea. Look at this beanie. Is it a) dry or b) really wet?'

'It's obviously wet,' he said. 'You didn't have to take it out in the rain to show me what a wet beanie looks like. You could have run it under a tap. Are you sure you wouldn't like to lie down?'

'Yes,' I said. 'And when we found it in the garden was it a) wet or b) dry?'

'Dry. I think that was option b).'

'So there you are,' I said.

'Where am I?' he asked.

'Yesterday,' I said, 'we found a bone-dry beanie. I wanted to check whether that was at all likely. So I went back to Muntham Court in the rain and placed the beanie on the same spot. It was soaked through in minutes. And what had the weather been like between the murder and our finding the beanie?'

'Mixed. It rained overnight and then—'

'It *rained overnight*. So what should the beanie have been: a) wet or b) very wet?'

'OK—I think I understand without your doing the a) or b) thing. Maybe you just put it back in the wrong spot.'

'Ethelred, think. You knelt down on the ground by it, yes?'

'Yes.'

'And were your knees a)—'

'OK, they were very wet,' he conceded, cleverly anticipating both options. Sometimes he's quite on the ball for a third-rate crime writer.

'This beanie did not fall from the head of an intruder in a blue suit. Somebody planted it in that spot—probably no more than a few minutes before we found it.'

'But it was just you and me and Annabelle and Dave Peart,' said Ethelred.

As far as we know,' I said. 'I suppose there could have been anyone concealed in the bushes. Still, the four of us, with the silicon-enhanced tart as the prime suspect, is still OK by me.'

'But why? Clive and John O'Brian both saw the intruder. Why plant a hat when you've got two reliable witnesses?'

'Why indeed? You have to admit it's interesting.'

Ethelred was thoughtful for a moment and then said: 'Actually, I had one or two pieces of information myself this afternoon. Jane Smith phoned to say that the murderer was Clive Brent, Clive Brent phoned to say it was John O'Brian and Gerald Smith phoned to say it was Felicity Hooper.'

The last of these interested me. I said so.

'Gerald said that Robert had phoned him,' Ethelred continued, 'and asked, in effect, if Felicity had any legal redress for a pregnancy and abortion some years ago. Gerald advised him that it was unlikely and he seemed much relieved. I'm not sure I believe it myself, though. Felicity said they had had a fling and that Robert had dumped her—but there was no suggestion of any fallout of that sort.'

'Or then again, maybe it did happen,' I said.

'But we've got no evidence.'

'That's all you know. One of the problems that you writers have is that you can't keep your personal lives out of your books. No imagination, that's your trouble.'

'Maybe,' said Ethelred guardedly.

'You remember I told you that Felicity Hooper sent me her first novel?'

'And?'

'It was about a rather naive girl training in physiotherapy at Oxford. She falls for some rugby-playing yob, who gets her pregnant and dumps her. So she goes off to London and gets an abortion. But it all goes a bit wrong and she finds she can't have any more children.'

'And then?'

'I wrote Hooper a note saying that I loved the book but unfortunately I wasn't taking on any new clients at present and so on and so on.'

'No, I mean what happens in the book? Does she go back to Oxford and murder the rugby player?'

'How should I know? I don't read to the end of every manuscript I'm sent and I certainly didn't read to the end of that one. It was drivel.'

'But,' said Ethelred, 'we know that Robert did read the book and arranged to meet Felicity soon after. Then, at about the same time, he contacted his lawyer with a strange query.'

'So,' I summarized, 'he knew and was afraid she could sue him or something. Whereas maybe what she had in mind was murder.'

'Maybe,' he said.

'What was the case against Clive Brent?' I asked.

'Robert double-crossed him—left him to carry the can for the bank's losses.'

'And John O'Brian?'

'Clive Brent reckoned he had some sort of hold over the family—at least, he was being paid rather more than a gardener might expect to be paid.'

'He was being paid by Annabelle for a few night shifts,' I said. 'Of course, that might mean that he and Annabelle did want Robert out of the way.'

'Annabelle was—'

'—devoted to Robert. Yes, you've said that once or twice already. It's such a shame that repeating things doesn't make them true. But if it was Annabelle who planted the beanie, then she's doing some covering up for somebody. I can't help feeling that the whole picture is there, but we just can't see it. You know those drawings that look like a candle if you look at them one way and a pair of faces if you look at them the other way? At the moment we're seeing the candle. But if we just look at it the other way, we'll see a face.'

'Two faces,' said Ethelred, who was a bit of a stickler for accuracy. 'One candle or two faces. At least we can rule the McIntoshes out of the picture.'

Then I remembered a piece of paper that I had found in the study and that must still be in my bag. I knew exactly where I had put it so it took me only ten minutes to locate amongst the sweet wrappers and empty lipsticks.

'There!' I said.

'It's some pages you've torn out of somebody's diary,' he said.

'Shagger's diary for last year. Hidden wisely but not too well in his desk drawer. And observe closely—what do you see?'

Ethelred ran his finger down the first sheet of paper.

'Dental check-up, car MOT, FM UCLH, dinner Ivy, boiler service, FM UCLH again…' Ethelred turned and looked at me.

'Exactly,' I said. 'FM UCLH. UCLH is where Fiona McIntosh works. It's Robert's diary for last year. He was running up to town to see Fiona McIntosh on a regular basis.'

'Not running up to town,' he said. 'He hadn't bought Muntham Court then. He would have just been meeting up with her. He was, after all, an old friend. Chelsea's not that far from Euston Road.'

I raised an eyebrow but Ethelred patently failed to see things as clearly as I did.

'Whatever,' I said. 'And what did Gillian Maggs say when you spoke to her?'

'She didn't phone,' said Ethelred.

'Then phone her,' I said.

'Annabelle said—'

'Annabelle said...' I repeated.

'As I have observed before, Annabelle doesn't speak in a silly whiny schoolgirl voice.'

'That was you I was impersonating, not Annabelle.'

'Even so, I don't have her number.'

'Do you have the Worthing telephone directory?'

'Yes.'

'Then I suspect, Ethelred, that you have her number. Look, why don't you go and make me a hot sweet drink and I'll phone and see when it would be convenient for us to drop round for a chat.'

'For *me* to drop round for a chat.'

'Yes, of course,' I said with all the girlish innocence I could muster.

As I expected, the number was there in the book and I dialled it.

'Hello,' said a woman at the other end of the line.

'Is that Gillian Maggs?'

'Do you want to speak to Mum?'

'If your mother is Gillian Maggs, yes. I'll hold.'

'You'll need to hold for a while then.' There was a note of condescending insolence in her voice that told me I was talking to a teenager.

'How long?' I asked, waiting for the punchline.

'A month or so. She's gone to Barbados.'

Not a bad punchline, all things considered.

'When?' I asked.

'This morning.

'Isn't that rather sudden?'

'I think she had some sort of special deal.'

'And she's staying there for a month?'

'Maybe longer.'

'On her own?'

'No, Dad went too.'

'Do your parents often take holidays of indefinite length in the West Indies?'

'It's usually an off-season week in Benidorm. Maybe they fancied a change.'

'Did somebody give them the money to go?...Hello, are you still there?'

'Why do you ask that?'

'I just wondered.'

'Look, I've told you all I know. Ring back next month.'

'Or did somebody threaten them?'

'Who *are* you? Are you the police?'

'No.'

'Why are you asking all this stuff?'

'I need to get hold of her urgently,' I said. 'I'm a friend.' I don't know why, but that last bit came out rather more creepily than I had planned.

'I'm putting the phone down now,' she said, a bit like somebody in a call centre when you've just told them what you really think of their service.

'If they were in danger, maybe you are too...' I said.

But the line had gone dead. I tried phoning back but just got the engaged tone.

Ethelred returned, holding two steaming mugs of something. 'Annabelle's cleaner's gone to the West Indies,' I said.

'Jamaica?'

'No, but I'm wondering if somebody else did.'

Chapter Seventeen

'Are you sure you're right?' I asked as I put the two cups of coffee down on the table.

'She's gone, and not on holiday, if you want my opinion,' said Elsie. 'The daughter sounded frightened—well, worried, let's say. Anyway, Annabelle said nothing about her being away this week, let alone going off to Barbados for an indefinite stay. Gillian Maggs has done a runner.'

'So somebody has threatened her? But who?'

'The murderer,' said Elsie. 'Gillian Maggs obviously knows too much about something. The problem is that she is the only person there that day who we haven't spoken to. With hindsight you should have obviously spoken to her first.'

'Possibly,' I said.

'So, if it was the murderer who threatened her, who is the murderer? We know that Felicity Hooper has a long-standing grudge. She was out of sight of everyone else for long enough.'

'Everyone was out of sight for long enough,' I said. 'That's the problem.'

'True. And John O'Brian and Clive Brent were both having an affair with Annabelle.'

'I think that's just Dave's vivid imagination,' I said.

'Look, Ethelred, I grant you your imaginary world is a much nicer and cleaner place than Dave Peart's but, back here in real life, Annabelle was running at least three men at the time of Shagger's death. One of the two who wasn't her husband might have decided things would be better with Sir Robert Muntham out of the way—and of the likely suspects, Clive had the added incentive that Shagger had cost him his career. John was allegedly being paid more than he should have been, which is odd but it sounds less like a motive for murder.'

I shook my head.

'Shake your head all you like,' said Elsie, 'but it won't change the facts. Anyway, there are others who could have done it. Gerald Smith, for example.'

'Based on what?' I asked.

'Well, Shagger had been sleeping with his wife.'

'But a long time ago,' I pointed out.

'True enough. Shagger's affair with Jane Smith was over long before Gerald met her. It's not much of a motive, unless there was more to it than we know. Still, the Smiths would have had an opportunity like the others. Maybe it was Jane Smith who harboured the grudge?'

'Or maybe it wasn't one of the guests at all. What about Mrs Michie?'

'She and Dave Peart confirm they were together in the kitchen when Shagger popped his clogs. Mrs Michie would cover for Dave up to a point, but I don't think her loyalty would extend to covering up a murder. I'm not sure Dave Peart would cover up for anyone, unless they were paying him double time plus expenses.'

'I think we can rule out the McIntoshes,' I said.

'Colin McIntosh was one of the few people who knew Shagger was dying. It would hardly have been worth the risk of killing him, even if he wanted to. The same applies to Fiona, I guess, whatever Robert's reasons for meeting up with her. Which leaves Annabelle—and don't say she couldn't have— wives do kill husbands sometimes. She too had her chance. And then there is the business of the secret passage. She knew it was there but, when Robert was killed, she didn't suggest we should try to get into the room that way.'

'You can't get in that way,' I reminded her. 'The mechanism is broken. You can use the passage only to get out.'

'Good point. Even so, Annabelle didn't mention the passage to the police,' said Elsie, 'even though the main argument for suicide was that there was no way out of the room. The following day, though, she was quite happy for you to "discover" it. That doesn't make sense.'

'No,' I said. 'It doesn't. So, it confirms that she didn't know the passage was there.'

'Or,' said Elsie, 'it confirms that there was a good reason why she didn't want anyone snooping around the passage straight away. So what, or who, was in the passage that evening?'

'But we were all there outside the library. By the time the police arrived, none of us could have been in the passage.'

'True.'

'The man in the blue suit?' I ventured, though I didn't quite believe it.

'No,' said Elsie, with a sigh. 'He doesn't exist. Clive and John were both lying. John wouldn't have let some random stranger wander round the garden. Clive added in that detail of the beanie, then planted that black hat, probably bought for the purpose, shortly before we found it.'

'And the cigarette butts?'

'Could be anyone—Dave Peart having a crafty drag, like as not.'

'And the scrap of blue cloth?'

'Yes, that's odd,' admitted Elsie, 'unless Clive planted that too.'

'So, if there was no man in a blue suit, who or what was in the passage?'

'I don't know, but I can't help feeling that almost everybody so far has lied to us and that Gillian Maggs is the one person who might have been able to tell us why they were lying.'

'And she's in the West Indies,' I said.

'Only if her daughter is telling the truth. And on the basis of our track record to date, what would you say the chances of that are?'

Chapter Eighteen

We were driving up to Muntham Court again.

We had earlier lunched at the Village House, one of my local pubs. I had had a steak sandwich. Elsie had said that she would have a light meal of poached salmon, but had defeated the object of the exercise by ordering triple chips. The chocolate pudding that she followed it with was also advertised as low-calorie, but that was presumably if you ate only one of them.

'All that red meat isn't good for you,' she said, gathering up a large spoonful of custard.

'Do you want me to drop you at the station after lunch or do you want to walk some of that off first? We could take a stroll up to Cissbury Ring, if you like—or to Chanctonbury if you're really feeling fit.'

'I've been thinking,' she said, wagging her spoon at me. 'The key to it all is that secret passage and why Annabelle was lying.'

'She wasn't lying,' I said, wiping the spots of custard off my jacket with a napkin. 'It's possible that she really didn't know the passage was there. Maybe the previous owners hadn't mentioned it.'

'Oh, yes, right,' said Elsie. 'That's really likely, that is.'

'I'll go and ask her then.'

'I'd better come too.'

'I thought you had important things to do in London?'

'They can wait.'

'It may not be a convenient time for her.'

'It's a convenient time for me.'

'I can manage on my own.'

Elsie did not even bother to contradict me. 'Let's go,' she said.

So, we went.

❰ ❰ ❰

I apologized profusely for the intrusion, but Annabelle graciously assured me that she wanted in any case to know whether I yet felt able to go to the police. So, over coffee in the conservatory, I told her about the morning's phone calls (tactfully skating over the detail of Robert's relationship with Felicity Hooper) and explained why I thought that the beanie might have been planted.

'I suppose anyone could have dropped the beanie there,' said Annabelle. 'Even if it has nothing to do with the murder, it doesn't mean that it was deliberately planted. The piece of cloth that Elsie so cleverly found is pretty clear evidence that there was somebody in the garden wearing a blue suit—or a blue pair of trousers anyway.'

'Did you know Gillian Maggs was planning a trip, by the way?' I asked.

'Is she?'

'Her daughter says she's gone to Barbados.'

'I think she did say something…I hadn't realized it was this week. It may have been an anniversary or something.'

I nodded. 'I guess that's about all then,' I said.

'So, about this secret passage then,' said Elsie, putting her cup down. 'You hadn't come across it before?'

'No, not until Ethelred found it for us. You've both been really smart.'

'The previous owners didn't mention it?'

'Not to me. I never met them. It was also done through agents. We had somebody looking for suitable properties for us; they, of course, had agents selling on their behalf. It wasn't mentioned on the survey report.'

'Thank you,' I said. 'Well, it's good to have cleared that up, not that it was an important point...'

'So it wasn't in the property details from the agent either?' asked Elsie. 'Strange, that. Interesting thing like a secret passage. Bit of a selling point really, unless you've got a totally crap agent.'

'Our own agent was alerted to the property before it went onto the market. I don't think a brochure was ever printed. Sorry—I can't see what you're getting at.'

'I think Elsie is asking if anyone else could have known about the secret passage,' I said. 'Presumably not?'

'No, not really,' said Annabelle.

'Not Gillian Maggs?' demanded Elsie.

'It's possible,' said Annabelle. 'She had worked for the previous owners. But as I've said, she wasn't there when Robert... died. I don't think she's at all important in any of this.'

'Her daughter was worried,' said Elsie.

'Worried? In what way?'

'She didn't want to tell me very much,' said Elsie.

'Surprise, surprise,' said Annabelle, glancing across at me. 'Well, don't be too concerned, either of you. I'll give her daughter a call and reassure her that Gillian is not in any way caught up in this case.'

'Thank you,' I said, happy that everything had been cleared up to most people's satisfaction. 'That's very kind of you. Now, I think Elsie needs to get back to London, so we'll leave you in peace.'

✦ ✦ ✦

'So, there you are,' I said to Elsie, as we walked across the gravel drive and back to the car. 'We have resolved that little problem. Annabelle has clearly been telling us the truth. Let's focus on this intruder in the blue suit.'

'Were you listening to nothing that she said?' asked Elsie.

'Yes,' I said.

'Then you will know that she is clearly lying through her teeth with every word,' said Elsie. 'Do I really have to explain everything to you?'

'Possibly,' I sighed. 'Possibly.'

'OK,' she said. 'Let's start again from lunch-time.'

Chapter Nineteen

We had lunched at the Village House. Ethelred had said that he felt like a change and that they did a good steak sandwich there. I wasn't that hungry and settled for a little snack of poached salmon and the merest suggestion of a sweet.

I really needed to get back to London, but Ethelred more or less insisted I went with him to Muntham Court. It was a good job that I did.

You could tell Annabelle was pretty pissed off that we had shown up out of the blue, but she put a good face on it (not too much of a problem if you have more than one face available to you) and made us coffee.

Ethelred then footled about as usual.

'I'm sorry to raise this with you, Annabelle, but were you aware that Robert knew Felicity at Oxford?'

'I think he may have mentioned it.'

'They were quite good friends.'

'Possibly. He always said he had lots of good chums at Oxford—including you, of course.'

'I think he was better friends with Felicity than he was with me.'

'Yes, he said he didn't see that much of you in those days. You didn't play rugby?'

'No, I didn't play rugby.'

'That would explain it.'

'That wasn't quite what I meant. Felicity didn't play rugby either.'

'I should think not indeed.' Annabelle tilted her head to one side as if to say she hadn't the faintest idea where all this was going. Since I hadn't the faintest idea either, I hoped Ethelred was working to some sort of plan and was about to be all manly and decisive.

'Er, yes, quite, absolutely...' he said decisively. 'Did Robert say that Felicity had been in touch with him?'

'They met up again recently,' said Annabelle.

'Yes, they did,' said Ethelred, leaning forwards in his chair. Perhaps he was about to spring his trap? 'He didn't say if they had talked about their time at Oxford and...just after?'

'I suppose they would have done. That's what you do when you meet somebody you haven't seen since university, isn't it?'

'Yes, indeed,' said Ethelred, sitting back again with a sigh. 'That's what you do.'

Well, I was glad Ethelred had broached the subject of the abortion so directly. That one was cleared up then.

He was equally good about the beanie, amiably agreeing that it might have floated down from heaven or somewhere; and he was willing to accept that Gillian Maggs really had taken it into her head to go off to the West Indies.

Somebody had to get a grip on proceedings.

'So, about this secret passage then,' I said, putting my cup down. 'You hadn't come across it before?'

Annabelle's jaw dropped. Eventually she managed to mumble: 'No, not until Ethelred found it for us. You've both been really smart.' She smiled weakly at me.

'The previous owners didn't mention it?' I asked.

Annabelle now looked like a rabbit caught in (my) powerful headlights.

'Not to me,' she said. 'I never met them. It was also done through...agents. Yes, that's right—I remember now—we had agents looking for suitable properties for us. So we never...met them...'

She was floundering so much that Ethelred tried to intervene but I was having none of that.

'So it wasn't in the property details from the selling agent either?' I asked.

'Our own agent was alerted to the property before it went onto the market. I don't think a brochure was ever printed. Sorry...I can't see what you're getting at [gulp].'

But she could. Her bluff was being called.

'I think Elsie is asking if *anyone else* could have known about the secret passage,' said Ethelred, offering a massive get-out.

'No, not really,' said Annabelle, gratefully.

'Not Gillian Maggs?' I asked.

Annabelle looked at me as though she was trying to weigh up the odds. How close to the truth would she go?

'It's possible,' said Annabelle eventually. 'She *had* worked for the previous owners. But as I've said, she wasn't there when Robert...died. I don't think she's at all important in any of this.' Another pleading smile.

'Her daughter was worried,' I said.

The jaw, which had assumed a normal sort of position for a while, dropped again. I was not supposed to have contacted the Maggs household. But I had.

'Worried? In what way?' she asked.

'She didn't want to tell me very much,' I said.

Annabelle briefly tried sarcasm, then thought better of it and offered to give the daughter a reassuring call, though I doubted myself that the daughter would be answering the phone.

'Thank you,' said Ethelred, after a fierce glance in my direction. 'That's very kind of you. Now, I think Elsie needs to get back to London, so we'll leave you in peace.'

><

'All right,' said Ethelred, when I had explained a few things to him as we sat in the car on the gravel drive. 'Maybe she *could* have known about the passage, but I really don't think she did.'

'If Gillian Maggs knew about the passage, why would she keep quiet about it?'

'We've no evidence that either of them knew.'

'Well, *somebody* knew, or else that was a self-cleaning passage. Self-cleaning houses and something that tastes in every way like chocolate but has no calories at all—those are the two inventions that mankind needs, but I don't think we have either of them yet. The daughter was edgy. Who made her edgy, and why?'

We drove back to Greypoint House and made more coffee, prior to my departure for London.

'Let's phone the daughter again,' I said. 'But this time, you do it.'

Ethelred shrugged. He pressed the redial button on the phone.

The ringing tone came through loud and clear, even where I was sitting on the far side of the room. It buzzed away for a minute or so.

'She's not in,' said Ethelred, putting the phone back.

'Try again in a while,' I suggested. 'I'll get a later train.'

We tried at hourly intervals until ten o'clock.

'She's there but not picking up,' I said. 'Let's go round.'

'It wouldn't be fair...'

'Bollocks,' I pointed out.

We checked the address in the phone book and then drove through the village and onto the bypass. After a bit, we turned off the main road and drew up in front of a nondescript sixties bungalow. It was like all the other bungalows in the road except that the place was in darkness. Complete darkness. And silent as the grave.

We stayed in the car outside the house until midnight. Nobody came. Nobody went. The lights stayed off. By that time the other bungalows in the road had joined in the lights-off thing, making the Maggs place absolutely identical with the rest, except its lace curtains were not twitching as people got a good look at us hanging around in a suspicious manner.

'They don't seem to be in,' said Ethelred.

'That's right,' I said. 'All the people who might have known about the existence of the passage have coincidentally vanished, one after the other. Of course, somebody else must have known too.'

'Who?'

'The person who made them vanish,' I said.

We drove back to Ethelred's. Once we were in the flat Ethelred locked the door. Then he bolted it. Then he double-checked he had bolted it.

'What now?' I asked.

'Go to bed,' he said. 'I'm going to stay up and see if I can write another chapter or so of the Master Thomas book.'

'Is it going well?'

'For some people,' he said.

A Clerk of London

'That doesn't tell us much,' said the Prioress, as Thomas finished his account. 'It could have been anyone really. A whole bunch of people knew you were coming down here. If we could just establish who wanted Sir Edmund dead...'

'Have you read Genesis lately?' asked Thomas.

'Maybe, maybe not,' said the Prioress. 'What's that got to do with anything?'

'The fruit of the Tree of Knowledge is dangerous,' said Thomas. 'The best plan is to eat of it only when you are sure it's yours to eat. Whoever wanted Sir Edmund dead is a great deal more powerful than I am. Sometimes it's easier not to know things.'

'I thought you were braver than that.'

'No, that's precisely how brave I am. I have got out of a dungeon, with some cleverness I should add, and now I plan to return, with equal cleverness, to my family in London. I have no idea whose innocence the Sheriff wished to establish using my testimony, but it makes no difference to me whatsoever.'

'And your conscience?'

'Is as clear as it needs to be. I had no choice but to sign. I also got a reasonably good breakfast (and lunch). When you became a nun, you signed up to do God's work and fight Evil. I am against Evil in principle too—I'm just not contractually obliged in the way that you are.'

'That's despicable.'

'No, that's how you survive in the real world that most of us have to live in.'

'What's that?'

'The real world?'

'No, that noise out there.'

And indeed there was a sound of scuffling and heavy boots on the stone floor.

'If they've come to arrest you again,' said the Prioress, 'don't expect me to pray for you this time.'

'You didn't pray for me last time.'

'And how right I was,' said the Prioress, turning indignantly to Thomas and thus missing the entry of the Sheriff and his two henchmen, plus a fourth man who did not appear entirely happy to be with them. This last-mentioned individual suddenly pitched forward, either having been precipitously released from their hold or perhaps having been deliberately flung onto the rush-covered flagstones. He groaned softly and pulled himself to his knees, where he remained. Thomas noticed that the man was dressed as a clerk and wore a dark grey hood. It was a bad choice of costume under the circumstances.

'I think,' said the Sheriff, addressing Master Thomas, 'that we have our murderer.'

The man looked imploringly at Thomas.

'I'm not sure…' Thomas began.

'Not sure?' repeated the Sheriff. 'You signed a statement to say that you saw clearly a man dressed as a clerk, wearing a dark grey hood. A hood the colour of summer thunderclouds, I think you said. Very poetic. This is just such a man. We also found a dagger…as close by as we needed to.'

'Only not my dagger,' said the man in a way that suggested he had said it a few dozen times before.

'It is to be expected that you would deny it,' said the Sheriff indulgently. 'There was fresh blood on the dagger.'

'If I were the murderer,' said the man, 'I would have cleaned my dagger straight away. It only takes a moment. Never let the sun set on dried blood—that's what my grandmother always used to say.'

'You know a great deal about murderers then,' said the Sheriff. 'Why should that be?'

'It's because he is one,' said one of the henchmen, with a genuine desire to be helpful.

'I hadn't thought of that,' said the Sheriff. 'Now, Master Thomas, could you just confirm that you saw somebody like this lurking (as I think you so skilfully phrased it) near the scene of the murder.'

'For pity's sake,' said the man, fixing Thomas with an imploring eye. 'Tell them the truth. Tell them that you did not see me.'

'But,' said the Sheriff, before Thomas could answer, 'Master Thomas has already signed a statement to say that he did see somebody exactly like you. He signed it…where was it now?…ah, yes, it was in Bramber Castle only this morning. I am sure that an upright servant of the King would not have committed the crime of perjury, carrying as it does so many heavy and painful penalties. Extremely painful penalties that it would make me quite nauseous even to describe. I am sure that Master Thomas would not wish to retract a statement of such importance to those who enforce the King's Law. I am sure that he would merely wish to confirm that you fit the description of the man he swears he saw, so that he can go peacefully on his way and have a trouble-free journey back to his family in London. Is that a fair summary, Master Thomas?'

Thomas did a quick count. That was two thinly veiled threats, possibly three. Obviously one good one was all you actually needed— say the one about waylaying him on the way home. That was easily good enough on its own.

'I am not retracting my statement,' Thomas began, 'but…'

'But?' asked the Sheriff, getting more meaning into a single word than most poets managed to get into several quatrains.

'I beg you,' said the man on the floor. 'I am innocent. They have dragged me out of a tavern, and taken me to some desolate spot that

I never visited before in my life. They have gone through a play-acting to find a knife dripping pig's blood, or some such thing, that I am supposed to have cast aside when I stabbed Sir Edmund. They have brought me here, to meet a man I have also never seen before. I thought it was a bit too good to be true when somebody made me a present of a nice new hood this morning. Talk about a complete stitch-up. Kind sir, if you are a Christian, I beg you. Tell them that you have never seen me.'

'He is a Christian,' chipped in the Prioress.

'Let me help you,' said the Sheriff to Thomas, in tones so mild and friendly that they struck fear into Thomas's very soul. 'If you do not wish to state categorically that this is not the man—as perhaps is the case—then I have the right to assume that it is the man. Do you follow me? You don't actually need to say a thing. Silence is fine. In many ways, silence is the best thing for all of us—except possibly for the guilty person snivelling in front of you.'

'They will torture me,' said the man.

'That's true,' said the helpful henchman.

'Only if he denies his guilt,' said the Sheriff, with a mildly reproving look. 'We are not savages.'

'Reverend Prioress,' said the prisoner, switching his attention away from Thomas. 'Can you not intercede for me?'

'How,' said the Prioress, squaring up to the Sheriff, 'do you know he is guilty?'

'We won't know until he confesses or we have tortured him or both,' said the Sheriff. 'But Master Thomas's testimony is admirably clear. You have no idea how grateful we are to him.'

'The man says he's innocent.'

'Well, he would, wouldn't he?'

'But—St Lawrence's lemons! —you could be torturing an innocent man. You imperil your soul, sir knight.'

'It rarely happens that we torture an innocent man. Almost all prove to be guilty—or so they tell us eventually. My lady Prioress, you must pray for the unhappy prisoner, which is what you do best, and leave us to do…what we do best. In view of Master Thomas's very conclusive silence, we shall be on our way.'

'Dolted daffe,' said the Prioress, though it was not clear which of the men she was addressing.

The Sheriff smiled. 'Pax vobiscum,' he replied.

The henchmen half-dragged, half-carried the prisoner to the door. With difficulty he turned his head towards Thomas one last time. 'Please?' he begged.

'I…' said Thomas.

'Take him to Bramber,' the Sheriff said. Then turning to Thomas he added: 'Bramber is many miles away and the walls are fourteen feet thick. Unlike me, you will not be troubled with this miserable wretch's screams. Probably. So I bid you both a very good night and a restful repose.'

The footsteps echoed again on the bare stones, then there was the crunch of boots on soft snow, then, at long last, blissful silence. The fire spat and crackled briefly, as fires will.

'Well, that was good,' said the Prioress with some of the heaviest irony Thomas had encountered in a person of religion.

'What was I supposed to say?'

'You could have said you definitely saw somebody but that wasn't the man.'

'I suppose I could…I just didn't think quickly enough.'

'Dolted daffe,' said the Prioress, thus clarifying who the remark had been addressed to earlier.

'What now?' asked Thomas.

'You have,' said the Prioress, 'just sent an innocent man to be tortured and hanged. Maybe drawn and quartered as well if it's not his lucky day. I have never seen anyone framed in a more blatant manner. You'd better come up with a way of springing him from gaol.'

'How?'

'Tell you what,' said the Prioress, 'I'll do what I do best: pray. You can do the rest of it.'

><×> ><×> ><×>

It was getting late. From what seemed to be a long way off, I heard Elsie's gentle snore from my bedroom (and indeed from my bed). I reread what I had just typed. The Master Thomas stories were normally quite light. This tale had suddenly become much darker—the moral dilemma that Thomas was in more complex—than in previous books. If writers draw constantly on their own experience, how did this relate to my own? Or was it just a story about fourteenth-century England?

I closed the lid of my computer, changed into my pyjamas and, pulling an inadequate blanket over myself, tried to find a sufficiently comfortable position on the sofa to allow me to sleep. There was no such position, but eventually I slept anyway.

Chapter Twenty

'Shouldn't you be back in London by now?' asked Ethelred (always the perfect host) over a fairly late breakfast.

'My place,' I said, 'is by your side.'

'I'm going up to London anyway,' he said, 'to talk to Fiona McIntosh. I phoned her earlier. I'm meeting her this afternoon.'

'But you're coming back?'

'Yes, I'll be back late afternoon.'

'Then I think I should stay until I'm sure you are absolutely safe,' I said. 'You need more butter, by the way.'

'I don't think any of us needs protecting,' said Ethelred. Outside, the sun was shining and there was the reassuring sound of the world going about its business. 'The Maggs girl was probably just out at some club in Worthing. That she wasn't home by midnight might worry her mother, but for teenagers these days, the evening is only just beginning round about then. It doesn't mean she's been murdered or that she's fled the country. If I need more butter, it's because you've eaten it.'

'That's what you are supposed to do with butter. Let's ring her later. What time do teenagers get up these days?'

'You must have been eating it straight from the tub with a spoon. If she's supposed to be at school or college or something, she should already be up,' said Ethelred, looking at his watch.

'I certainly did not eat it with a spoon. I licked it off the knife—the one you were using to spread your toast. We could go and doorstep her again,' I said.

'Or,' said Ethelred, putting his knife to one side, 'we could ask Mrs Michie what she knows. They work together, after all. If Gillian Maggs had a trip planned, she ought to have known. We've time to see her before I catch the train to London. I'll also ring Gerald Smith later and see what was in the envelope that I forwarded on Robert's behalf.'

◄ ◄ ◄

Mrs Michie's number was equally easy to track down and, with more or less good grace, she agreed to see us before she went off to work at Muntham Court. Her bungalow in Findon Valley was neat and almost identical to all of the others in the road.

'No,' she said, eyebrows raised, 'I didn't know that Gillian Maggs was planning to go anywhere. She should really have checked with me first that it was convenient. Still, if Her Ladyship knows and approves, who am I to question it?' I think it was what is called a rhetorical question, in the sense that she ended it with a sniff.

'Barbados would be a bit expensive for her?' I asked.

'Her Ladyship doesn't pay any more than she has to.'

'Would that apply to John O'Brian as well?'

'I can't say. She certainly doesn't overpay Gill Maggs, or me come to that.'

'Does Mrs Maggs's husband have a good job then?'

'Doesn't have any sort of job at all. Who says that's where she's gone anyway?'

'Her daughter.'

This time Mrs Michie just sniffed, but it was an eloquent sniff.

'What does the daughter do?' I asked.

'Same line of work as the father.'

'So not likely to be able to afford a trip to the Caribbean at short notice?'

'What do you think?'

On the subject of the passage she was more contemplative.

'Everybody in the village knew there was supposed to be a secret passage. It's even mentioned on the village website,' she said with a frown, 'but I thought it was just a story. I never saw it myself. If Gillian Maggs knew, she never said nothing to me.'

'Could Gillian Maggs have discovered it—while cleaning, say?' I asked.

'Could have done, I suppose. She worked for the previous owners of Muntham Court too. She could have known about it for a long time.'

'And not told anyone?'

'She'd have told Her. Maybe not Him.'

'Why do you say that?'

'Just a feeling. I sometimes thought Gill Maggs was a bit too pally with Her Ladyship.'

'Why?'

'Just because,' said Mrs Michie, as if the answer was obvious, except to somebody who used the subjunctive on a regular basis. 'Anyway, Her Ladyship might have found a secret passage quite handy.'

'Why?' repeated Ethelred, though again the answer was pretty obvious to some of us.

'Good place to hide one of her boyfriends if Sir Robert came back unexpected, eh?'

＜＞＜ ＜＞＜ ＜＞＜

Back at the flat, Ethelred made coffee for himself and hot chocolate for me.

'I need to get some more coffee,' he said, inconsequentially, as he handed me my own steaming mug. 'I've still got plenty of decaffeinated, but I never drink it myself.'

For a while we consumed our respective hot beverages and thought about the late and much-missed Sir Shagger Muntham.

'Look,' I said, 'this business with the passage. It's all starting to make sense. Annabelle knew about the passage. So did Gill Maggs. When questioned on the night of the murder, Annabelle said nothing to the police about a secret route into the library.'

'*Out of* the library,' said Ethelred.

'Whatever,' I said. 'Then, the next day, it's suddenly vital that the passage is discovered, and we go through the farce of having to discover it for her.'

'Even allowing the unlikely premise that Annabelle knew about the passage beforehand, it still doesn't make sense.'

'Yes, it does. Annabelle knew Robert was going to be murdered and she knew who was going to do it, because she was in on it. She'd told the murderer about the secret passage. After he had strangled Robert, he slips away into the passage. Annabelle is in the dining room in the full view of half a dozen people when the deed is done, so that's a perfect alibi. She then raises the alarm. But she can't tell anyone about the secret passage because her accomplice could, for all she knows, still be hiding there. Once he's gone, the existence of the passage can be made known, but she now can't admit that she knew about it before and failed to mention it to the police. So she goes through that bit of play-acting. But, she still has a problem because Gillian Maggs might let slip to the police that Annabelle had been well aware of the passage for some time— possibly also that one or other of her lovers was aware of the passage too. So, the one person who could give the whole game away then conveniently vanishes. When you start to question the daughter, the daughter vanishes too, having also gone to "Barbados".'

'Yes, they went to Barbados,' said Ethelred. 'In the West Indies.'

'No,' I said, 'they went to "Barbados" in inverted commas. Mrs Michie said they hadn't got the money for that sort of trip. All three of them are probably somewhere off the coast of Sussex with heavy weights attached to them.'

'So, who is the accomplice hiding in the passage?' said Ethelred, with a note of sarcasm that he would regret when I was proved right.

'Clive Brent or John O'Brian.'

'If it was Clive Brent, Annabelle knew exactly where he was. By the time the body was discovered he was right beside her. She wouldn't have needed to lie about the passage.'

'John O'Brian then,' I said, slightly reluctantly. 'He claims to have left before the murder occurred. But who knows where he was? It all fits together.'

'No, it doesn't fit together at all. If you have just conspired to murder your husband, and if the police are convinced it's suicide, then surely you'd say: "Yes, thanks, suicide, I'll take that." You wouldn't spend the next two days trying to persuade everyone it was murder and get the police to open up the case again. Above all you'd keep the secret passage secret.'

I ran through my argument again. There did seem to be a small flaw in it.

'Something happened,' I said, 'between the discovery of the body and our conversation with Annabelle in the library the following day. Whatever it was caused her to change her mind about keeping the existence of the passage to herself. If we just knew what that thing was then we'd know...well, we'd know a lot more than we do at the moment.'

Ethelred sighed. 'Maybe Fiona McIntosh can throw some light on it all this afternoon. In the meantime, I'm going to the post office to buy some coffee,' he said. 'Is there anything I can get you?'

'You need butter,' I said.

It was while Ethelred was out purchasing essential groceries that his phone rang. I obviously answered it, but the caller got in the first word.

'It's Lady Muntham. Is Ethelred Tressider there?'

A little formal for one of Ethelred's closest friends?

'No,' I said. 'He's just popped out. Butter crisis.'

'Well, when he just pops back, could you give him a message?'

'Of course.'

'Tell that evil lying little shit that I never want to see him again.'

'Is that the whole message?'

'You can add that he'll hear from my lawyers shortly.'

'Got that,' I said. 'Have a nice day now.'

I put the phone down. I wasn't quite sure what Ethelred had done but, whatever it was, I definitely approved.

Chapter Twenty-one

'No,' I said. 'I've no idea what she meant.'

'Well, you must have done something right,' said Elsie. 'She absolutely hates your guts.'

'You must have got the message wrong,' I said.

Elsie said nothing but her smile was deafening.

'There's clearly been some terrible misunderstanding,' I said. 'I'll go straight over and sort it out.'

'I'll come with you,' she said.

'No,' I said. 'This time I'm going on my own. Aren't you needed back in London?'

Elsie shrugged. 'Fine. You can drop me off at the station first.'

'It's not on my way to Muntham Court.'

'I never claimed it was.'

❦ ❦ ❦

I drove back from the station as quickly as the traffic regulations allowed. As I turned off the main road onto the gravel drive that led to Muntham Court I felt my heart beating faster than usual. I couldn't imagine how the misunderstanding had occurred, but the sooner I saw Annabelle, the sooner we could resolve it. I was ready to counter recriminations. I was ready to laugh about some miscommunication. I was ready to apologize for anything I had done or indeed not done. By the time I arrived at the house I had rehearsed almost every eventuality other than the one I encountered. The house was shut up. Nothing stirred. Nobody answered my repeated sounding of the doorbell. I walked round to the back of the house, but the garden too was deserted.

I checked my watch. I could remain here until Annabelle chose to return or I could still just get to London in time for my meeting with Fiona McIntosh. I hesitated a moment, then drove back into Worthing and parked close to the station. I bought a day return and was soon seated in a train pursuing Elsie's towards Victoria.

⮜ ⮜ ⮜

I had arranged to meet Fiona McIntosh in a cafe close to where she worked. For some reason I had expected her to opt for a skinny wet mochaccino or something else that would demonstrate urban sophistication, but she just asked me to order her a black coffee.

'I've no idea what half of those things up on the board are,' she said. 'I suspect the people who work here don't know either.'

I returned to our table clutching two large mugs.

'They're called Americanos,' I said.

'I wonder when people stopped drinking coffee,' she said. 'So, unless you've travelled up to London just to buy me an Americano, what can I do for you in return?'

'I just need to know slightly more about the discovery of Robert's body,' I said.

'Well, entering as you did via the window, you beat me to it by a good thirty seconds. I guess you already know at least as much as I do.'

'I didn't examine him as closely as you did.'

'Yes, but you'd probably had less to drink than I had. Quite a lot less, actually.'

'You would still have seen things I missed. I'm not a doctor.'

'So you're not,' conceded Fiona McIntosh. She put her coffee down and looked me in the eye. 'Very well, Robert died of asphyxiation as a result of a thin cord being wound tightly round his neck. No doubt the CSI people would have preferred me to leave it in place, but trying to save lives gets to be a habit unless you're careful. So, there'll be no photographs of the ligature in situ, I'm afraid, and only my hazy recollection of events to help you. I do remember, however, that there was a pencil inserted in the cord, which had first been used to tighten the noose and then fixed behind Robert's ear to hold it in place. It's not the commonest form of suicide, but there are recorded cases. It's quite effective if you can get a few minutes to yourself and there are no busybodies around to revive you. With the cord removed, you could see there were slight abrasions of the neck, entirely consistent with the apparent cause of death. No petechiae on the skin or eyes, as I recall, but that doesn't really prove anything one way or the other. Death by strangulation, without any doubt at all.'

'Annabelle doesn't...'

'...doesn't like to think it was suicide? Yes, I know. But for it to be murder, as I think Colin pointed out, surely there should have been some sign of a struggle? A chair overturned would have been good, if slightly clichéd. Everything was, however, remarkably tidy, down to the pen on the desk.'

'I was thinking— perhaps Robert knew his killer? Perhaps he was overcome before he realized what was happening?'

'Well, as you are aware, people do tend to know their killers a lot of the time. Strangers may murder you for the cash in your wallet, but the potential for pissing off your friends is considerable. Still, you'd have to know somebody very well indeed before you'd let them wind a cord round your neck and tighten it with a 3B pencil.'

'Facetiousness to one side,' I began.

'Who's being facetious? I can't say I'm into that type of game myself. I don't think Colin is either, though if he ever brings a length of cord to bed with him, I'll probably decline. But some people do get a kick out of asphyxiation, so I'm told. Unfortunately, it's the sort of game that can go badly wrong.'

'You're not suggesting…'

'…that a member of the British aristocracy would engage in kinky sex? No, I'm sure that's never happened before. Especially to one with the nickname "Shagger".'

'Facetiousness, as I said, to one side, there was no evidence…'

'…of any sexual practices, deviant or otherwise? You're quite right. He died with his boots on and his trousers in place. In summary, there was no evidence either that Robert had resisted or that he had welcomed the killer's attentions. Where does that leave us?'

'I don't know. Where does it leave us?'

She paused, doubtless summoning up the key points from some long-past course on How to Break Bad News.

'It was suicide, Ethelred. Suicide, pure and simple. Nobody could have got out of that room.'

'There is a secret passage,' I said.

'So, that's the solution to the locked-room mystery? A secret passage? How boring.'

'The solutions to most locked-room mysteries tend to be a bit of a let-down. It's rather like having a conjuring trick explained to you.'

'Well, that does open up other possibilities, I suppose. Assuming there was somebody who, one way or another, could get the rope round Robert's neck, they could have rendered him unconscious in ten seconds or so. They would not have needed to hang around until he was dead—just left him as he was and hopped back into this secret passage and off to the billiard room. She could have been back with the other guests in no time,' said Fiona.

'She?'

'Or he, of course, but I'm still thinking of Robert not objecting while somebody playfully ties a rope round his neck.'

We both contemplated this image for a moment.

'Annabelle says she didn't know the passage was there,' I said. 'We discovered it after Robert's death.'

'Did Robert know it was there?'

'I don't know— one end was in his library, after all.'

'It's a shame he can't just tell us.'

'Yes,' I said, thinking of the trail of obscure clues he had laid for me. 'Yes, it would be good if he could just do that.'

'Well, if that's all I can do for you...' Fiona began.

'Almost,' I said. I paused, wondering how to get round to the main purpose of my visit. It hadn't troubled me when Elsie had first mentioned it, but it had weighed on my mind since.

'You and Robert saw a lot of each other last year,' I said.

'Is that what he told you?'

'No, I saw the entries in his diary.'

'I didn't know he kept one.'

'Just a simple appointments diary, but "FM" appears quite often.'

'He was an old friend,' she said. 'We would meet up for coffee. Very often we would meet up exactly here. This cafe, this table.'

'Twice or three times a week?'

'Yes. He was lonely, Ethelred. He had problems he didn't seem to be able to discuss with anyone else. Sometimes he just wanted to talk about the past to take his mind off the present. After the bank sacked him he was a bit of a lost soul. Didn't he ever drop round and have coffee with you for no apparent reason?'

'Quite often,' I said. 'Decaffeinated.'

'There you are then,' she said. 'And Ethelred...'

'Yes?'

'It was suicide.'

'I'll bear that in mind,' I said.

><× ><× ><×

I left Fiona to return to her hospital and to her operating list for the afternoon. I had a second visit to pay, close by.

I walked along Euston Road to the British Library. I wanted to consult a paper by Professor Keith Simpson in an old volume of the *International Criminal Police Review*. The Internet is all very well, but it lacks the authority of a leather-bound tome, read within the hallowed walls of one of the greatest libraries in the world. Professor Simpson had described in detail six cases of suicide by self-strangulation. In one case a son had narrowly avoided conviction for the death of his mother, so like murder had it seemed. Another case involved the use of a pencil to tighten the ligature. I also wanted to remind myself of the circumstances surrounding the death of General Pichegru—one of Napoleon's generals, found strangled under similar circumstances and another suicide.

Fiona McIntosh seemed as keen to believe that it was suicide as Annabelle seemed keen to believe it was murder. Though it was easy to understand why Annabelle would not wish it to be suicide, it was difficult to see that Fiona's conclusions were based on anything other than the medical evidence. Of all the guests assembled that evening, she at least seemed to have no axe, or any other type of murder weapon, to grind.

Chapter Twenty-two

It's a long trip back to London from Worthing, and it gave me a bit of thinking time. My theory about Annabelle conspiring with John O'Brian obviously needed a bit more work.

Though I was convinced that Annabelle had lied about the passage, there was another flaw in my argument that Ethelred had generously not pointed out. There is nothing so irritating for any wife as to find that you have just murdered a husband who only had a month or two to live anyway. Annabelle must have suspected how ill Shagger was, even if he hadn't told her the whole story. Calculating bitches don't chip their nail varnish unless they absolutely have to. Annabelle would have just let things take their natural course, not hastened them with a bit of rope.

I couldn't help feeling, though, that this murder had a woman's hand in it somewhere. Men shoot each other or bludgeon each other to death. Strangulation with a slender cord wound tenderly round the neck has that feminine touch sadly missing from so many modern-day killings. What I really needed to focus on was which of the women, other than Annabelle, might have wanted Robert dead. Felicity Hooper was, when you thought about it, the one with the motive—cruelly abandoned and left to the mercies of some backstreet abortionist. Why shouldn't she have resented

Shagger Muntham's rise to fame and riches? Why shouldn't she have earnestly wished him dead? And she had no way of knowing that Shagger was on his way to the Happy Hunting Ground without her help. So, to conclude, why shouldn't she have taken the opportunity to strangle him—having first loudly pointed out that the lack of security at Muntham Court could have allowed any number of murderers in? And, thinking about it, having cleverly ensured that Ethelred and I would remain in the dining room...

The best way to tell what a writer is thinking is to read their books. But I had foolishly returned the relevant MS half-read. My life as an agent has been singularly without regrets, but in this case I now realized I had been over-hasty. I urgently needed to find out how that novel had ended.

🐟 🐟 🐟

It was the work of a moment to slip into WH Smith at Victoria and locate a copy of *Abandoned!* by Felicity Hooper. I wasn't sure whether the curvy but slightly dishevelled young lady on the front cover was supposed to be modelled on La Hooper when she was just a chit of a girl—but I rather suspected that it was. I flicked quickly to the end, but the heroine was just sitting on a cliff-top, reflecting on the fact that things could have gone worse. I worked backwards looking for the murder of a rugby-playing tosser and—bingo!—somebody was being taunted and then pushed off Folly Bridge into the swirling floodwaters below. *'One arm, encased in the sleeve of a Balliol rugby jersey, rose briefly above the foam, then I saw nothing except the powerfully flowing Isis. "Bobby!" I exclaimed.'*

'Are you planning to pay for that or just read it?' asked the assistant in the nasal tones of South London.

'Worth every penny,' I said, slapping a fiver on the counter (the book was, inevitably, on special offer).

'She's good, isn't she?' confided the assistant, handing me my change. I've read all her books. Did you know she's signing copies of her new best-seller at our shop down the road this afternoon? You should go along.'

'I might just do that,' I said.

$$\text{✦✦✦}$$

It looked like a pretty average book-signing. There was no queue of any description in front of the small table at which Felicity Hooper was sitting. A sign propped up close by featured her photograph and quoted (under the banner 'Praise for Felicity Hooper') some of the more enthusiastic reviews for earlier work. She was slowly and dutifully autographing a pile of books that would later go on the shelves with a label saying 'Signed by Author'. Excellent—I would be able to get her full attention. I approached the table like a silent but deadly nemesis and thrust the book under her nose.

'Who should I put that it's to?' she asked, glancing up. 'Oh, it's you.'

She gave me a look as though I was a complete arsehole.

'I was just passing,' I said. 'I thought I would get you to sign my copy of *Abandoned*! I did so enjoy it—especially the bit just before the end.'

One of the conventions of a book-signing is that you have to sign the books, even for complete arseholes. She shrugged and was scribbling her name when I said: 'I'd also like you to write a line from the book.'

Book collectors like their 'signed, lined and dated' copies, so she expressed no surprise but just replied: 'Which line?'

I opened the book close to the end. 'I thought this bit, where you say: "*You pillock, did you really think I'd let you get away with that?*" It's just before she pushes him off the bridge.'

'He overbalances and falls. He's drunk. She doesn't kill him—though she does blame herself. There's not really any need for her to feel guilty. One useless man fewer in the world—no great disaster. Anyway, if that's what you would like me to write, it's your book.' She applied her pen to the page and started writing the quotation.

'Is that what you said to Robert?'

'To Robert?' She stopped writing and looked up at me.

'In the library.'

'By the time I got to the library, Robert was dead. I didn't say anything to him as far as I remember.' She put down the pen and looked me in the eye.

'The second time you went to the library that evening, maybe, but not the first time,' I said.

'What do you mean?'

'Did you take the rope with you or was it there already?'

'I think you'll find it's *Cluedo* in which the weapons are randomly scattered through the house. Elsie, I went to the library once in my life and once only. Are you implying that I killed Robert?' She looked round the shop. It was almost empty, but this clearly wasn't the type of conversation writers, or their publishers, want overheard by paying customers.

'Didn't you kill him?' I asked. No point in beating about the bush, I always say.

'Why should I?'

'He abandoned you.' I put a lot of emphasis on the word 'abandoned'. I indicated the cover of the book in front of us in case she missed the point.

'Yes. You can stop tapping the book like that—I do get the literary allusion.'

'You were pregnant.'

'I was on the pill. I wasn't that stupid.'

'You had an abortion.'

'Have you been drinking?'

'I've read the book.'

'I know. I sent you the manuscript.'

'It is clearly based on your own experiences.'

'In my latest novel, the heroine wins the Badminton Horse Trials. I'm not claiming anyone's mounted me with a whip and bridle.'

'But this was your first. All writers put their own experiences into their first book. It's like dogs returning to their own vomit, but slightly less uplifting.'

'I was a physio in Oxford. That's about it for autobiographical content. Oh, and I do actually like Liebfraumilch, an authentic bit of seventies detail.'

'No pregnancy?'

'No pregnancy.'

'No abortion?'

'Difficult without the pregnancy.'

'You had the opportunity to murder Robert.'

'Yes, but I opted for a pee instead. I'd do the same again.'

'Huh! So you say.'

'You never give up, do you?'

'No.'

'God, Elsie, you get on my tits. Would you like me to sign them for you?'

I turned round. A customer was politely hovering, two new hardbacks in hand.

'Yes, could you sign them, please? Could you make this one out to "Darren". He's my boyfriend. I don't read your books myself. The other one's for my mother. She doesn't read you either but she does like signed books—you'd be amazed at the rubbish she's got.'

Felicity Hooper smiled weakly and handed me back my copy of *Abandoned*! As I was leaving the shop I checked the signature. It read: *'For Elsie. You pillock. Felicity Hooper.'* Well, that should sell for more than a fiver on eBay.

Chapter Twenty-three

On the Tube back to Hampstead, I glanced at my new purchase from time to time and reminded myself of the basic plot—a girl seduced and betrayed by a rugby-playing bounder who later meets a sticky end. As I had suspected—not really all that auto-biographical then. Perhaps however it was, quite coincidentally, somebody else's story? I knew that Jane Smith was a former, but much more recent, girlfriend of Shagger's. Had I been barking up the wrong tree? Was it Jane Smith who harboured the murderous grudge and had a bit of rope she wouldn't need again?

I knew the Smiths lived in Crawley. Possibly they were back from their autumn break, or whatever it was. The online phone directory gave eighteen people called 'G Smith' in the Crawley area. Most of them were in that evening and I had pissed off thirteen people by the time I got lucky.

'Hello,' said a voice that I recognized as Jane Smith's.

'Elsie Thirkettle here,' I said, as I hadn't on thirteen previous occasions.

'Oh,' she said.

Then there was silence. Guilty conscience?

'I thought I'd give you a call,' I said.

'Is there some news? About Robert's death, I mean.'

'In a sense,' I said. 'You see, Jane, I know all about you and Robert.'

'Yes, I told Ethelred,' came back the urgent whispered reply. I guessed that Gerald might be in the next room.

'Yes, but I know *all* about you and Robert,' I said. 'Not just the bit you told Ethelred.'

Another silence. Somebody was trying to work out what to do.

'What do you want?' she hissed down the line.

'Meet me tomorrow,' I said.

'Where?'

'Crawley.'

'Whereabouts exactly?'

'Somewhere we can talk in private. Your place if Gerald won't be around.'

'Fine. My house. Around ten then.'

'So that Gerald will be at work?'

'That's when Scott has his nap.'

I confirmed the time. She gave me directions. I'd clearly struck gold. Now all I had to do was work out what it was I might know about her that Ethelred didn't.

◆ ◆ ◆

The Smith place was a comfortable Georgian detached residence on the outskirts of town, with a large garden. A number of trees, already beginning to look a little autumnal, peered over the wall. In the eighteenth century, some Crawley merchant had announced that he had made it in this world by putting together a large brick collection and turning it into the ultimate statement of solidity and respectability: classical, double-fronted, perfectly symmetrical, glowing smugly in the September sunshine. Heavy curtains with rose silk linings arced across upper corners of each gleaming window. The brass door knocker shone.

Though Scott would scarcely be walking yet, a large and colourful climbing frame was already in place in an otherwise tranquil and tasteful setting. I caught a glimpse of a paddling pool away under the trees. It seemed very likely that the rose beds would in due course be replaced by a trampoline and the pergolas by goalposts. This already had the feel of a kingdom ruled by a small and demanding tyrant.

Jane Smith ushered me into the sitting room and offered me a drink, treating me with the sort of tight-lipped politeness you normally accord a potential blackmailer.

'I'm not here to blackmail you,' I said, wishing to clear that one up straight away. 'I just want to know why Robert died.'

'Well, I didn't kill him,' said Jane, doing her own bit of clearing up. 'I'm not some sort of strangler or poisoner.'

'I'm pleased to hear it,' I said, putting down my half-finished mug of hot chocolate. 'But you did have a strong motive.'

'I told Ethelred that I'd had an affair with Robert. It's in the past. It's not a secret. Gerald knows all about it.'

'Not *all* about it,' I said. I had no idea where this was all going, but blundering ahead with no clear plan often works quite well in my experience.

'How much do you know?' she asked.

'Everything?' I suggested.

Jane Smith made a noise that went: 'Ha, ha [sharp intake of breath], waaaaah!' Derisive laughter to uncontrollable tears in roughly four point two seconds. So, my technique was working then.

She applied copious snot to my proffered hanky and then added: 'You are a complete moron and you are way off track, but I've got to tell somebody or I'll go mad.'

I nodded. Neither of us wanted her to go mad.

'It all started when I was Robert's secretary. You get to see your boss a lot as a PA. You work late together. He said he saw more of me than he did his wife. You have lots of excuses to be together. Nobody thinks anything of it if you go off to conferences together.'

I raised my eyebrows momentarily. That last statement was taking naivety one stage further than usual, but I let it pass.

'One thing led to another as they say. He took me out to dinner. We...slept together. I got pregnant.

'You didn't take precautions?'

'I must have forgotten...I can be so stupid...when I told Robert I thought he would be pleased.

'Pleased?' My eyebrows wouldn't go quite high enough to express my views about this one, so mere words had to suffice. Even then, I could only manage two. 'Bloody hell,' I said.

'We *loved* each other. This was *our* child.'

'And he was pleased?'

'No.' She pouted and continued: 'He asked me who else I had told, then he arranged for me to go to a private clinic that afternoon.'

'For an abortion?'

'No, for a pizza and fries.'

'That's probably a joke?'

'Yes, that's a joke,' she said. She turned and looked out of the window. We could just see the bright red upright of one corner of Scott's future climbing frame. It really was an eyesore. 'They said that they thought I could still have more babies but...'

'They'd screwed up?'

'Gerald and I tried to have children. He'd always wanted children. He really, really wanted children of his own. Maybe that was what attracted me to him after...Robert. We tried to have children for a long time. Then we adopted Scott.'

'Does Gerald know about the abortion?'

'I can't tell him...I just can't...'

'Were you afraid that Robert would tell him?'

'Gerald said that he had had a strange phone call from Robert a while back. He'd been asking about a girl he'd got pregnant and who'd had to have an abortion and who might sue him.'

And you thought he was asking advice about you?'

'That would be weird, wouldn't it? Asking Gerald for legal advice in case I sued him? No, I don't think it was quite that. I think it was Robert trying to find out whether I had told Gerald anything. When Robert worked out I hadn't he just let it drop.

That was what Gerald couldn't understand—why it was so important one minute and not at all important the next. But I knew what was going on as soon as Gerald told me.'

'And that was that?'

'Yes,' she said. She returned my well-used hanky. 'I don't think I need that any more. Thank you.'

She gave me her strong-independent-woman look—the one I've seen so many of my friends give shortly before asking for the hanky back.

There was, however, still an unanswered question. It's tricky accusing somebody of murder when you've got a pocket full of their snot, but I looked her in the eye and said: 'Nevertheless you had a motive. You must have wanted that bastard dead?'

'I loved him,' she said.

'That doesn't rule out murder.'

'But Scott does,' she said. 'Scott rules out murder. Do you think I would take that sort of risk when I have Scott? I *loved* Robert. I *love* Scott.'

'You said "I" rather than "we". About Scott, I mean, not Robert obviously.'

Jane Smith shrugged. 'I didn't kill Robert. Gerald and I were together the whole time that evening'

'That's not true. You had the opportunity. You and Gerald were briefly separated when everyone was looking round the house. You were both alone for long enough that either of you could—'

She shook her head vehemently.

'Hang on a bit!' I said. 'What you're really worried about is that Gerald could have done it, aren't you? You're worried that he could have found out about the abortion and decided to get his revenge.'

'No,' she said. But her theory that married bosses and young attractive secretaries could go off to conferences together without arousing much comment was really far more convincing.

'If it's any comfort,' I said, 'I don't think it was Gerald. Probably.'

She looked at me gratefully for a moment, then sniffed and said: 'You don't still have that hanky, do you?'

I checked it out and told her she could keep it.

It struck me that what I should do next was go to Gerald Smith's office and ask him one or two pertinent questions. I had taken the precaution of furnishing myself with the address before leaving London. I parked my car in the centre of town and walked the hundred yards or so from the nearest parking space to a glass-and-concrete edifice, part of which his firm occupied. I was standing in front of it, trying to decide whether to use the same successful tactics that I had with Jane Smith, when the front door opened and Ethelred staggered out with a goggle-eyed expression on his face. It wasn't that much of a coincidence, in the sense that I knew he had plans to talk to Gerald Smith. Still, it was good timing and I thought he'd be pretty impressed by what I had managed to discover.

When I called him, however, he just looked uncomprehendingly at me, then he blinked a couple of times and said: 'Elsie! Thank God you're here. You won't believe what I've just found out. I still don't quite believe it myself.'

So we went off to a café and he told me.

Chapter Twenty-four

The train journey back from London gave me time to ponder things. Annabelle had, when you thought about it, no motive at all for killing Robert. Nor did I agree with Elsie that she had behaved oddly over the discovery of the passage. It seemed to me that Annabelle had been as surprised as I was when the panel had slid to one side—more surprised perhaps. Increasingly I felt that Elsie's views on Annabelle were somewhat harsh and unfair. She was allowing her personal feelings to get in the way of more mature judgement.

The more I thought, too, the more I agreed with Clive Brent that it was John O'Brian who had the shakiest story. He had been around the whole evening, but had been working alone. He would have been able, from the garden, to see Robert enter the brightly lit library. He had an unrequited passion for Annabelle. And, if Clive was right about the payments to him, he seemed to have some strange hold over the family. After I had spoken to Annabelle I needed to speak to him.

⤙ ⤙ ⤙

I drove straight from Worthing station back to Muntham Court. The front door remained closed and unyielding as before, but this time my walk to the back of the house was not entirely in vain.

John O'Brian was busy putting tools away in the garden shed.

'She's gone off somewhere,' he said, arranging some forks against the wall.

He did not seem entirely happy. I pointed this out.

'I am no longer in Her Ladyship's employment,' he said. 'As of this morning. She has reluctantly let me go. I came back this afternoon to pick up a few things and leave this place tidy for whoever replaces me. Once I've done that, which will be very soon indeed, I'm out of here for good.'

'Fired?' I asked.

'I'd have said so,' he replied. 'I've been told to leave the premises forthwith and that any money owing to me will be sent on.'

'Did she say why?'

'I hoped you could tell me,' he said. 'I do, however, have a bottle of good Irish whiskey hidden away in that corner. I could take it with me, or we could drink it here. So, why don't we have a chat and see whether we can work it all out?'

Apart from a comprehensive selection of clean and well-cared-for tools, a small tractor for cutting the grass, and a range of killers of animal and vegetable life (in liquid and solid form), the shed contained a couple of old garden chairs and a small wooden table. John O'Brian went to a cupboard marked 'POISONS' and took out a half-full bottle of Bushmills and two drinking vessels.

'So,' he said, as he swilled his whiskey thoughtfully in a Thomas the Tank Engine mug, 'it would seem this is my farewell drinks party. Her Ladyship's not here to make a speech, but she made a brief one this morning and I'll have to make do with that. Between you, me and that mower over there, I've had enough of this place anyway, but I was just wondering whether you had even the faintest idea what I'm supposed to have done.'

'Not what you've done nor what I've done,' I said. 'I too am apparently off the case, as far as the murder investigation is concerned.'

'Women!' he said, and raised Thomas the Tank Engine to his lips. I did the same with my Flopsy Bunnies tea cup (saucer missing).

'People think you were sleeping with Annabelle,' I said.

'Well, that's the truth anyway,' he said.

'Were you?' I asked, surprised.

'I suppose, thinking about it, sleeping was one of the few things we didn't do—but we did have sex all the time. I can't even say we went to bed together—to use another euphemism—this place was as good as any for her. Then there was this funny passageway that leads from the billiard room to the library...'

'You knew about that?'

'That's where she really liked doing it. Preferably with himself in the library a few feet away from us and completely unaware, though he occasionally must have thought the mice were having a pretty good time behind the oak panelling.'

'You weren't...you weren't in the passage the evening of the dinner party?'

'I was nowhere near it. It's funny though. That afternoon Annabelle suggested she might slip away from the party and join me for some fun in the secret passageway. She said I should wait for her there.'

'But you didn't?'

'I thought she was joking. In any case, I wasn't going to wait around for hours in the dark on the off chance. It wouldn't have been the first time.'

'But she might have thought you were there?'

'You'll have to ask her.'

It was of course very unlikely that Annabelle would have made any such arrangement. I shrugged and said: 'Annabelle thinks that the murderer might have escaped that way.'

'Does she? How would an intruder have known about the passage, then?'

'Who did know?'

'Well, Annabelle and me, as you will gather. Gill Maggs— Annabelle liked to have the passage clean, even if she was planning dirty work there.'

'Anyone else?'

'Annabelle preferred to keep it all on a need-to-know basis, for obvious reasons. Of course, I've no idea who needed to know. It might well have been half the male population of West Sussex.'

'I think that's a little unfair.'

'Is it? Fine—then let's say it was just Annabelle, me and Gill Maggs.'

'That means you would have been one of a small number of people who would have known how to get out of the library, leaving it apparently locked,' I said. 'Your movements are also unaccounted for round about the time of the murder.'

'So, are you saying I'm the killer, then?' he asked, topping up my Flopsy Bunnies cup with a generous slug of golden spirit. 'That's a little harsh in view of my hospitality.'

'Don't you think you have an opportunity and a motive?'

'What motive?'

'You wanted Robert dead so that you could marry Annabelle.'

'Hang on—who said anything about marriage? Look, I've worked in a few big houses over the years. This isn't the first time the lady of the manor has taken a fancy to the rough son of the soil in her employ. It happened to me more often when I was younger, but neither then nor now did anyone mention making it a permanent position. Anyway, I'd seen how she treated Sir Robert—not a great inducement to form a permanent relationship. If he hadn't died, I might have stayed around a bit longer—Her Ladyship was paying me better money than I've had anywhere else. But I'd nothing to gain from his death.'

'Why did she pay you so much?'

He laughed. 'I suppose she thought Sir Robert had stacks of money and she might as well throw it around.'

'But he doesn't have stacks of money?'

'Lately I got the impression not. She didn't really confide in me much. I was only staff—just like Gill.'

'Gillian Maggs has vanished.'

'Yes, I know.'

'Gone to Barbados.'

'So they tell me.'

'You don't believe it?'

John O'Brian pulled a face. 'It's not cheap, that sort of thing. Sir Robert and Annabelle—they were always going there. I can't see the Maggs family taking off for Barbados at short notice.'

'What if they were threatened?' I asked. 'What if they needed to get away?'

'It's still not an obvious place to go, is it? And if I were running scared, I wouldn't tell people where I was going—not the real place anyway.'

'Could Clive Brent have known about the passage?'

'Annabelle could have told him, I suppose,' said John O'Brian. 'He also had a motive.'

'He was in love with Annabelle?' I asked.

'Love? We're into euphemism territory here again, aren't we? But he had a perfectly good motive apart from that. Sir Robert had stitched him up badly. He'd destroyed his career. That might be enough for some people to start thinking about murder.'

'Of course, there's also the stranger in the blue suit. You saw him.'

John O'Brian looked very uncomfortable. 'You'd better talk to Clive Brent about that too,' he said. 'He's the one who really saw him—so he says anyway.'

'What do you mean "really saw him"?'

'Look—Annabelle asked me to do it, right? She told me that Clive Brent had seen this guy hanging around that evening, but that the police wouldn't take it seriously if Brent was the only witness. So she got me to agree I'd say I'd seen him too. I felt a real fool telling you about him, when I'd never seen a thing. But it seemed harmless enough to say I'd glimpsed the same guy—after all, if Clive Brent was that sure, what harm was there?'

'So that was it—no real explanation—she just told you to do it?'

He smiled. 'I'm used to it. You'd be amazed how good I am at taking orders. Now, could those Flopsy Bunnies of yours do with another slug of the hard stuff? I'm not planning to take the bottle away with me and I apparently won't be coming back to this bar again.'

Chapter Twenty-five

I knew that Clive Brent now occupied a small cottage in the grounds of the boarding school of which he was bursar. It was within walking distance of Muntham Court, which bearing in mind the amount of whiskey I had drunk, was just as well.

The children I encountered thought that it was only mildly odd that a strange man smelling strongly of alcohol was looking for their bursar on a Monday evening. They were very helpful and I found the cottage without too much trouble—a two-storey building, scarcely wider than its Gothic front door, and situated close to what seemed to have been the stables of the main building.

'Oh, it's you,' he said, when he had responded to my knocking. 'You'd better come in, whatever it is you want. Have you been drinking?'

'With John O'Brian. Is it that obvious?'

'You are surrounded by an almost visible haze of Irish whiskey. What can I do for you?'

'The investigation...' I noticed I was having difficulty pronouncing that word. 'The *search* is getting complex.'

'I'll get you another drink then. I've only got beer, I'm afraid. Is that OK? Just keep talking. I'll fetch a couple from the fridge.'

He seated me in a chair in the ground-floor sitting-room-cum-dining-room-cum-kitchen. Upstairs, I guessed, there would be room for a bedroom and a small bathroom. It was one of the few houses I have ever seen that made my flat look big.

'The police,' I said, 'say that it must be suicide because there was no way out of the locked library. But it transpires there is a secret passage.'

'So Annabelle says.' Clive shut the fridge door with his foot and carried two bottles over to the sink to open them.

'Did you know about the passage?'

'Not until Annabelle told me yesterday.'

'She never mentioned it before?'

'No.' He handed me the opened bottle and a glass.

'Not the sort of thing that a total stranger would have known about,' I said.

'No.'

'A stranger like this man in a blue suit, for example?'

Clive Brent looked awkward. 'You'd need to talk to John O'Brian about that.'

'I have.'

'Then you'll know all there is to know.'

'He says that Annabelle asked him to say he'd seen the man to corroborate your account.'

'Are you serious?'

'That's what he says.'

'That may be what he says, but that's not what happened— or it's what happened but completely the other way round. It was John O'Brian who got a good look at him. Annabelle then asked me to say that I...Hang on, are you saying she told both of us that the other had definitely seen the guy and that she just needed a second witness to make it more credible? And we both fell for it? Well, I'm a bloody fool and you can tell John O'Brian he's one too.'

'I can't tell him anything. He's gone. Annabelle sacked him.'

'Did she? Well, that's a minor tactical mistake if she wanted him to continue to perjure himself for her.'

'Looks like a change of plan. Maybe not for the first time.'

'No, not for the first time.'

We both drank beer in silence for a while, then I remembered why I had come.

'You had a motive for killing Robert,' I said. 'He stitched you up over that futures thing.'

'True enough. Still, he found me this job.' Clive Brent waved his hand at the sitting-room-cum-dining-room-cum-kitchen. It took only a brief wave to encompass it all. 'Bastard.'

'You wanted to get revenge.'

'Very true.'

'You had the opportunity to kill him.'

'On an almost daily basis. I could have lain in wait somewhere along the drive to the house and bludgeoned him to death with something from his own garden shed as he walked back with his newspaper under his arm. I didn't need to do it in a house full of his friends.'

'So it wasn't you then?' I said.

'I like your questioning technique. Very straightforward.'

'Thank you.'

'No, it wasn't me,' he said. 'What good would that have done? I was having my revenge twice a week on average with Annabelle—in a good week several times in one afternoon—and it was a lot more fun than murder. In the meantime there was at least an outside chance that Robert would actually deliver on his promise of something better than a part-time bursarship. I had no reason to want him dead.'

'Was Robert having an affair with anyone?'

'In all likelihood. It was pretty much what he did. I wasn't actually aware of anyone lately, though.'

'Fiona McIntosh thinks it was suicide, but she also suggested that he might have been killed by somebody he was having an affair with—somebody he might have trusted even though they were playfully knotting a cord round his neck.'

'There are many things that I would have described Robert as, but "trusting" isn't one of them. I'll get you another beer. It won't help you decide how Robert died, but it will help put things into perspective.'

When Clive returned, I raised another question that had been hovering at the back of my mind.

'Now Robert is dead, I assume you and Annabelle will...'

'There's no me and Annabelle. There never was a me-and-Annabelle in any meaningful sense. Annabelle has spent her life using people. It was fun to feel I was using her for a while, but the novelty has rather worn off. No, I never had plans to make any permanent arrangements. If John O'Brian is out of the picture too...well, Ethelred, I'd watch my back if I were you.'

'Me?'

'Oh yes, I think you'll find you're next on her list.'

'Quite the reverse. I've got my marching orders too.'

He nodded. 'Yes, I can see she might have taken it that way.'

'So,' I said, trying both to work out what he meant by that and to summarize at the same time. 'No man in a blue suit. Nobody with any real motive. If we want to know who the murderer was, what we really need to find out is who benefits most from Robert's death.'

Clive Brent looked at me incredulously. 'Well, the answer to that question's pretty obvious, surely?'

'No,' I said. 'Who?'

He gave me the sort of look you give people when you're not sure whether they are being very cunning or very stupid.

'Well, you do, of course,' he said with a laugh. 'You do.'

><{{{º> ><{{{º> ><{{{º>

The Blue Death

'I've got a plan,' said the Prioress. 'We can rescue this man that you have arranged to have falsely imprisoned.'

'It wasn't me...' began Thomas, but he stopped, knowing how little use the explanation would be.

'Do you want to help him or not?'

'I don't see how we can get through fourteen-foot-thick stone *walls, grab the man from his cell and fight our way out,' said Master Thomas reasonably.*

'Of course you don't see,' said the Prioress. 'You are thinking like a man. It's all about penetrating things and getting into a fight.'

'And your plan?'

'We'll talk our way in, then we'll talk our way out again. Only, when we talk our way out, there'll be three of us.'

'And you've thought this through?'

'Yes.'

'Does it require divine intervention at any stage?'

'No more than, as a prioress, I can reasonably expect.'

'I don't mean to be rude, but have you ever done anything even remotely like this before?'

'Dozens of times,' said the Prioress, not quite looking Thomas in the eye. 'Piece of honey cake, frankly. Now if you can get Lady Catherine's men to provide us with a couple of horses, we can get over to Bramber while there's still time.'

'It will have to be tomorrow,' said Master Thomas.

'Tomorrow it is then,' said the Prioress.

The following day, the snow had started to melt, but the journey was, if anything, harder than it had been through fresh snow. The horses slipped and slithered over the half-frozen surface. Though they had started early, it was late morning before they reached the castle. Its walls, thought Master Thomas, looked every bit fourteen feet thick—no way through them or over them. Hopefully the Prioress was a very good talker.

'So what is this plan exactly?' asked Thomas.

'You'll see,' she said.

When challenged at the gate, the Prioress smiled demurely and said: 'We have come to visit the prisoner lately brought hither and to pray with him.'

'Can't be done,' said the guard. 'It is more than my position is worth to do that.'

'Would you endanger his immortal soul by denying him the word of God in his hour of need?'

'Can't see why not,' said the guard.

'Would you imperil your own soul in the process? Deny him succour and you risk the flames of Hell.'

'I'll chance it,' said the guard, who unfortunately didn't seem all that religious.

'How much?' asked Thomas.

'A shilling,' said the guard, taking a bit more interest in the conversation, 'but you'll need to be quick about it—the Sheriff is due back at midday.'

Money was transferred from Thomas's purse to the guard's and one nervous clerk of the customs and one sweetly smiling Prioress passed through the gateway. There was a further guard beyond, who also felt his soul was safe enough without the Prioress's blessing, and another shilling changed hands before they were led down into the dungeons that Thomas had left so thankfully a short time before.

The prisoner greeted them with suspicion, as the cell door slammed behind them and the gaoler's footsteps receded down the passageway.

'What are you two doing here?' he demanded.

'Fear not,' said the Prioress. 'We have come to free you. Though you are but a miserable wretch, and less well washed than I had hoped, we shall escort you to liberty.'

'You have a warrant from the Sheriff?'

'No,' said the Prioress.

'You have a royal pardon?'

'Not as such.'

'You know how to burrow through a fourteen-foot-thick wall?'

'I admit I haven't done it recently.'

'You know how to seduce the guards?'

'Of course, but it won't be necessary.'

'So, what's the great plan?' asked the prisoner with an amused sneer.

'The plan,' said the Prioress, 'is this. I have in my pouch a blue dye, with which I will paint your face with convincing blemishes.

Master Thomas will then bang on the door bleating like a lunatic: "Plague! Plague! This man has the plague! Let me out!" I will then say calmly that as a nun it is my duty to care for the sick, and that I shall take him to our house nearby to look after him. The Sheriff will be delighted to see the back of him and we shall ride away.'

'OK, just a couple of points there,' said Master Thomas. 'Is there any particular reason why it has to be me who bleats like a lunatic and you who are the calm saviour of the castle? I have after all trained as a doctor.'

'And your second point?'

'How will a few blue spots convince anyone he has the plague?'

'Have you seen anyone who had the plague?'

'No.'

'There you are then. It's well known that the French call the plague La Morte Bleue. We just have to make him blue enough.'

'Only an idiot,' said Thomas, ten minutes later, 'would believe that this gentleman has the plague.'

'That should be good enough then,' said the Prioress. 'Now, are you going to shout or do I have to do everything myself?'

'I've got a better plan,' said Thomas. 'We'll wait for the Sheriff to return, I'll explain that I did see somebody but I am now certain this isn't the man I saw. He will have no choice but to release him.'

'And then won't he ask why he is painted blue?'

'We'll wash it off.'

'Do you think I would try a trick like this with washable dye?'

'I don't know. Would you?'

'Absolutely not. We'll be able to frighten children with him for days if we're lucky. So, let's try it my way. Yell at the guard. Oh, and do try to sound deranged with fear.'

Thomas walked over to the door and, through the small barred opening, yelled: 'Guard, guard, come at once!'

After what the guard clearly considered a decent interval, a shuffling footfall announced his arrival.

'You and your nun done enough praying?'

'Yes…no…this man is very ill. I think he has the plague.'

The guard's shuffle slowed considerably and he tried to peer through the opening from a very long way away.

'What makes you think he has the plague?' he asked.

'Can't you see? He's covered in blue marks,' said Thomas.

'Can't see anything from here, master clerk, but if you say that turning blue means he's got the plague, then I reckon I'll take your word for it.' The guard was starting to back away.

'Let us all out, and we can take him to the Prioress's house to be nursed.'

'If he's got the plague, he's as good as dead already. So are you two. So am I if I go anywhere near that door.'

'Then just throw us the keys,' suggested Thomas.

'The plague!' yelled the guard at the top of his voice. 'They've got the plague!'

'The keys!' yelled Thomas at the rapidly retreating figure. 'You've got the keys!'

The footsteps increased in velocity but decreased in volume. Somewhere, a very long way off, a door slammed. The silence that followed was the deepest and most complete that Thomas could ever recall.

'I don't call that bleating like a lunatic,' said the Prioress. 'Nobody would have believed you had anything more than a borderline personality disorder. The guard—now he really did sound deranged, but you…Next time, remind me to do it myself.'

'You were rubbish,' confirmed the prisoner. 'I'd have done it better than that. Now look what a mess you've made of things. Next time—'

'I have no plans that there should be a next time,' said Thomas. 'If either of you ever do this again, it will be with somebody else entirely.'

'Since you wrecked my plan,' said the Prioress, 'perhaps you'd like to tell me, by St Benedict's bacon, exactly what we do now?'

'Well,' said Thomas, 'the way I see it, we are locked in a dungeon. The gaoler has fled. He will report that one of us has the plague already and that the other two of us are likely to have the plague very soon. His companions may decide to descend to our cell and check or, equally, they may decide it is wiser not to do so. If somebody is coming to unlock the door, then I suspect that they will do so quite soon. If, on the other hand, we have induced the blind panic that you were intending to produce, then they may not unlock the door for some days, or indeed years.'

'They may have tortured me,' said the prisoner, 'but at least they were feeding me regular. Now, because of you, I'm probably going to starve to death.'

Thomas cast his eyes round the cell, looking for any ray of hope. 'All we have is that flagon of water and that portion of a stale loaf,' he said.

'No,' said the prisoner, 'all I have is that flagon of water and that portion of a stale loaf. You, sadly, have nothing at all.'

The torch, fixed to the wall outside the cell, spluttered and went out. For a while the glowing end of the torch gave a very, very small amount of light. Then it didn't.

So, where next for Master Thomas then? Of course, he was not trapped for ever in the dungeon, but I enjoy setting myself problems of this sort. The easiest way out would be for the three of them to discover a secret passage, but I hesitated to introduce anything so unimaginative. A more interesting line would be that Thomas was far more valuable to his captors than he knew—and that a minion would be sent, reluctant and trembling, to unlock the door. That introduced all sorts of new possibilities concerning the real purpose of Thomas's journey and the perfidious plotting of the obnoxious Geoffrey Chaucer. Thomas had to be kept alive because…because…well, it would come to me later. Or, and this appealed to me most of all, the solution to their problem was that the door to the cell was not locked at all. I would need to check but I was pretty sure that I had not said in the preceding paragraphs that anyone had actually turned the key in the lock. The Prioress, having prayed in the most irritating manner possible for their deliverance, would simply touch the door lightly and it would swing open. That would provide an opportunity for her to be very smug and self-satisfied. Thomas would know the door could not have been locked, the reader would know the door could not have been locked, but both would have to endure a page and a half of the Prioress congratulating herself on the excellent PR she had put in with the deity over the years that had now paid such handsome dividends. They would then successfully escort the prisoner out of Bramber Castle and back to safety.

Did Thomas and the Prioress then return to Muntham Court and confront Lady Catherine? Probably. But I was no longer convinced that she would have been complicit in her husband's murder. I needed to go back and revise the first chapter that I had written, which now appeared forced and unsubtle. It was far too obvious that Lady Catherine already knew of Sir Edmund's death. It seemed to me that in the scene of Thomas's arrest I had sacrificed both characterization and plot for a cheap laugh. Perhaps in putting a similar sentiment into Thomas's own mouth I had been trying to tell myself something?

I was more confident of the ending. Once the party was safely back in London it would be revealed that the prisoner was, after all, the murderer (on the instructions of the Duke of Gloucester). Thomas and the Prioress had been thoroughly duped. The prisoner, for whom incidentally I still had no name, would admit as much and then depart rapidly and with only the briefest and most insincere speech of thanks. The Prioress would immediately remind Thomas that the whole escape business had been his plan all along, and that hanging, drawing and (possibly) quartering would now be his fate when it was discovered that he had aided and abetted a felony. To the extent that she herself might have been considered a minor accessory, she would fortunately be tried in a church court and sentenced to no more than a dozen or so Hail Marys—say two dozen absolute max. At this point, however, Chaucer would intervene and save Thomas, to avoid indictment himself for his own role in the affair. Thomas would be spared hanging, and the Prioress spared excessive prayer, but at the dreadful cost of Thomas's eternal indebtedness to Chaucer. Master Thomas would finally be allowed to return home, only to discover that he had forgotten the stories he had made up for his children en route for Sussex. He would therefore be forced to make up a new story for them, which he begins with the words: *'There was 'tis told a Nun, a Prioress, That of her smiling was full simple and coy, Her greatest oath was but by Saint Loy...'*

But would I ever complete the story? And should I? How many years did I have left to write the masterpiece for which I would always be remembered? Of course, I still had only the vaguest idea what my great literary novel would look like. And if I stopped writing crime novels, what precisely would I live on during the two or three years that I felt it would take me to produce it? I needed money. I needed a large and unexpected windfall.

I realized with a start that it was two o'clock in the morning and that I had to be in Crawley and thinking clearly in eight hours' time. I saved what I had just written and headed off to sleep—this time in my own bed.

Chapter Twenty-six

I awoke the following morning with a headache that Elsie might have put down to excessive whiskey, but that I knew was simply the result of working late and spending too much time staring at a computer screen. As the milk splashed deafeningly onto my cornflakes, I reviewed what had happened the previous day.

My drinking buddy, Clive Brent, had refused to elaborate on his claim that I was the main beneficiary of Robert's death. He seemed suddenly to decide he had said too much. Whatever I said after that, he blocked by saying I must speak to Gerald Smith.

Perhaps, if I had not had one or two whiskeys with John O'Brian and three or four beers with Clive Brent, I might have pressed harder for an explanation. As it was, I had been sent out into the autumn evening, to sober up by easy stages on my walk home—and to resolve to phone Smith in the morning.

As it happened, when I got home there had been four messages from Smith asking me to call him urgently, the last giving a mobile number. He too had been enigmatic when I finally tracked him down.

'Had you read the document you kindly forwarded to me, you wouldn't need to ask. I guess it's good news, but I need to talk you through it properly. Ten o'clock tomorrow suit you?'

⤙ ⤙ ⤙

So, 09.59 precisely saw me stepping through the entrance of a glass-and-concrete building in Crawley and being directed to the first floor.

'Did you know what you had passed on to me from Robert?' asked Gerald Smith, ushering me into a leather chair in front of his desk.

'No, I just posted it as requested.'

'It was a new will,' he said. 'Robert has left everything to you, pretty well. He's obviously had to make some provision for Annabelle, and his debts are fairly impressive. There are some very small bequests to obscure and possibly fictitious charities—we're checking which ones are jokes on Robert's part. The National Society for the Prevention of Children thankfully proved to be fictitious; it seems likely the Lupin Pooter Foundation for Distressed Stockbrokers is equally imaginary. Anyway, what's left at the end of it is basically Muntham Court. It's yours, free of death duties, encumbrances and so on and so forth.'

'And you say Annabelle...'

'...would like to kill you,' said Gerald. 'She is convinced that you have somehow persuaded Robert to do this.'

'It would explain the message she left with Elsie,' I said. 'And Robert didn't discuss this with you?'

'He must have got some solicitor in Worthing to draw it up for him. No law against that, of course. I have already phoned the firm to check that there's no chance this is a forgery. They confirm he came in and got them to draw up precisely this document. Clive Brent, Colin McIntosh and I are still the executors—I've already explained to them what has happened.'

'Look,' I said. 'Do you think Annabelle had any idea that Robert was about to change the will?'

'Because that would give her a motive for wanting him dead before he could change it? No, I don't think she did know.

It seemed to come as a complete shock when I phoned her yesterday. Are you worried she might have been the one who strangled Robert?'

'No,' I said. 'She's the one person I've never suspected.'

'Meaning you might have suspected me?' he asked. 'Let me tell you frankly that the fact that he was a former boyfriend of Jane's did rankle sometimes. Not often but sometimes. He knew Jane had told me and enjoyed reminding me. Then there was that time he phoned me about the girl he got pregnant.'

'Yes, you said.'

'It didn't make sense then, and it still doesn't.'

'But it has no bearing on Robert's death.'

'I keep wondering who this girl was. You don't think it could have been Jane?'

'Does that really worry you?' I asked.

'Yes, of course,' he said.

'Even if it's all in the distant past?'

'Yes.'

'And you want to know, even if knowing is of no possible use to you and could make you very unhappy?'

'Why not?'

'One of the things about being an author,' I said, 'is that people expect you to know something about the human condition and Life with a capital L. You don't, of course, but every now and then you are typing away and you suddenly get some strange insight.'

'And?'

'You are a very fortunate man, Gerald. You are successful in what you do—at least in as far as I can judge—and you have a wonderful wife and a son who, from the accounts I have heard, is very nearly perfect.'

'That's it? The great insight?'

'No, the great insight is this. You can be as fortunate and successful as you wish, but it's of no value to you at all if you lack the ability to enjoy your fortune and success. Like one of those Danish stoves that can heat the room with a few small smouldering logs, you can make do with very little if you know how to do it. Or you can have heaps of good dry logs and let the heat go straight up the chimney. On second thoughts, maybe that's not as great an insight as I thought, but it's still true. *Carpe diem* as they say. Seize the day, because it's the only day you've got, and tomorrow will deal you the same shitty hand whether you enjoy today or not.'

'Is that what *carpe diem* means?'

'Yes,' I said. 'That's exactly what it means. Don't believe anyone who tells you different. It's not about hope, just about damage limitation.'

'That's what you think, having just inherited a small stately home? You're a very fortunate man yourself.'

'I've never had the ability to enjoy the moment,' I said, 'with the possible exception of a few weeks last year—and then I had somebody watching me pretty carefully and checking that I did it. Go home. Love your wife. Love your son. It's something I doubt I'll ever have the chance of doing now—my own wife and son, I mean, not yours. Study me carefully, then go away and be something else entirely.'

After I left Gerald Smith's office, with a copy of the will in my pocket, I sat for a moment in reception and dialled Colin McIntosh's number.

'I suppose,' said Colin McIntosh, 'I should congratulate you on your good fortune. That's several million pounds' worth of property you've inherited. I'll make sure my fellow executors get a move on.'

'And Annabelle?' I asked.

'Legally, Robert couldn't avoid making provision for her, and so he has. The house was in his name alone, but she may contest that. Still, our job as far as I can see is to deal with the will we have. If she wants to fight it, then it may get a bit expensive for all concerned.'

'Did Robert tell you why he was leaving the house to me?'

'Not a word. Annabelle may know of course and, if she's speaking to you, she may possibly tell you.'

'She's not.'

'Ah well—small mercies and all that. Any more sighting of the mysterious stranger in a blue suit?'

'No. I don't think we'll see any more of him.'

'It was suicide, you know, Ethelred.'

'Fiona told me the same thing. But why?'

'He was ill.'

'That doesn't explain it.'

'Without a suicide note, it's as close as we'll get.'

'There is a note somewhere to me from Robert, but he hid it too well. I can't find it.'

'Why did he hide it?'

'It's a long story.'

'Robert's usually were. Well, I hope you find this note, whatever it is. I'm going to have to go now—I've got a surgery full of patients who want me to write them a sick note. One or two may actually be sick. Good luck with the hunt for the missing note. *Carpe diem*, eh?'

'Absolutely,' I said. '*Carpe diem quam minimum credula postero.*'

I shut my phone and put it in my pocket, then, with a nod to the receptionist, I pushed open the glass door and stepped out into the street. For a moment the strong sunlight made me blink. I needed to sit down and talk to somebody properly about all this and sort out my thoughts. Then, inexplicably a familiar face hove into view.

'Elsie! For God's sake, what are you doing here? Still, you won't believe what I've just found out. I still don't quite believe it myself.'

Chapter Twenty-seven

'So,' I said, summarizing the main part of Ethelred's announcements. 'You will be part of the *Sunday Times* Rich List, even if you will never be part of the Best Seller List.'

'Rich List? Not by a long way,' said Ethelred, stirring the remains of the skinny wet mochaccino that he had for some reason chosen to order. 'I wouldn't even be a footnote on the Rich List. Still, it's probably enough to allow me to stop writing historical detective stories for a bit and concentrate on what I really want to do.'

'And what about Master Thomas?'

'I'm going to leave him to his moral dilemma.'

'So we'll never know who killed Sir Edmund?'

'It was the suspicious stranger. The solution is the obvious one that everyone will have rejected because it was the obvious one. But more to the point, we're no closer to knowing who killed Robert. Nobody quite has a motive. Clive Brent was ruined by Robert but claims to have had his revenge already. John O'Brian had the best opportunity and knew the passage existed, but has no trace of a motive. Gerald Smith might have had a motive if he had known the whole story of Jane's abortion, but I'm now certain he doesn't, even if he suspected something. Jane Smith does know the whole story, but I believe her when she says it wouldn't have been remotely worth the risk. The same with Felicity—it was all too long ago and not worth it. And why would Annabelle kill Robert when she would have known he was dying anyway? Gillian Maggs knew about the secret passage, and her disappearance is odd to say the least, but what possible motive could she have? Colin and Fiona McIntosh both have their money on suicide—but I don't understand why.'

'Possibly to save Annabelle pain,' I said.

Ethelred nodded thoughtfully.

'On the other hand,' I continued, returning to reality, 'let's factor in that Annabelle has lied and lied and lied, and see what that does to the general picture. She led us up the garden path, in the most literal meaning of that term, over this man in a blue suit. We know that she was well aware of the secret passage when she first spoke to the police, but said nothing. We know that she tried to get both Clive Brent and John O'Brian to lie too. She has probably also murdered Gill Maggs and her husband and daughter—I can't see why anyone except Annabelle would want them out of the way. So that's the case for her being guilty. You may argue for her innocence but I fear your case rests mainly on short skirts and fake tits. It won't convince a jury, unless it consists entirely of middle-aged males.'

'Her skirts aren't that short,' said Ethelred.

'For her age they are.'

'She's not that old.'

Time to change the subject. 'It all comes back to why she was happy for the passage to be a secret at first, and then desperate for people to know about it later on,' I said.

'Maybe, like Master Thomas, I should just let this drop. I have a horrible feeling that, when I get to the solution, I may not like it that much anyway. I'm a writer, not a detective.'

'On the other hand, we're pretty close and Annabelle probably does know the ending to this story.'

'You're right. I'll go and see her and sort this out.'

'I'll come with you,' I offered.

'No, I can do this on my own.

'Ethelred, you will not be safe on your own. You've no idea what havoc a woman like that can wreak on a poor innocent lamb like you.'

'I'm not that innocent.'

'All the sex scenes in your books, such as they are, end "dot, dot, dot".'

'I don't do sex scenes.'

'You are not going to Muntham Court unchaperoned.'

'Yes, I am.'

For a moment it looked as though we might have a shoot-out in a cafe in Crawley. Then I figured, how much harm can she do in one brief meeting? She had been pretty pissed off. She might not even agree to see him.

'OK, drive me back to Findon,' I said. 'I'll wait for you back at the flat. I guess you're old enough to look after yourself.'

Even as I said it, however, I knew Ethelred would never be quite that old.

Chapter Twenty-eight

It was with no little trepidation that I approached Muntham Court and rang the bell. The door opened quickly and Annabelle was standing there, dressed modestly but elegantly in a straight black skirt and crisp white blouse. A single strand of pearls adorned her neck.

'I'd like to come in and explain,' I said.

'Perhaps you'd better,' she said rather severely.

She led me, in silence, to a small sitting room that I hadn't seen before. The thought crossed my mind briefly that this, along with all of the other rooms, passages, rose beds and tool sheds, was now mine. At her invitation, I sat on a comfortable damask sofa. Annabelle sank down beside me, her knee almost touching mine.

'Go on, then,' she said, smoothing her skirt with her hand. 'Make it good.'

'I didn't ask Robert to leave the house to me,' I said.

'I know,' she said suddenly. I looked at her. There was both sadness and understanding in her eyes. 'To be perfectly honest, Ethelred, it will be a relief not to have to worry about this huge place any more. It's just that...' She turned away briefly, struggling to get the words out. 'I feel so alone, Ethelred. So very alone.'

'I'm sorry...' I said.

She turned back to me and placed her fingers gently on my arm. 'Ethelred, I can count on you…as a friend…can't I? I wouldn't want this house or anything like that to come between us. You've always been very special.'

'Always?' I said.

'Since I met you, obviously,' she said, withdrawing her hand. She looked at me as though I was an imbecile—something I've grown used to over the years in my dealings with women. 'You know what I mean, for God's sake.'

'Of course,' I said.

'And you will help me to sort out this mess?' Again, a hand on my arm, this time more firmly.

'I thought I was off the case?'

'I need you, Ethelred,' she said. 'I've been so stupid. So very stupid.'

'You've lied to me,' I said, finally getting round to what I'd intended to be the important part of the conversation.

'Oh, I know. I know. Can you bear to forgive me? Dear Ethelred, can you?'

'Annabelle,' I said. 'Just tell me what happened. This time, just the truth. No evasions. No red herrings.'

She leaned forward. Her knee accidentally brushed against mine for an instant. I felt the warmth and the roughness of the nylon against my trouser leg.

'You are aware that Robert was very ill,' she began.

'Yes,' I said.

'He knew that I would be distraught when he…passed away…but in his very caring way he had insured his life some time before, so that I would not be left completely destitute as well as…distraught. And so on. Then, as you know, he committed suicide. I couldn't understand it, but I think he wanted to save me the pain of the last days of his illness—watching him slowly decline and slip away. I'm sure that was it.'

'So, it *was* suicide.'

'Oh yes.'

'But…'

'...why did I tell the police it couldn't be?'

'Yes.'

'Ethelred, dear sweet Ethelred, Robert, in his great kind-ness, had not thought things through. The insurance policy paid out if he died of *an illness*...or passed away in some terrible accident...but not if he committed suicide.'

'And you checked the policy...'

'...constantly. I was going to be left penniless, Ethelred. It was so wrong of me—I see that now. I told the police that it *couldn't* be suicide. I had to. Then when they didn't believe me....'

'You got me to discover the passage, so I would tell them there was a way out of the locked room.'

'Yes.'

'Then you invented this man in a blue suit. You invented a murderer.'

'I didn't want to get one of Robert's chums arrested. So I had to invent somebody who didn't resemble any of them. I thought that bit was quite clever.'

'A hiker in a blue suit?'

'I never claimed he was a hiker. Anyway, if I'd said that this person was in an anorak and jeans, just think of all the people that the police might have arrested.'

'Then you got John O'Brian and Clive Brent to lie, telling each that the other had definitely seen this person.'

'They were so keen to help me, Ethelred. They were really sweet. And when I thought about it, it was so much more convincing having two people see the killer.'

'Then you planted that material on the rose bushes.'

'A bit of one of Robert's old suits. I destroyed the suit itself so it wouldn't be traceable.'

'And the cigarette butts.'

'From that gardening boy we employ, whatever he's called. He leaves them all over the place.'

'He's called Dave Peart.'

'Is he? Yes, of course. So he is.'

'You said he didn't smoke.'

'A slip of the tongue.'

'Didn't it worry you that DNA testing might incriminate him? It would have been easy for the police to identify who had smoked them.'

'Might it? You know so much about these things. I certainly had not planned for him to come to any more harm than was absolutely necessary.'

'And you planted the black beanie.'

'It was a pound at a shop in Worthing.'

'The price is immaterial,' I said.

'I'm sorry,' she said. 'Clive or John, I can't remember which, came up with the bit about the beanie. I thought it was jolly good so I went straight into Worthing...but I really am sorry, Ethelred. I realize now that was wrong too. I should have taken you into my confidence so much earlier. Dear Ethelred, I do so need your help.'

I realized that her hand had been on my knee for some time, but couldn't remember her placing it there.

'What did you do with Gillian Maggs?' I asked.

'Nothing. Well, not much. She was the one who told me about the secret passage. She'd worked for the last people who lived here. After they both died and the family put it on the market, she was possibly the only person alive who knew about the passage. She told me, of course. I've always got on well with Gilly. Anyway, I realized that it might be awkward for her if she had to talk to the police...I didn't want her to feel embarrassed in any way...and Robert and I have a little place in Barbados. So I sent her there for a short holiday. Or possibly a long one, depending on when this silly business is all cleared up.'

'And the daughter?'

'She phoned me to say that she was worried by the questions you and Elise had been asking.'

'And?'

'I told her to stay put until the courier arrived with a first-class ticket to Barbados.'

'Annabelle, I'm sorry to ask you this, but were you…in a relationship…with John O'Brian or Clive Brent?'

'Ethelred, I swear on Robert's life—or my mother's life if you prefer. No. Absolutely not. They are both dear boys and I think that they may have both been just a teensy bit in love with me—but I adored my husband. Ethelred, you couldn't imagine, even for a moment…'

'Why did you sack John O'Brian?'

'Didn't he explain? I just couldn't afford him any more. I couldn't keep him on and not pay him. Perhaps I explained myself badly—I was cross about the will and with you and perhaps with men generally. I may have been a little abrupt with him.'

'It wasn't that you had just ended an affair with him…'

'Oh, Ethelred. An affair? You are too cruel, too…I couldn't bear it if you thought that badly of me.'

Suddenly she flung herself at me and started weeping uncontrollably. I felt her hot tears run down my own cheek.

'I don't think badly of you, Annabelle,' I said, though her hair was all over my face, making clear speech tricky, and she was holding onto me quite tightly. Her cheek rubbed damply against mine. Somehow our mouths touched. I tasted the salt of her tears and inhaled her perfume. Again the image of a Venus flytrap unaccountably crossed my mind.

'Ethelred,' she breathed into my ear, as though something had just occurred to her. 'You can help me. You know that, don't you?'

'How?' I asked.

'We've still gathered lots of good evidence, haven't we? All you need to do is to take it to the police. Tell them where we found it. And about the secret passage that you so cleverly found. And then perhaps say that you saw a stranger in the garden—that you had thought nothing of it at the time, but now you remembered.'

'But it wouldn't be true,' I said, briefly disengaging myself.

'Some of it would be.'

'It's called perverting the course of justice. At the very least it's wasting police time.'

'Wasting their time? Not if it helps them get back my insurance money for me. If I'd had a cheap ring stolen, the police would spend time looking for it, wouldn't they? Well, I've lost my insurance money, and that's a jolly sight more important. What do I pay my council tax for?'

'It doesn't work like that,' I said.

'Please?' she said. She kissed my cheek. 'Please?'

'Annabelle, I'm not sure we should be doing this…or that…and certainly not that…though obviously I'm very flattered that you should…'

'I've always been so fond of you, Ethelred. Ever since we met. I've always found crime writers irresistibly attractive. Most women do.'

How could I doubt her sincerity? I looked at her. She looked at me.

Then, very slowly, she started to unbutton her blouse…

Chapter Twenty-nine

'Y ou took your time,' I said, as Ethelred came through the door, looking a little bedraggled. His shirt was buttoned up all wrong (which strangely I had not noticed that morning) and his hair was a complete mess, even for him. He slumped down beside me on the sofa.

'Sorry,' he said. He looked tired, poor lamb.

'What's that aftershave you're wearing?' I demanded. 'It smells a bit girly.'

'I'm not wearing aftershave,' he said.

'I can smell something on you,' I said.

'Maybe just the soap I used at Annabelle's.'

'Expensive soap then—smells just like Chanel,' I said. 'Did you get a good look round the place?'

'Just a sitting room and a bedroom,' he said.

'So, what did she say?'

'She admitted to faking the evidence. She wants me to lie to the police so that she can get the insurance money. The insurance people won't pay up if it's suicide.'

'So, that's what it was all about.'

'From beginning to end.'

'Excellent, let's get on the phone to the cops now and grass her up.'

'Would you like some coffee?' asked Ethelred, ignoring my suggestion.

'No, I'll have some chocolate,' I said.

'Sorry—I forgot to get any. There's just regular coffee and decaf.'

'Decaf then.'

'I've got plenty of that. Haven't touched it since Robert last came round.'

'Hold on,' I said. 'Where does coffee come from?'

'Tesco,' said Ethelred.

'I mean which countries?'

'I don't know—it probably says on the jar. Kenya? Brazil?'

'Ethelred—think back. Shagger's poem—"*What you must seek is not so very far, From Andes hills or Afric slopes, a jar*"— that has to be it. *How did it end?*'

'Something, something, something "*crave*"—"*You shall receive where formerly you gave*".'

'And where did you give Shagger coffee?'

'I'll look in the kitchen,' said Ethelred.

'I'll do it,' I said. Ethelred could fall around for ever. I took the jar of decaf from the cupboard, removed the top and upended it over the work surface. Nestling snugly amongst the rich brown grains was a tightly folded sheet of paper.

'Robert must have hidden it there when he was last at the flat,' said Ethelred.

'OK,' I said, carefully unfolding what proved to be an A5 sheet, closely written on both sides. 'This is the piece of evidence that you've had all along, and that would have saved us three days of arsing around, had you found it straight away. Which you didn't.'

And, with no little curiosity, we proceeded to read Shagger's Last Note.

Chapter Thirty

Dear Ethelred,

   If you are reading this, then you have cleverly cracked the clues—or more likely you just felt like a mug of decaf.

   Anyway, as you will have gathered, the point of this letter is that I want to make sure things don't go wrong. Let's do a bit of explaining then, in case you haven't picked up some obvious points on the way—you never were the brightest of my chums, but hopefully you won't make a complete pig's ear out of this.

   First, it won't have escaped your notice that my good lady is hopping in and out of bed with a number of my other chums. Second, you will have been told that I have only a month or two to live—even without my clever little wheeze (about which, more in a moment). Finally, you will have probably worked out that I am flat broke. I've still got plenty of wonga tied up in Muntham Court and the places in Chelsea and Barbados, but the point has come where I have no ready cash whatsoever, and banks like a contribution towards one or other of your mortgages from time to time. They are threatening to foreclose on Muntham Court. I never did like bankers.

   Annabelle's solution to the problem has been straightforward enough. She made me take out a large life insurance policy—before I found out that I was poorly, by the way, so it's all kosher. Now she's *sitting there waiting for the money to roll in so she can go off with Clive or John or whoever takes her fancy.*

Then I thought—why let her get away with it?

I considered cancelling or defaulting on the insurance payments, but I reckoned some officious insurance clerk would immediately alert her to what I had done and she'd say it was a mistake and just get Clive to stump up for a month or two until I snuffed it. So, I examined the small print and—what do you know?—the policy is invalid if I commit suicide. Well, Colin has told me that the time I've got left won't be much fun anyway, so I can kill two birds with one stone, as it were—one of the birds being my good self. Of course, a low-key private suicide might be rigged to look like natural causes or even murder, and I can't have that.

So, I am planning to kill myself in a way that will leave nothing open to doubt. I shall invite round a few chosen chums to my Last Supper. Annabelle won't know or appreciate it, but I'll be serving some decent wine, including my last magnum of Lafite, which I've been saving up for a suitable occasion. At some appropriate point in the evening, happy and well refreshed, I shall go off and do away with myself—I haven't quite decided how, though I am of the opinion that shooting is messy and that most poisons are not half as much fun as Agatha Christie makes out. Anyway, it will take place in a locked room that no murderer could have escaped from and with lots of good reliable witnesses. You'll be one of them. I do hope you all have a nice evening.

Of course, there'll be a bit of money left, when everything is sold up, that Annabelle might still get her dirty mitts on—but I've got a plan for that too. I'm leaving Muntham Court to you, free of encumbrances and death duties. You don't particularly deserve it, and I won't pretend I ever really liked you, but I think that good fortune should fall on people as randomly as possible without any regard to merit. So, enjoy it—you are now Lord of the Manor.

Of course, the upkeep will probably bankrupt you and Annabelle will hate you for ever—and you rather like Annabelle, don't you?—but that won't be my problem.

Oh, and there's one other sting in the tail. The obvious solution to Annabelle's problem is to marry you and to continue to be the

Lady of Muntham Court. She usually gets what she wants and you're pretty spineless, so my money, if I still had any, would be on your not resisting for long. You know that she'll treat you no better than she's treated me, but I think you might still be sucker enough to go through with it. You have no idea how my final days have been enlivened by the thought of the trouble I shall cause when I die. It's such a shame I can only do it once.

It was about this time of year that Annabelle and I used to start planning our next trip to the West Indies. Autumn's on its way. I've had my fun and it's not such a bad time to be throwing in my hand. I've never been keen on English winters. So, whatever you do, don't start feeling sorry for me. I'll be thinking of you from another place—quite possibly a warmer one than Barbados.

With fondest wishes from your old chum,

Shagger

'Friend of yours, was he?' asked Elsie.

For a moment I said nothing. Though in some ways I felt deeply insulted, I could at least feel rich and insulted, which was better than usual. I took the letter from Elsie and read it again.

'So, that was the plan,' I said. 'There was something in Robert's speech that always struck me as a bit odd—do you remember what he said about going off into the next room? It's from a poem, *"Death is Nothing at All"* by Henry Scott-Holland, but the actual words are "I have only slipped away into the next room" —that's why I didn't recognize it at the time. Robert never was much good at quotations, and if you change a word or two of a poem...Anyway, I think that, from what Colin McIntosh said, Robert didn't make a definite decision to go ahead with his plan until that evening, after Colin confirmed there really was no hope for him. The letter had already been sent to me. The clues had been planted. So, he slipped away and his game could begin. He was giving us all clues from the very beginning—even if some were a bit garbled.'

'But the game went a bit wrong,' said Elsie.

'Yes, Annabelle got to the body first. I knew there was something missing when I looked round the library—it was the suicide note. The pen was there on the desk but no sign of whatever he'd been writing. Annabelle must have realized the moment she saw the body that she was about to lose the insurance money. So she pocketed the key piece of evidence while I was unbolting the door.'

'But,' said Elsie, 'in that case, why not tell the police about the secret passage straight away? That way murder would not have been ruled out.'

'I think her mind just wasn't working that fast. Or maybe she reasoned that only she, Mrs Maggs and John O'Brian knew about the passage. It would not have looked good for John O'Brian under the circumstances.'

'Or had she arranged to meet John O'Brian there that evening? Did she think he was actually waiting in the passage?' Elsie asked.

'I don't know,' I said. Yesterday I would have said such a thing was too far-fetched. But yesterday was yesterday and today was today. 'The point is that, at the time, she was reluctant to draw people's attention to it. It was later that she came up with the idea of a mysterious stranger, who would have clumsily left multiple clues. But it was too late then to suddenly tell the police that she had remembered the passage existed. So she got me to "discover" the passage. She also got John O'Brian and Clive Brent to say that they had seen the stranger—but I've told you about that. Gillian Maggs might have given the game away, so she and her husband were offered an all-expenses-paid trip to Barbados until the investigations had finished. When it became clear their daughter was already revealing too much information to casual callers, she was offered the same deal, provided she left there and then.'

'So, we've basically been following a trail of red herrings, from the library to the billiard room via the secret passage, and on out into the garden. Just like *Cluedo*. Except, of course, that you have to play *Cluedo* strictly by the rules. There's nothing more tedious than finding somebody you ought to be able to trust has been cheating all along.'

'Yes,' I said, slowly. 'Though I'm still not sure the secret passage on the *Cluedo* board goes—'

'It could be worse, though,' said Elsie, folding the letter away. 'You can sell Muntham Court and buy yourself a nice flat in North London, where I can keep an eye on you...the painted tart will be thrown on the street...she'll probably have to go and live on a proper estate with graffiti and lifts that only work every other Tuesday...or she might become a bag-lady and get spat on by total strangers...she'll have to sit in shop doorways drinking the sort of sweet sherry she served to her guests for so many years...yes, it could be so much worse.'

'That's not what Robert wanted me to do, though,' I said, thoughtfully. 'Reading between the lines he's really asking me to take care of Annabelle...'

'Reading between *which* lines? The lines on your arse? He would scarcely have gone through this whole business so that Annabelle would end up with the house and the insurance money and you.'

'He says he thinks I'll end up marrying her.'

'If you aren't careful, yes, you could.'

'But I do think he wants me to keep the house.'

'You mean you'll hang onto a ruinously large house, that even a rich banker couldn't afford to maintain, so that Annabelle isn't made destitute?'

'You could look at it as a sort of trust,' I said. 'The house passes to me so that I can help somebody else. And it need not be ruinous. I'd have the house, unencumbered as the lawyers say, I can sell this flat and Annabelle would have some money from the insurance so long as—'

'You're not planning to lie to the police?'

'I wouldn't need to lie exactly—we would just tell them what we found.'

'And the man in a blue suit?'

'He's probably not essential. I suppose you wouldn't like to say you saw him?'

'Spot on. I wouldn't. You can get into big trouble once you start saying things like that.'

She said it with feeling and I wondered if she had been reading the (now abandoned) Master Thomas story. It was perfectly possible. My computer had no password protection. 'I'm sure Annabelle and I can manage anyway,' I said.

'Manage in what sense? Ethelred—I am not letting you throw yourself away on that bitch...'

'I didn't necessarily say I'd do it,' I said.

'So, what did you say?' asked Elsie.

For a long time I stared at the empty jar that had once held decaffeinated coffee.

'I just said: "Perhaps"...' I said.

Chapter Thirty-one

'What do you mean, "Perhaps"?' I asked.

'Only kidding,' said Ethelred. 'I'm not such a total tosser that I'd marry some painted tart like that. I learned my lesson with Geraldine. You were right all along—what a bitch she was.'

'So, you've finally come to your senses after all these years?'

'Absolutely. Let's go and celebrate at the Village House. They've invented an amazing new pudding. It tastes in every way like chocolate but it contains no calories at all, not that you need worry about calories with a figure like yours. You don't know how jealous Annabelle is.'

'Is that true?'

Absolutely,' said Ethelred. 'All of this is true. Let's go eat chocolate.'

Chapter Thirty-one

'What do you mean, "perhaps"?' asked Elsie.

'Just that I haven't quite made up my mind,' I said.

'Well, make it up quickly then. Annabelle's just like Geraldine,' said Elsie. 'I mean, in a good way. She's beautiful, kind, considerate. She was devoted to Robert—as indeed Geraldine was to you, with one trivial exception. I think you should marry Annabelle—if she'll have you, which I'm sure she will. Frankly, you're a bit of a babe-magnet.'

'Annabelle implied that all crime writers were irresistibly attractive,' I said.

'I think,' said Elsie, 'that she just meant first-rate crime writers, like you.'

'So, I should hang on in Findon,' I said. 'Not sell up and move to London?'

'Absolutely,' said Elsie. 'Stay here. It's the perfect place to write a great literary novel.'

'Do you mean all that?' I asked.

'Of course,' said Elsie. 'I've given up being cruel and sarcastic at your expense. And I'd be honoured to be a bridesmaid at your wedding. Do you think I should wear acid lemon or puce?'

'Why don't we let Annabelle decide?' I asked.

'What an excellent idea,' said Elsie. 'She has such perfect taste.'

'How true that is,' I said, 'how very true.'

And this is why I sojourn here
Alone and palely loitering,
Though the sedge is wither'd from the lake,
And no birds sing.

John Keats,
'La Belle Dame Sans Merci'

Acknowledgments

I needed to consult various sources for the historical sections of this book. They included *Richard II* by Nigel Saul, *England in the Late Middle Ages* by A R Myers, *London the Biography* by Peter Ackroyd, *Chaucer's Language* by Sim Horobin, *The Age of Chaucer* by Valerie Allen, *The Oxford Book of Mediaeval Verse* (ed. Celia and Kenneth Sisam) and Neville Coghill's translation of the *Canterbury Tales*. And, of course, that essential standby for twenty-first-century writers—*Wikipedia*.

The descriptions of Muntham Court were inspired by the excellent articles by Valerie Martin on the Findon Village website, and on additional material on the house and family that lived in it from Norman Allcorn. I am very grateful to both. Neither is to blame for any unintended inaccuracies on my part or (more to the point) for any deliberate changes that I made to the geography of the original when creating my fictional Muntham Court.

As ever I am grateful for the help I received from my publisher, Pan Macmillan, and in particular from my editor, Will Atkins, copy editor Mary Chamberlain and publicists Sophie Portas and Philippa McEwan. A writer could not reasonably ask for a better team.

Finally I must thank my family for their continuing indulgence that I spend so much time on something as unprofitable as writing books.